PENGUIN BOOKS

DR MUKTI

Will Self is the author of three short-story collections, *The Quantity Theory of Insanity* (winner of the 1992 Geoffrey Faber Award), *Grey Area* and *Tough, Tough Toys for Tough, Tough Boys*; a dyad of novellas, *Cock and Bull*, and a third novella, *The Sweet Smell of Psychosis*; and four novels, *My Idea of Fun*, *Great Apes*, *How the Dead Live* (shortlisted for the 2000 Whitbread Novel of the Year Award) and *Dorian*. Together with the photographer David Gamble, he produced *Perfidious Man*, a sideways look at contemporary masculinity. There have been three collections of journalism, *Junk Mail*, *Sore Sites* and *Feeding Frenzy*. Most of his books are published by Penguin.

Will Self has written for a plethora of publications over the years and is a regular broadcaster on television and radio.

DR MUKTI
AND OTHER TALES OF WOE

WILL SELF

PENGUIN BOOKS

PENGUIN BOOKS

Published by the Penguin Group
Penguin Books Ltd, 80 Strand, London WC2R ORL, England
Penguin Group (USA) Inc., 375 Hudson Street, New York, New York 10014, USA
Penguin Group (Canada), 10 Alcorn Avenue, Toronto, Ontario, Canada M4V 3B2
(a division of Pearson Penguin Canada Inc.)
Penguin Ireland, 25 St Stephen's Green, Dublin 2, Ireland
(a division of Penguin Books Ltd)
Penguin Group (Australia), 250 Camberwell Road,
Camberwell, Victoria 3124, Australia (a division of Pearson Australia Group Pty Ltd)
Penguin Books India Pvt Ltd, 11 Community Centre, Panchsheel Park, New Delhi – 110 017, India
Penguin Group (NZ), cnr Airborne and Rosedale Roads, Albany,
Auckland 1310, New Zealand (a division of Pearson New Zealand Ltd)
Penguin Books (South Africa) (Pty) Ltd, 24 Sturdee Avenue, Rosebank 2196, South Africa

Penguin Books Ltd, Registered Offices: 80 Strand, London WC2R ORL, England

www.penguin.com

First published by Bloomsbury Books 2004
Published in Penguin Books 2005

2

Copyright © Will Self, 2004
All rights reserved

The moral right of the author has been asserted

Printed in England by Clays Ltd, St Ives plc

ACKNOWLEDGEMENTS

'161' was commissioned by Neville Gabie and Leo Fitzmaurice for their Up in the Air project, using funds kindly donated by Liverpool Housing Action Trust. Thanks are due to the residents of Linosa Close, Kensington, Liverpool, and also to Colin the Caretaker. 'The Five-swing Walk' was commissioned by Dominic Gregory for the Ilkley Literature Festival in 2001. A primitive version of 'Conversations with Ord' was published by Suzy Feay in the *Independent on Sunday*. The other stories were written with this collection in mind.

WWS, London, 2003

For Liz Calder

CONTENTS

DR MUKTI

DR REICH

You don't know that rumour of schizophrenia? Oh yes. That was spread by Fenichel. Oh yes. Now, today, nobody believes it. It was quite a thing, quite a thing. I doubt that you never heard that I'm paranoiac, schizophrenic.

DR EISSLER

No, I didn't.

DR REICH

Sure?

DR EISSLER

Sure, I didn't.

DR REICH

You want to see the documents? Shall I give them to you?

DR EISSLER

Well, I mean, if you would —

DR REICH

All right, yes!

Reich Speaks of Freud

Part One

Dr Shiva Mukti was a psychiatrist of modest achievements but vaulting ambition. Not that he would've admitted it. Even if his oldest friend, David Elmley – a man of true mildness – had put it to him thus: Shiva, you're a psychiatrist of modest achievements but vaulting ambition, an absolute tirade of denials would've ensued. Whatdoyoumeanby-that? Modest by whose standards? By what measure? As for vaulting, why'dyousaythat? Because I dare to think that I should have a better job than this piss-poor consultancy at St Mungo's? Is that a little too unEnglish for you? Not quite cricket, old boy?

The situation wasn't hypothetical – even though Elmley wished it so. Wilting under this downpour of self-justification he began to issue qualifications. 'Oh c'mon, Shiva, you know I didn't mean it like that. Don't take it so personally, don't be so intense, if anything Indians like cricket more than the English.'

But this only changed the direction of Mukti's monsoon, which under the influence of a gale of resentment now began to drive into Elmley's lugubrious lantern jaw. 'Cricket! India!' he spluttered. 'You know nothing about either of them. I tell you, David, if you'd had a father like mine you wouldn't say these things –'

'What things?' Elmley was quick to be slow on the uptake.

'Vaulting ambition, modest achievement. You've no

bloody idea what my childhood was really like, the pressure I laboured under, the sheer weight of expectation I had to endure. I wasn't even allowed out by myself at night until I was in medical school, until I was twenty! My dad placed the whole burden of his own frustrated ambition on my shoulders, all my life I've been struggling along with that silly old fool's delusions about reason and progress and science loaded on top of me like a bloody bag of cement! David, all my childhood he was on my case, don't do this, Shiva, don't do that, Shiva, shouldn't you be studying, Shiva? Haven't you got an exam coming up, Shiva? Now you say my ambition is vaulting, I tell you this is being restrained, this is being modest! If I hadn't internalised that shit I wouldn't even get out of bed in the morning, let alone drag myself along to this bloody hive of pestilence!'

Mukti stared wildly around at the long Formica-topped tables of the St Mungo's staff canteen. It had suffered a forcible conversion five years before, when the hospital was gobbled up by the behemoth of an institution that was Heath Hospital. The conversion took the form of thin sheets of this or that being pinned, bolted or even nailed across the superfluous niches and fake embrasures which had given the neo-Gothic building what little distinction it possessed. Advancing columns had been boxed in, while flying buttresses were brought down in a welter of chipboard. Much paint had been shed, and yet all that had been achieved was to incubate a disorientating fever in this already sick establishment. It was now impossible to tell the floor from the ceiling, or one wall from the others. The gleaming blue table-tops looked like oversized strip lights, while the wan strip lighting appeared to be the tops of upside-down tables fixed to the roof. The food was dished up by a crew of Samoans, their yellow faces looming out of the smelly steam like full moons peeking through scudding clouds.

David Elmley worked near to St Mungo's in Cleveland Street. He'd occupied his small neat office for twenty years. Together with his partner he designed architectural ironmongery – latches, railings, letterboxes – Elmley himself specialised in hinges, the demand for which had been resolutely consistent since he left college in the early 1980s. Were he to have had even a weak sense of humour, doubtless the kind of thing Elmley would've said about his calling was, 'Opening doors has always been an open door to me.' But he didn't say this because he had no sense of humour at all. No perceptible one anyway, but deep inside himself he cherished a black and destructive absurdism.

Strolling towards Charlotte Street during his lunch break, and finding himself temporarily out of pocket, rather than prolonging the walk as far as the cash point on Tottenham Court Road, Elmley would often divert his gangling stream of limbs into the hospital, and take the option of eating cheaply with Mukti.

David Elmley knew all about Shiva Mukti's childhood. They'd attended the same secondary school. The two families had also lived only a few doors apart in Kenton Park Crescent. Not that the older Muktis and Elmleys had much to do with each other, but David and Shiva had formed one of those friendships which, despite being between temperamental opposites, often drag on into middle age, and eventually endure for a lifetime.

The basis of their friendship was mutual dislike. Had they been capable of acknowledging this it would've made them a very truthful duo indeed; and perhaps, instead of terminating their association, the revelation might've provoked the kind of honesty and soul-searching that true amity is founded on. But they weren't that honest, and there was much else about them worth reviling. Elmley had the aching parsimony of an only child mummy's boy who refused to grow up. Now in his early forties, he still affected a wide-eyed, raring-to-go manner. If anything novel was proposed Elmley would say, Oh I must do that/get one of those/go there. But the truth was he never did anything new at all, and this performance – with its obvious staginess – was the very guarantee of his timorous inflexibility.

Mukti, who was also a prodigious example of arrested development, and also an only child, took exactly the opposite approach. Under the cover of a threadbare cloak, cut from you-take-me-as-you-find-me cloth, and embroidered with I-am-what-I-am, he was both mercurial and a confirmed neophyte. Mukti made up for his strictured childhood when he reached medical school by becoming a serious carouser and a committed womaniser. He had even married out during his second year. Out meaning without the say-so of his parents and the family astrologer. Out of caste, out of race and effectively out of this world.

In one fell stroke he had laid waste to thousands of years' Brahminical observance. That the new Mrs Mukti was pale and blonde was well known to his fellow students, because she was one of the cleaners in their hall of residence, but less perfectly understood was what then happened to her. One week Mukti was to be seen strutting the hallways and corridors of the college, showing off his new bride, the very next the senior Muktis were in evidence.

He was small yet oddly intimidating in lungi, suede shoes and a quasi-regimental blazer (the crest was in fact that of the Kenton Horticultural Society); while she was bulky and perfectly aggressive despite her diaphanous sari and non-existent English. The Muktis didn't fit anyone's image of submissive Hindus, at a time when the popular view of them – under the influence of a recent biopic of Mahatma Gandhi – was as a nation of passively resisting corner-shop proprietors. And one week after that anaemic Sandra was gone, never to be seen again. There were rumours of a child – aborted, adopted, perhaps ascended to heaven – but Shiva himself said nothing about the affair, and since those close to him were so only by virtue of physical proximity, they decided not to raise the matter and risk his notoriously explosive temper.

Yes, Shiva Mukti was a snaky changeling; a bilingual, first-generation immigrant who stuck one of his tongues out at his elders, while employing the other to lick the ice cream the world had given him. He bowed down to novelty, worshipping American movies, Japanese gadgets and Italian cars. He was a small, fastidious man, with lustrous blue-black hair which grew densely on the slopes of his mound of a brow; and his extended lobes – widely believed, in India, to be a mark of divinity – were covered with a filigree of black hairs. When he was a young man, breaking away from his family, charging towards life with his arms wide open so as to grab as much as he could, Shiva Mukti's countenance had been at once chirpy and engaging, but with time had come overwork and thwarted expectations, which like swing doors slammed back into him, bruising and distorting his face.

As Mukti sat opposite David Elmley in the staff canteen at St Mungo's, and ranted for the hundredth time that year about how ill-served he was by the local NHS trust, his smile, at one time charmingly lopsided, was now set in a permanent grimace of burnt-out dissatisfaction.

Why did Mukti and Elmley persist in their charade of

intimacy? Insecurity. Grey, gritty insecurity which is poured into the foundations of so many relationships. 'I wouldn't even get up!' Shiva reiterated, and sat back heavily in his plastic stacking chair, while spooning an individual plastic pot of chocolate mousse with angry little digs of his plastic spoon.

'I see your point,' Elmley replied, 'but what does Swati have to say about it?' But truly he didn't see his friend's point at all. If David Elmley had woken up next to Swati Mukti he wouldn't have required any justification to stay in bed for that morning and for all mornings to come, until the Last Trump sounded and the long-dead, fish-belly-white corpses dug themselves up, and like so many grocery souls were weighed in the balance.

David Elmley knew, without needing full visual confirmation, that Swati Mukti's long, almost tubular breasts were capped by large, smooth, blue-brown aureoles; and that surmounting each circlet was a long, pinky-brown teat, purpose-made to suckle Elmley himself. When Swati had been breast-feeding Mohan, the Muktis' only child, Elmley felt as if he would liquefy with love for her. The several odours of breast milk, rose water, henna and incense, the tiny coffee-coloured head lost in the loosened folds of her sari, Swati's expression – at once imperious and touchingly vulnerable – all of it engendered in Elmley the small miracle of tearfulness accompanied by a massive erection.

Henceforth David Elmley had worshipped at the shrine of Swati. He would've liked to do a daily puja before her, bringing her whatever she desired in the way of exotic fruits or expensive flowers. He would've liked to awaken her by playing haunting airs upon an ancient flute, then bathe her shining limbs, then dress her in the finest and whitest of cloth, then sit all day long in the Muktis' airless house, fanning her with an ostrich feather dyed black. When evening came Elmley would distribute the remains of the offerings to the Goddess's other worshippers – Shiva, Mohan, old Mrs Mukti, the aunts and uncles – before mounting his foldaway bicycle and pedalling off in the direction of Tooting, where he lived emphatically alone.

What David Elmley never suspected – mostly because he himself had only been married for six months to a Japanese doctoral student seeking British residency – was that Shiva and Swati's sexual relationship had long since driven out into the desert, torched its car, put a pistol in its mouth and pulled the trigger. Of course, all intimacies die like this, in remote and lonely places, and by their own hand.

They still felt attracted to each other, because between them there was so much attractiveness. Even if Shiva had looked like Quasimodo, Swati could still have made good the deficiency. In part it was the child, who at seven still slept in their bedroom. They hadn't even got Mohan out of their bed until he was six, and even now he reclined on an air mattress at their feet, as if he were one of those oddly humanoid dogs who guard the tombs of medieval knights. But the child was also a pretext, the way they are all too often. This alone explains why so many people feel so inauthentic as adults and as parents.

In fairness to the Muktis, there wasn't really anywhere much for Mohan to go. The house in Kenton Park Crescent had always been a short-term lodging for relatives angling in from the four corners of the earth where the Hindu diaspora had taken them. Old Mr Mukti – although a martinet to his son and his neighbours (for many years he felt that his chairmanship of the local horticultural society gave him a perfect right to tell them what bedding plants to put in) –

nonetheless took his role as paterfamilias extremely seriously. Dilip Mukti was the eldest son of a deeply conservative priest at the world-famous Durga Temple in Varanasi. He had shocked the Brahmin community by decamping to North-West London where he became a regional manager for London Transport. Dilip Mukti hadn't even the paltry justification – in the eyes of his own father – that he was going to study the vastly inferior Western metaphysics at first hand. And as for his fellow immigrants who worked under him on the buses, they had two kinds of hatred for Dilip. The enmity of subordinates, and the much more keenly felt disdain of those who are compelled for those who've made a free choice. For he loved every aspect of his job, and loved the buses themselves in particular.

Between them his parents had twelve siblings, and such was the throng that Shiva grew up among that in early childhood he'd thought all households had the utilitarian character of his parents', where meals were served on thin metal plates at two long refectory tables. As for the sitting room – it was just that: a square room stuffed full of mismatched armchairs and sofas, so as to be capable of housing some twenty pan-chewing, raga-humming, telly-watching relatives. If one chair was moved then all the others had to be as well, so to clean the room was like doing a giant puzzle.

Now, thirty years later, the situation had changed – but not drastically. Left behind after the gold rush that had seen the Mukti clan stake claims all over Kenton, Harrow, Wembley, Stanmore and Burnt Oak were a selection of the most intractable and economically non-viable relatives. Termed collectively in the family argot as 'the aunts and uncles', their actual degree of relatedness was dubious in the case of two and non-existent as regards the other three. Be that as it may, they took up two bedrooms, while old Mrs Mukti occupied a third, leaving only one remaining for the titular master and mistress of the house.

But anyway, whatever the constraints and accommodations of their family life, the stark fact was that Shiva had never seen his wife naked. If David Elmley had known this he might perhaps have stopped feeling jealous of his friend altogether. If Elmley had had possession of Swati such would've been his anxiety – lest she betray him, or unman him, or simply ignore him – that he would've felt compelled to send photographs of her posing naked to a suitable publication, 'Immaculately Beautiful Asian Babe Wives', if it existed.

No, Shiva had never seen his wife naked. At the very outset of their relationship – shortly after all the sticky ceremonial of their marriage at the Neasden Temple, he'd attempted to unwind her sari in broad daylight in the doubtful privacy of their new sleeping quarters. She'd laughed in his face and bolted out the door. This wasn't a shy, modest or nervous laugh, a laugh that could at least be interpreted to mean that in the best of all possible erotic worlds she would've both happily and noisily allowed him to mount her while they leant against the soft concavity of the bizarre, zip-up, quilted-nylon-covered, freestanding wardrobe which in 1972 old Mr Mukti had thought would be the future of clothes storage. No. This was a brazen, in-your-face, how-dare-you-imagine-you're-man-enough laugh. A laugh that spoke volumes of sexual control and confidence. Which was strange, because so far as Shiva knew Swati had only had one partner before, her wayward cousin Jayesh. It was this liaison that accounted for desirable and highly eligible Swati being available at all, and further explained why her parents agreed to her marrying a young man as compromised as Shiva Mukti.

13

When their lovemaking did eventually begin, a pattern to it very quickly arrived and then became as securely set in stone as any erotic temple-carving; save for the fact that no self-respecting erotic stonemason would've troubled to depict a scene of such stasis. In the double darkness, beneath the duvet, Shiva's index finger whirred back and forth over Swati's clitoris as if it were glued to a joyless buzzer, while two of his minor digits scuttled in and out of her vagina. After a half-hour or so of this she would either orgasm, feign orgasm, or at least become sufficiently aroused to allow him to enter her; and by now, terminally frustrated, Shiva required only two or three strokes before he died. Uhn! After Swati became pregnant the penetrative aspect of these earthworm encounters in the loamy gloom of their marital bed disappeared altogether, and was replaced by a couple of cursory tugs with her slim fingers, as if Swati were a bored temple maiden milking a not so sacred cow.

Shiva, who'd spent his early twenties romping like a small brown satyr through a sylvan glade of Caucasian flesh – ginger-freckled, mole-bedizened, golden-furred, blue-veined – had always assumed that when he finally settled down with a good, high-caste Indian girl (and this assumption persisted throughout his brief marriage to Sandra), he would discover as yet undreamed of sexual pleasures, lovemaking of an ancient and contorted athleticism of such a high order as to make him weep with the sheer joy of being alive. He'd taken it for granted that the good Hindu girls – the Reenas and Lakshmis he'd shared honey pakoras with, and chased squealing through the shrubbery at family gatherings – would, while he was away at medical school, have been sequestered in the upstairs bedrooms of their parents' bland, suburban semis, in order to receive instruction in the subtlest – and yet most extreme – methods of bringing pleasure to their future husbands. In the meantime he'd had to endure the seemingly limitless willingness of white girls for all manner of odd couplings: for cunnilingus and fellatio until his chin was rubbed raw and his penis was scoured out; for stinky sodomy; for the occasional whipping; for anything – in short – that could conceivably turn them on.

But his older male cousins had, it transpired, been lying when they told tales of the astonishing delights and infinite joy of their own marital beds. This was – Shiva realised with the terrible acuity of a man sentenced to a lifetime's imprisonment on hearing his cell door slam behind him for the first time – the brave, silly face that these men put on the manner in which they were compelled to live, with, all things being equally fertile, their wives' bellies rising and falling with all the serenely indifferent power of the sea.

But Shiva didn't even get that. He didn't even get the respect which still accrued in his community to the father of a large and tumultuous brood. Once Swati was pregnant with Mohan it was all over so far as she was concerned – how else could he interpret her passivity? And when Shiva came to consider the whole shape of his life – and those of other British Hindus of his generation and class – it struck him that he and his wife were in the very vanguard of social change, breasting the sluggish demographic current, as they advanced into the placid pool of population stagnation, their son held out in front like a small lithe float.

If only the same could've been said of his career, if only Shiva had been in a psychiatric vanguard as well, then at least the disappointments of his home life would've been counter-balanced. But his career – which in its initial stages had accelerated with all the pokiness of a little red Alfa Romeo

– had stalled at St Mungo's. St Mungo's where the dimly lit corridors smelt so suitably bad; St Mungo's where the staffing levels were so low that Shiva found himself fitting straitjackets on to his own acute patients, as if he were a bespoke tailor of psychotics; St Mungo's where the lobbies and waiting rooms were hung with placebos of watercolours. St Mungo's where Shiva saw his patients in a cold stone niche, so that it was no surprise when they thought he was a gargoyle.

He thought they were as well. The man with the white onion head, filiform hair dangling over his swollen forehead; the man with the top lip which bulged in such a way as to suggest that he'd managed to swallow his own bushy moustache; and the woman – just one of many – with the face harrowed by distress, who had great furrows dragged down her cheeks by the clanking, clattering machine of her auto-destruction; and who yet, perversely, continued to inscribe perfect Cupid's bows of lipstick on her unloved and unlovely mouth. This was the human material he had to work with, and it was hard for Shiva to mask the contempt he felt for them. Not that any of his colleagues saw this for a second – outwardly Dr Mukti was exactly the same conscientious, hard-working physician that he'd been as a junior doctor and then a registrar. But internally he burned with the injustice of his job title. Consult with whom, and about what? Surely not with this human rubbish, dumped outside his door in their plastic-bag clothes? What could such a consultation really be like? Do you want voices or tremors? Tachycardia or incontinence? Mania or the inability to sit still in a chair because I've prescribed you a tranquilliser so strong that it's turned your muscles to meaty jelly?

In the first year or so of his appointment Mukti had tried. He'd taken copious notes and worked late into the night, labouring over the minutiae of these 'consultations'. In departmental meetings he argued about funding and made himself a nuisance with the Trust's administrators. His energy appeared inexhaustible – for he was but a human vehicle driven hard by the demon of ambition.

Soon enough Shiva Mukti understood that there was no point to any of it. He might bone up endlessly in the hope of encountering cases of Capgras syndrome (strangers taking on the identities of the sufferer's family members), or De Clerambault syndrome (peculiar to relate, this deluded woman is passionately adored by the current French Foreign Minister), or even epidermozoophobia (subject is infested by sea lice, or the parasites of still more exotic animals), but the harsh fact of the matter was that the vast majority of the patients who walked through his doorway – or were man-handled, or even steered – were endlessly inventive – but for all that painfully repetitive – schizophrenics.

Schizophrenics, with their metaphor-free descriptions of labyrinthine conspiracies, alien abductions and kraken jailbreaks; schizophrenics, with their tiresome grandiosity and their even more annoying self-deprecation; schizophrenics, with their gurning and their craning and their stooping to scope out hidden listening devices hidden underneath Mukti's desk; schizophrenics, who, like mad mendicants, are always among us, and who – Mukti was still a good enough and honest enough psychiatrist to admit – he could do very little for.

Sure, he could palliate and he could section, he could ensure that the outreach team was up to speed and that the poor devils didn't self-medicate themselves into total oblivion, but he couldn't cure them – that was up to God or gods, fate or the Fates. And if it was in the hands of a deity then it was a jocose one, who in disposing of their souls observed the same rule that was commonly applied to very bad gags, namely the Law of Threes. A third of them were untreatable, a third could be medicated into a shambling semblance of normality, and the final third would spontaneously recover.

Schizophrenics – what could Dr Mukti possibly do with them that was original? After all, there were whole research institutes taken up with the problem, as well as therapeutic communities staffed solely by dedicated professionals; as fields went this was a crowded one, with little left to graze on. Besides, all parties were in agreement now that, when the breakthrough eventually came, it would be a pharmacological one. No shrink-of-all-trades such as himself was going to make a significant contribution. There was no novel way of talking to people who believed that by picking their scabs they healed them, just as there was no revolutionary diet for those who thought that all foodstuffs were prepared deep down in the insect mines of Minroad.

How Shiva Mukti wished he had been practising in an earlier era, when the psychiatric field was yet to be enclosed. When across the open savannah of mental disorder ranged small bands of nomadic doctors, bagging whatever prey they could. Then no one had the temerity to stop any qualified man doing exactly as he pleased. Hypnotism, electricity, water jets – whatever took your fancy could be turned into a perfectly respectable therapy. Hell, Freud himself had even championed the curative properties of cocaine, administered in huge injections, for the treatment of drug addiction! And for that matter, how would Freud's own 'talking cure' have fared had it been introduced into the current age of anxiety, with its pill-pushing practitioners in vassalage to their pharmo-corporate overlords? No doubt the Viennese would be tarred, feathered and run out of town on a couch-shaped rail. Even in the 1960s – when Shiva was a little boy, barking his shins on Kenton fences – the likes of R.D. Laing and Zack Busner were able to get away with denying that schizophrenia was an organic disease at all.

To think of Laing, out there on the periphery of London at Shenley – that industrial-estate-sized assembly line of aberration – taking LSD with patients who already saw far more than they wanted to, upon whom hallucinations were positively *wasted*, made Mukti's blood curdle with sour indignation. And that absurdity Busner! Not only did he run a bogus 'Concept House' in Willesden, but he also egregiously marketed an 'enquire within tool' – The Riddle – which sold so well that the fat fraud was able to afford the substantial detached house in Hampstead where he resided to this day. Busner – who anyone would've supposed to have utterly compromised his reputation with such antics – had even appeared on celebrity game shows, mouthing his asinine catchphrase: 'Well, we're not helping anybody sitting here, are we?'. And yet despite – or, more upsettingly, because of – all this, Busner had been allowed to resurrect his reputation again and again. It was almost as if the medical establishment, rather than being personified as a courtly, reserved, silver-haired figure of uncommon rectitude, were instead a credulous slack-jawed hebephrenic. Even now, aged seventy, Busner still retained his consultancy at Heath Hospital, sitting like a fleshy plug on top of a geyser of younger psychiatric talent. Busner, who, like an eminent jester, still pranced about the wards of the hospital, smiting the unfortunate inmates with his pig's bladder full of hot airy chutzpah.

Of course Shiva Mukti knew this was an unlikely device – the pig's bladder full of chutzpah. Because although he never let himself formulate the thought – best that it remain inchoate, or he'd be stuck fast in stupefying bigotry – it was obvious that Busner was a Jew, and as such he must have access, if not to illuminati who ensured his advancement, at any rate to a number of sympathetic friends in very high places, who made certain that he maintained his position.

There was no Hindu old-boy network in the Royal College of Psychiatry, or if there was it wasn't one that had seen fit to extend a helping hand to Shiva. Anyway, it was next to impossible to imagine what such a thing could be like, given that there were as many different kinds of Hindu as there were gods in the Vedic pantheon. Hinduism – Shiva both ruefully and proudly acknowledged – didn't even begin to exist as a self-conscious body of religious doctrine until the twilight of the British imperium in India, and it wasn't like these monotheisms, a pyramid-selling operation whereby a god with a big stick flogged humble acolytes their own little sticks. Oh no.

Shiva supposed there might be some Hindus who identified with the zealots who handed out leaflets at the Neasden Temple, and who urged the normally peaceable inhabitants of North-West London to get on a plane, fly to Delhi, switch to an internal flight, land at Varanasi, get in a taxi and go and level a mosque with their own bare hands. However, he couldn't connect these people with the kind of steady assistance that Busner and his people had received for their entire working lives.

So, Busner perched in his eyrie of an office, up on the tenth floor of Heath Hospital, only swooping down to deliver a prestigious lecture at the Royal Society of Ephemera, or attend a book launch, or even appear on television once more but this time as a respected leonine head, who could talk so that the viewers understood him just enough to imagine themselves clever and well informed.

Busner looked out over the verdant Heath and was able to picture himself – or so Shiva pictured him – as the lord of an urban manor, surveying his own parkland. Meanwhile lowly Mukti crouched in a monoxide-filled trench, buried in a dugout of dusty brick and phlegmy mortar; a subaltern who served impossibly long hours in the front line of the mental-health war, with no recognition, either from his colleagues, society, his patients, or his family. His father had always seen fit not to mention the fact that Shiva was a psychiatrist, communicating his disapproval by the sneaky – yet devastating – tactic of showering with praise the work of heroic surgeons, who – to hear old Mr Mukti talk – chopped bits out of people and replaced them with bits chopped out of other (dead) people, as casually as if they were working in a quick-fit exhaust centre.

Still, all of this – the lousy patients, the crumbling infrastructure, the inadequate pay, the lack of status – would still have been bearable, were it not for the fact that Zack Busner, far from ignoring his lowly colleague, was intent on cultivating a relationship. If Busner had blanked him, Shiva could've happily loathed him from afar, but at a conference on affective disorders the older man had, seemingly, made a point of coming up to Shiva and introducing himself. 'You must be Shiva Mukti,' he'd boomed. 'I'm your neighbour up at Heath Hospital . . . Zack Busner.'

How Shiva despised the way Busner left his name until the very end of his sentence. Typical of the famous, always prodding and probing the nerve of recognition in their interlocutors, as if they were veritable dentists of celebrity. 'I know,' Shiva replied.

'We get a fair few patients up at our place who rightfully belong to you – I expect you have the same problem?'

'Yes.'

'I expect you also take the same approach that we do, and treat them by way of saving on paperwork.'

'Sometimes, or if they appear particularly intractable or difficult we send them up to you.'

'Ha-ha,' Zack Busner said rather than laughed. 'I think I'm going to like you, Mukti.' And he rolled and unrolled the furry end of his mohair tie while grinning broadly. Shiva registered that Busner also had that idiotic trait of the truly conceited, believing that any falling off from the sycophancy usually manifested by those who danced attendance on him represented a deeper, more sincere level of respect.

What a prat, Shiva thought, taking the flaccid white hand that was offered to him. He moved away from Busner into the herd of mental-health professionals, who bumped and re-volved around the cavernous precincts of the conference venue, and who – to a jaundiced eye – looked not unlike those who they professed to treat.

Part Two

Busner began to send patients to Shiva Mukti for second opinions – and this the younger psychiatrist could not believe. When he went out into the vestibule where onion head and his pals awaited, he'd find stranger strange faces, new boys and girls who'd approach him respectfully, the folders containing their medical notes held out in front of them like buff warning flags. The missives Zack Busner had appended to the front of these disease narratives were short, chatty and – to Shiva's mind – oddly gnomic.

Dear Shiva –

This is David Juniper, he's under the impression that he's a creosote man, both made out of creosote and with a mission to bring creosote ideas to the rest of mankind. He's undoubtedly schizoid, but he also has certain atypical symptoms consistent with hormonal imbalance. I happened to see your article in the BJE[1] and thought you might be prepared to venture a second opinion in this case.

Thanks in anticipation,

Zack

Unbelievable! The barefaced cheek of the man! The utter, self-serving, lazy, presumptiously familiar, self-regarding

1. *The British Journal of Ephemera*, Issue 19, Vol. 73.

nerve. Shiva Mukti looked at Creosote Man, who stood in the odd position – like an upright foetus – that was typical of the pseudo-Parkinsonism associated with antipsychotic medication. Creosote Man looked back, his eyes devoid of anything, their irises like brown rings of creosote around the rotten black cores. 'You'd better come in,' Shiva said reluctantly and eventually.

Back inside the niche Shiva sat down while Creosote Man shuffled in, his marsupial paws clutching at the chilly air. To occupy himself during this mini-marathon Shiva flicked through the notes, scanning the completely stereotypic case history. Could – he dared to wonder – Busner be sending him this patient in all sincerity because he'd absorbed the full import of the paper and genuinely respected Shiva's views? Shiva thought back to the content of 'A Note on Endocrine Imbalance and Symptomatic Embellishment in Schizreniform Disorders'. His argument had been simple but potentially highly disruptive of traditional diagnostic techniques.

Moffat, a doctor on one of the medical wards, had asked Shiva to take a look at a young woman who'd presented initially with weight gain and terrible acne, but who had then returned as an acute admission suffering from left-sided headache, drowsiness, nausea and double vision. All of these were consistent with pituitary apoplexy and Moffat had assumed a tumour was involved. However, scans had revealed only the tiniest of intercranial haemorrhages, altogether insufficient to account for the patient's severe symptoms.

But she was also – and this explains why Moffat had called for Mukti – flamboyantly delusional, clamouring that a mighty pillar of sugar was being slowly extruded from her vagina.

'What d'you make of it?' asked Moffat, a diminutive ginger

ball of Scottishness, as he stared down at the pallid spotty pillows of the patient's cheeks.

'How big will the pillar of sugar be?' Shiva asked the young woman conversationally.

'Ooooh,' she moaned, 'a mighty size indeed, surging up and over, arching at the top, then plummeting back down to the earth, and in its sides will be drawers for things and people and places.'

'Is it a good thing, this pillar?'

'Good as gold,' the woman fluted, clutching pleats of hospital sheet between all of her outstretched fingers, 'and twice as neat for boys to play with.'

In the next bed along a woman whose bulging eyes and jaundiced skin marked her out as a gall-bladder patient clutched a fluffy teddy bear to her scrawny neck, while directing an appalled expression at Shiva.

'Her command of English,' Shiva said to Moffat when they were standing in the grotto alongside the nursing station which housed a fire extinguisher, 'is really very good.'

'Well, she's an English teacher by profession,' Moffat replied. Shiva flicked through the notes – the young woman had no history of mental disorder.

'What do you think you'll do with her?'

'Unless you have any other ideas I'll start her on a gluco-corticoid.'

'Mmm . . .' Mukti mused. 'Perhaps the glucose has some-thing to do with the sugar pillar.'

'What?'

'Only a thought, but maybe she realises – not at a conscious level, but in some portion of her brain – that she has a sugar deficiency. It's just a hunch, but I've seen patients in the past who've presented with symptoms including a psychotic fixation on a particular substance, and when it's been provided they've been alleviated.'

'You think this will happen here?' Moffat looked at Shiva quizzically.

'We'll see, after all you were going to give her the glucocorticoid anyway. Keep an eye on her and tell me if the pillar retracts.'

A week or so later Moffat called by Shiva's niche to tell him that the pillar had indeed retracted. 'She's now entirely lucid, it was uncanny, as the solution went in so did the pillar.'

'Well, as I said, I've seen similar things happen before, but this is the most dramatic example so far. Perhaps . . .' He had decided to like Moffat on the sound basis of expediency. 'We should write a paper together. You could handle the physiology, I'll do the psych stuff. I've got a friend at the *BJE* who might consider it.' Moffat agreed at once to this and as an afterthought Shiva asked him, 'What's the prognosis for the pillar woman?'

'Oh, she's a gonner, I'm afraid. There was a tumour after all, just not in her head. Shame, nice woman.'

But Creosote Man was a different matter altogether. Unlike Moffat's patient he had plenty of form – the disease came off him in palpable crime-waves against sentience, each of which threatened to leave Shiva Mukti pinioned in his seat. There were these and there were also the emanations of shit, the percolations of piss, the wafts of vomit – and worse. Creosote Man was as rank as a fox and as crazy as a stoat. He clucked and twitched while a steady stream of monotonous chit-chat about creosote issued from his letterbox-shaped mouth.

Creosote eh, what was that? A naturally occurring antiseptic – or was Creosote Man perhaps preoccupied with its wood-preserving capabilities? Shiva leant forward and tuned in to the radiophonic drone: 'Yellowy stuff spread it on yellowy stuff . . .' said Creosote Man. 'Doesn't soothe but helps. Get it from the bush, burn the bush, crush it, do it to make the creosote that gets put in the little brown bottles and sold at the old chemist's shop in Chittlington, the one at this end of the village, not the one by the pub.'

'Is that right?' Shiva probed.

'Comes in little brown bottles, hand-labelled, cheap at the price. You,' he said pointedly, 'should try it.'

'I might well do that,' the psychiatrist mused.

Close to the poor fellow smelt even worse: there was a putrid tinge braided with the other, denser stinks. He'd have to do a physical examination, he couldn't risk missing what was wrong, not with a referral from his arch-rival. How Shiva wished he had a nurse – or better still a decontamination unit – to deal with this one. But instead he stolidly pulled plastic gloves from the dispenser and expertly rolled them on. 'Now,' he addressed the reeking shell of a human being, 'I want to give you a proper examination, Mr' – he glanced at the notes – 'Juniper. Could you slip out of your clothes?'

He could do nothing of the sort. He required firm, strong hands to unlash trousers cinched with packing tape. He demanded a solid shoulder to lean against as he tottered out of the collapsed huddle of cotton and serge, he needed skilful goading before he could be detached from the wadded nylon which had formed a cast of his upper body. Then Creosote Man was revealed to be a knock-kneed and abandoned human scrap in a dank moleskin shirt. The smell of decay was now so strong that a passing nurse stuck his head into Shiva's niche to see if he needed any help. Together they laid Creosote Man face down on the examination couch and gingerly pulled up the shirt.

He hadn't been burbling senselessly about antiseptic, he needed some desperately. Dr Mukti couldn't remember seeing an infection this bad ever before. It was unthinkable that human flesh could be corrupted in such a manner, not right here, right now. This was a Fourth World infection, the kind that afflicts children made out of lolly sticks glued to beach balls, who can't make it to the nearest diseased water hole because they're blinded by trachoma.

Together Shiva and the nurse laboriously cleaned the foot-square raw patch and removed the blobs of pus. The nurse plied the antiseptic wipes, while Shiva used a pair of tweezers to prise off the septic divots of lint left behind after some earlier, ineffectual attempt at treatment. Creosote Man remained surprisingly calm, he kept still and merely muttered into the paper-wrapped headrest, 'One, two, maybe three coats will be necessary if you want to ensure all-year-round protection for wood with a rougher grain . . .' his breathy — and well-spoken — exposition agitating the paper so that it produced a kazoo-like vibrato to accompany his maunderings.

When they were done Shiva and the nurse got him upright. Shiva taped on a temporary dressing and sent the nurse to get a gown. Creosote Man persevered '. . . bought three bottles in the chemist's and a three-inch brush from old Mr Pindar the ironmonger, but it wasn't enough for the job, after all the fence runs the whole length of the churchyard and then there was the lychgate to consider . . .' while Shiva did the necessary paperwork for the admission. Moffat would countersign the section when Creosote Man arrived down on the ward. By rights Shiva should put him on the small psychiatric ward — but there was this jigsaw he was doing with Moffat, and maybe — just maybe — Creosote Man was another piece.

The following day Shiva went to see how his new patient was getting along and found Moffat in attendance. 'Did Busner send you this two-by-four?' He jerked his ruddy-duck head in the direction of Creosote Man.

'Mr Juniper? Yes, he's come from Heath.'

'I only ask because I have a suspicion that you're going to try and fit him into your little theory.'

'I don't see how.' Shiva bent down to look at Juniper's face, but the erstwhile Creosote Man appeared to be asleep. 'He has a comprehensive history of schizophrenia, I hardly think his creosote delusion is to do with a creosote deficiency.'

'You say that, Mukti, you say that, but the fact of the matter is that when he arrived yesterday he was perfectly lucid. He then deteriorated throughout the night – although I now believe that may have been the fever caused by the infection, and we gave him – so to speak – a second coat after ward round this morning. He picked up considerably and was able to tell me all about himself, it seems he's a church warden up at some village in Buckinghamshire.'

'That figures.'

'Well, what d'you make of it?'

'Nothing at all,' Shiva said moodily. 'The English teacher had a sugar deficiency all right, but she wasn't mad to begin with. If you're saying Juniper went on and on about creosote because of the infection on his back, how the hell do you explain this' – he brandished the case notes in Moffat's face – 'twenty-year history of mental illness?'

'I dunno, but it could be that this symptomatic embellishment happens regardless of any underlying pathology. Anyway, I'm only suggesting that you keep an open mind.'

'I will. And why don't you keep an open bathroom,

Moffat? Look at the state of this man's feet.' Shiva pointed at the blackened heel poking from between the sheets.

'Oh I know,' Moffat sighed, 'but you try getting agency nurses to bathe these patients – we'd be better off hiring zoo keepers.'

Later in the day Shiva sat beside David Juniper's bed. 'How are you feeling?' he asked, his tone – as ever – perfectly pitched so as to convey dispassionate caring.

'Much better, thank you, Doctor,' Juniper replied. 'I think this bloody infection on my back must've quite turned my mind. Was I talking a load of rubbish when I came in yesterday?'

'Well, some of what you said was . . . how can I put it . . . inappropriate, but it all made perfect sense. You were attaching particular importance to creosote.'

'There's no mystery there, Doctor, I do use a good deal of creosote in my work, fixing up the church and so on.'

'Yes, yes, I understand, but when you saw Dr Busner at Heath Hospital – you remember seeing him? – you were convinced that you were a "creosote man" with a calling to bring knowledge of the stuff to the whole of mankind – as if it would prove to be our salvation.'

'There may be no mystery there either, Doctor . . . Doctor . . .?'

'Mukti. I'm the consultant psychiatrist here at St Mungo's.'

'I mean to say, I'm a lay preacher as well as the church warden, p'rhaps I got my duties mixed up in the feverish state?'

'Perhaps,' Mukti mused.

'Mukti!' Moffat hailed him as he was striding off the ward. 'What d'you want me to do about Juniper's medication?'

'What's he been prescribed?'

'Heaps of the stuff – haloperidol, carbamazepine, quazepam –'

'Take him off it.'

'You can't be serious, I checked with Juniper's GP and he's as nutty as a fruitcake.'

'Even so, why not taper him off a bit, it's worth a try. Let's see what happens with his delusional symptoms. If they get bad we can whack it back up again, and anyway the poor guy could probably do with a shit – the amount of stuff he's on he can't have had a good one in months.'

'Isn't this course of action a little unethical, Shiva?' Moffat called after him, and even though Shiva quickened his pace the words kept up with him, flapping about his ears like admonitory bats as he regained the gloomy security of his Gothic niche.

Unethical. Waiting for him he found a severely depressed adolescent. Her eyebrows were pierced, her lips were pierced, her cheeks were pierced with industrial-style rivets, but her ears weren't. Shiva supposed this was because she considered this sticking point too prosaic. Shiva thought of the emerald he'd stuck in Swati's nose. It'd cost him three months' salary but was worth every penny – any lesser jewel would've looked tawdry set in her flawless face. The depressed adolescent inveighed against her white liberal parents, her dirty T-shirt was pitted with the tiny black-fringed holes of hash burns, as if she'd been peppered by .02-calibre rifle bullets. All Shiva felt like saying to her – if only to check her unforgiving flow – was that if she kept on the way she was going she'd end up in piercing hell. Piercing hell, where the demons would remove the nuts and bolts from her robotic face and feed her on to a long skewer. Piercing hell, where she'd squirm for eternity on Belial's barbecue, together with hundreds of millions of other dumpy adolescents. But instead he reached for his pad and wrote a note to a psychotherapist.

*   *   *

31

At the end of another long day, Shiva's skin crawled with the pins-and-needles prickle of his computer screen as it shut down. He walked through the late-afternoon hubbub of St Mungo's – the dinner trays slapping, trolleys clashing, mops slopping – and out of its grimy portals into the grimy twilight of the Tottenham Court Road. Down a narrow gully in the cliff face of the building, Shiva could see a biffed-about wheelie bin, and beside this lay a cardboard box. The lettering stencilled on its side – '100 PREMATURE TEATS' – seemed to him to cohere meaningfully with the single squashed orange on top of it. The psychopathology of everyday rubbish. By the tube station a small flock of street junkies were roosting, their flapping, ragged coats giving them the appearance of threadbare crows. Pickle them in methadone, Shiva bitterly ruminated as he barrelled past aiming for the ticket machines.

At home in Kenton the aunts and uncles were eating rice and dahl at the long table in the kitchen. White cotton stretched to transparency over scrawny brown hands as they reached out to ball grain and pulse, then folded into opacity as they potted the balls of food into their pink baskets of mouths. Uncle Rajiv chewed a chaw of pan, turning from time to time to the frosted-glass kitchen door, which he opened with a slippered foot, so as to spit expertly into the dark passage which led to the back garden. Swati, ethereal in a mauve sari, wafted from hunched uncle to bent aunt, refilling their grooved plastic tumblers with water from a stainless-steel jug. In the next room could be heard the chuckle-speak voices of the Simpsons and Mohan's answering giggles. Shiva sat and fiddled with his food, trying to imagine what it would be like to live in a home that didn't resemble a bus-station canteen. A home where Swati, Mohan and he would sit down to eat alone, the china plates set in front of them neatly segregated into compounds for meat, green vegetables and potatoes. White middle-class families always looked formally dressed to Shiva – whatever garish apparel they affected – when set beside the loose bundles of his own family.

After he'd eaten Shiva announced that he was going to take a walk around the neighbourhood. Although these walks were a recent development they aroused no comment, because Shiva was frequently absent – even when he was present. So far as Shiva was concerned he had no part to play in Mohan's bedtime, and the way the child ran himself down into uneasy sleep was just another example of Swati's lackadaisical approach to child-rearing. So, Shiva shut himself up in the tiny study he'd fashioned out of the old scullery. Here he would 'catch up on things'. Early on in his career Shiva had kept up, wading his way through journals, papers and books, laboriously cross-referencing malaise with theory with treatment, until his head spun in a whirlpool of supposition. But now . . . well, what? Surely these academic theories were only hessian sacks stuffed full of dry-as-dust language then thrust in the path of the great inundations of despair which afflicted real patients? As his thwarted ambition – like a deformed toenail – grew into the very quick of his soul Shiva had some moments of clarity: perhaps what was happening to him was more than simple burnout? Could he himself be a neurotic? But if so what could he possibly do about it? Turn himself into his colleagues, the thought police? Or pay someone less qualified and less perceptive than himself to sit in a room and think about his problems? For that was what – in the first and last analysis – such psychotherapies amounted to.

Or maybe he should reconnect with the Brahminical traditions his father had so decisively driven the bus away

33

from? Visit the temple more and offer to tote the gods on their annual bumpy perambulation. Or should he embrace the way of a sannyasin, casting off all worldly goods so that he could busk for enlightenment with a begging bowl? The idea was preposterous. Some of the aunts and uncles had the fussy and aloof neatness of the high caste, but Shiva felt himself – during his happiest moments – to have been sanctified by his contact with the earth, not defiled.

No, Shiva Mukti preferred to construct his own therapeutic regime, to sidle about the crescents and avenues of this North-West London suburb as if he were an electronic particle mapping out the contours of a giant cerebellum of green privet and red brick. He liked to saunter from cemetery to cemetery – Wealdstone to Harrow on the Hill, Harrow on the Hill to Pinner. Some nights he would venture as far west as Horsenden Hill, and, losing himself in the scrubby bushes which overlooked the Park Royal industrial estate, he'd feel touched by a quicksilver inspiration. Maybe – he dared to consider – maybe I am more potent than I care to acknowledge? And spying a furtive secretarial figure hurrying home from the Harvester Inn across the playing fields, he'd grab at the cord of paranoia that connected them. She turning, sensing his watching eyes upon her, as he crouched in the musty tangled thicket, where scraps of toilet paper were snagged on the trunks of silver birches like shitty little prayer flags.

And when orange dusk had become maroon night, Shiva Mukti liked to seek out obscure cafés, where he could sit unknown and unobserved. Shiva compared these interludes to those pregnant moments when the thermostat clicks and the fridge – which you've long since forgotten was humming – falls silent. A non-smoker, he relished sitting in the smoking sections of pubs and restaurants, sipping with his blueish lips on the brownish vapours which had so recently been inside other people's lungs. It helped him to think – and then again, not to think at all.

This particular evening, his head resting against the cool flank of a clunking trivia-quiz machine in the lounge bar of the Cruel Sea on Honeypot Lane, Shiva thought about Creosote Man – and Busner. How arrogant of the older psychiatrist to have sent this severely ill patient to him, without even troubling to give the poor man even a cursory physical examination. Could it be that Busner actually believed that Creosote Man's symptoms substantiated Shiva's ideas, or was it rather that he was toying with them both? There could only be one way to probe Busner – and even jab at him. Shiva would hang on to Creosote Man for the duration of his section – whatever the progress of his condition – and he would, in turn, send Busner one of his own patients for a second opinion. He had one in mind. Some psychiatrists – and Busner, Shiva knew for a fact, was one of them – had patients who they kept with them for years, transferring them from hospital to hospital as if they were treasured ornaments. And in a way they were, because they decorated the practitioners' pet theories. Shiva, however, didn't have any pet patients, he hadn't the leisure to walk them or the notoriety to feed them. In their place he had patients who were unhealthily fixated upon him, and who despite being exiled to the therapeutic gulags on the periphery of London – or even transported further afield – nonetheless returned to St Mungo's, homing in on Shiva's niche with the unerring accuracy of racing pigeons guided by instinctive internal voices.

Rocky, a six-foot-seven would-be Rastafarian, was one of

these. He adored Shiva with the pathetic doggy affection of a child bullied by its peers who is lent an ear by a sympathetic teacher. He was a classic schizoid type, alternating between severe catatonia and egregious mania. About every six months he went away for one, to Edgware or Friern Barnet, or some other echoing airforce base for the mentally ungrounded. For the rest of the time Shiva kept an eye on him through the hospital's outreach team. Rocky had a one-bedroom council flat on an estate north of the Euston Road, and he managed fairly well there by himself. The neighbours knew him and also knew that he was harmless enough. Shiva – although he couldn't abide Rocky – had nonetheless grown curiously protective of him over the four years that they'd been seeing one another. So much so that on a few occasions he'd visited Rocky's flat. There, Rocky had served him with milkless, sugarless, over-stewed tea in a diminutive spotted tooth mug, and while Shiva sipped dubiously at it, he recounted the history of the table-top standing stone which was the centre-piece of the living room. This was a votive object, a house-hold god, and even the source of its worshipper's moniker. 'It tell to me of its time in Babylon, brought outa Babylon carried into the holy land of Zi–on. It speak to me – the Rock.' Rocky's adoring gaze swung from his doctor to his namesake, which to Shiva looked suspiciously like a breeze block that had been hacked at with a crude adze.

'See here now, Doc-tor Mukti, see here now the 'scription on the Rock.' Shiva bent forward obligingly. 'What it say now, tell to me what the Rock says.' Scrawled unevenly across its rough surface was the legend, 'BABYLON 10,000 YEARS'. Shiva dutifully read it out. 'That what it saying!' Rocky grinned extravagantly. 'The Rock know its 'istory, thass why for it come 'ere now to speak troo me . . .' and on he would go, and on some more. Despite all the trappings of his breeze-block fundamentalism it would've been unfair to Rastafarians to number Rocky among them. Even though he had dreadlocks which gushed from his high forehead like jets of gingerish flocculent water, Rocky's grasp on the doctrine remained distinctly hazy, while use of the sect's quasi-sacrament – marijuana – sent him into still dizzier and more vertiginous spirals of delusion.

Rocky would stop by Shiva's niche on a weekly basis and extemporise reams of what he called 'prophecy'. Like many schizophrenics' Rocky's meticulously envisioned alternative worlds were unutterably prosaic, perfectly realised in all their fantastic mundanity, and like nothing else but themselves. It was as if – Shiva had reflected in the days when he still bothered to speculate on such things – the delusions of the disease were the very leaching away of the sufferer's imagination. And perhaps it then followed that it was the very ability of the sane to see the moon as a face that prevented them from looking too deeply into its craters-for-eyes?

But what Shiva Mukti also knew was that Rocky was a conundrum walking around inside a banality. With his great height, dirty combat fatigues, shambolic gait, gurning face and elemental hairdo, he seemed the very acme of violent craziness; yet he was, of course, statistically less likely to be dangerous than the mousiest of men. Any good psychiatrist would know this. However, after some idiot had misguidedly fed Rocky a few tokes on a joint the previous summer, the apostle of the Rock – firmly convinced that it was a behemoth of Satan – had attempted to preach to the two fat ladies of the Number 88 bus which was rollicking along the Hampstead Road. Since then his behaviour had taken a distinct turn for the worse. At the end of each month, when the stores of chlorpromazine Shiva had laid up in his muscles ran low; in place of Rocky's threatening – but harmless – ebullition, came episodes of genuine rage. He'd twice had to be restrained, and on the second occasion severely bit a policeman's ear.

Busner didn't know any of this. Shiva would send him Rocky, a humanoid time bomb with a frontal-lobe lesion which sent his serotonin levels through the floor. Send him Rocky along with a note reading:

> This patient displays an uncannily consistent ametaphoric tendency. His total inability to enact analogous or comparative speech modes called forcibly to my mind your 1978 paper 'Intentionality Refracted: Schizophreniform Disorders and the Re-embodied Poetic'. I've no real belief that anything can be done for him, but thought that the intervention of a more experienced and perceptive therapist than myself might nevertheless throw up some interesting insights which might be applicable in other cases.

This would be the kind of titivating obsequiousness – Shiva hoped – tailor-made to appeal to Busner's grotesque intellectual vanity. The older man would kick some sad hebrephrenic out of her bed and find Rocky a place on his chronic ward. Rocky would, obligingly, transfer his fixation to Busner and who knew what might happen then? Shiva Mukti could acknowledge that this was a test of Busner, a test of his credentials as a diagnostician, but in the murkier, St-Mungo's-like recesses of his mind, he hardly dared to admit that it was a far more primitive justiciary act – a trial by ordeal. If Busner neglected to map out those frontal-lobe lesions, he would be entering terra incognita, with the angry, maddened Rocky menacing him from its shadows.

So be it. Rocky was dispatched up the hill to Heath Hospital, while his capacious case notes were stuffed in the internal mail. Then Shiva waited for he knew not what, some sign or portent perhaps? A cloud of smoke rising up over the Euston Tower that would tell him his rival's guilt had been confirmed.

He waited and he treated and he palliated and still there was no news. He walked to the tube, was blown through it by the city's meaty breath and then walked home. The next morning it was suburbia's turn to waft him back on an exhalation of wet privet and fresh tarmac. Each journey felt to Shiva like another crease scored into the sagging skin of his ageing life. Mr Double – a patient so called, by Shiva, because of his extreme repetitiveness – came to see him twice, and then twice again. The detergent rain soaked the leaves of plane trees on Charlotte Street, soaked them until they dried up, fell off the branches and were mashed to urban loam by the hurrying feet below.

At home, in Kenton Park Crescent, the Mrs Muktis, together with the more active aunts and uncles, made preparations for Divali. Strings of fairy lights were uncoiled from their attic boxes, food was cooked in the kitchen, an ablebodied uncle was sent to the newsagent to buy sparklers and fireworks, Mohan's embroidered waistcoat was taken to the dry cleaner's. It was Shiva's part in all this to do the household accounts. This was the Hindu tradition, and, while it was more zealously observed by the merchant caste than by his fellow Brahmins, it still used to give Shiva a buzz when he was younger. The tallying of income against expenditure, and the calculation of how much the family could afford to spend, give away and prudently save had confirmed him in his role as paterfamilias. He'd even put the figures on to a computer spreadsheet, but this year he sat in his cubbyhole staring sightlessly at the blank screen, haunted by images of Busner thrashing about in the tentacular grasp of Rocky's dreadlocks. When old Mrs Mukti asked him how much they should donate to the Temple's fund this year, Shiva came up with a figure off the top of his hot head, hazarding that it might be a little more than the previous year's.

The Mukti family were becoming only too accustomed to Shiva's desultory moodiness and hair-trigger temper. He knew he lost it sometimes – slapping Mohan's stick-thin thighs when the boy pestered him once too often to be allowed a computer game – but what he wouldn't see was that his angry tension surfaced in other ways as well. Like a reserve of oil it flowed to the joint between every impulsive thought and ill-considered action, lubricating Shiva's hands and feet so that they shot off at unexpected angles. He knocked over mugs, stabbed himself with biros, and on more than one occasion lanced his thigh with a hypodermic.

A fortnight after he'd sent Busner Rocky, Shiva was sitting in the staff canteen lunching with David Elmley. The hinge designer paused, his mash-smeared knife held aloft, and pointed it at Shiva's hands. 'You've got a lot of cuts and scratches – what's the problem?'

'Oh I dunno.'

'Some people say minor accidents are always an expression of repressed rage.'

'I KNOW THAT!' Shiva exploded.

'All right, all right, keep your fucking hair on.'

Elmley went back inside his cottage pie, while his friend's

gadfly gaze flitted about the gloomy room, alighting here on a tarnished strip light, there on a greying face. Two tables away from the resentful duo a more than usually animated knot of healthcare workers was dining. They weren't in uniform, and Shiva recognised the Assertive Outreach Team from Heath Hospital. Presumably, he thought, they've been doing a client nearby and come in to get a subsidised lunch. He tuned in to their jolly-sounding banter, only to discover that it was nothing of the kind. A tall man with sallow, acne-scarred cheeks who was the team's psychiatrist said, 'I don't think you can entirely blame the old man, after all this guy was bloody huge –'

'And bloody mad,' put in a curly-headed blonde who Shiva could tell just by looking at her was the nurse.

'That's as may be.' The thin nervy black man in the regulation jeans-and-leather-jacket of a psychiatric social worker leant across the table brandishing an accusatory finger. 'But the fact remains that the patient is dead. Everyone knows it was Busner what administered the drugs, and I'll tell you one other thing that everyone knows for nothing, and that's that whatever the outcome of any investigation – not that there's likely to be one – he'll get off scot-fucking-free!'

Some of the others murmured in assent, while the shrink began talking in a serious, measured fashion about malpractice, its whys and wherefores. But Shiva wasn't really listening any more: at the mention of Busner a heavy hum had begun in his ears. He felt chilly and crossing his arms hugged himself the way people do in cold weather.

'What's up now?' Elmley was batting about his last few wayward peas.

'N-nothing,' Shiva chattered, 'I–I gotta go.' And leaving behind his own half-eaten lunch – chicken pie, craven cabbage, pusillanimous potato – together with his wallet, he scampered out of the canteen.

When, five minutes later, Elmley tracked Shiva down to his niche, he found his friend still shivering and turned that very particular shade of beige that brown-skinned people go when they're subjected to shock or sudden illness. Shiva was on the phone, speaking to a porter at Heath Hospital, a man who owed him a big favour over some wayward codeine. Shiva had – after swearing him to complete secrecy – easily obtained the shocking details of the incident.

Busner had been paged – because his senior registrar was unavailable – to deal with a patient who'd become violent on the ward. 'Fucking big Rasta geezer,' the crooked porter wheedled through the ether. 'I'd seen 'im round the place. Anyway he went completely tonto, took four of 'em to restrain 'im, then Busner slaps the tourniquet on an' bangs a hypo full of how's-yer-father into 'is arm without taking the torq off first. So, when 'e does the Rasta gets the whole hit in one go like. Maybe it wouldn't've done for another geezer, but they reckon this bloke wasn't too clever in the brain department – if you catch my drift, Dr Mukti.'

'M-meaning?' Shiva managed to mumble.

'Meaning that the word is that the Rasta 'ad an 'ead injury. I've heard at least two SHOs say Busner should've known about it. That, together with the botched shot, makes it look pretty bad for the old man, wouldn't y'say?'

Shiva didn't venture an opinion, he only reminded the porter of exactly how big his debt was, and that this intelligence was only part-payment. Then he broke the connection. 'What was all that about?' Elmley's lantern jaw dangled overhead in the dim light of the niche.

'Nothing,' Shiva said taking the proffered wallet.

'Funny kind of nothing, I'd say,' Elmley began, but then seeing Shiva's maddened eyes he went no further. On his way out he caught the considerably saner eye of the receptionist. They both glanced at Shiva's office door and winked, although what exactly they were complicit in Elmley had no idea.

That night the Mukti family were due to visit the Neasden Temple and then go on to the Ambika Sweet Centre in Southall. Here the oldest and youngest members would gorge themselves on sticky-sweet and gelatinous confections. Shiva got ready to go robotically. With every leaden step he took he became more convinced that the following day would see him arraigned in the dock with Busner, accused as an accessory before the terrible fact of the old charlatan's fatal malpractice.

The Muktis had a seven-seater people carrier, which Shiva kept in the garage alongside the house, together with his father's old gardening equipment and various other tools – drills, spanners, plumbers' rods – that he didn't know how to use. Dilip Mukti's passion for gardening and DIY had been a calculated affront to his own Brahminical background, but his son had reverted – in this respect at least – to being the kind of man who factored his ignorance of the material world into a little religion of superiority.

For a long while this evening Shiva sat behind the wheel of the car and listened to the muffled rumble of the engine as it reverberated against the windows, while the blue-grey of its exhaust fumes obscured the dusty coils of hosepipe and rusting spades. But the sheer practicality of suicide defeated Shiva even before he could get started. How exactly would he remove the nozzle from the hose and attach it to the exhaust pipe? Surely it was far too long for the fumes to pass along it? And if so what could he use to cut it? After five minutes he got out and, coughing and spluttering, opened the garage door. The aunts and uncles were already waiting on the driveway, their best saris and suitings peeking out from beneath the hems of their utilitarian coats. His mother chuckled indulgently as Shiva emerged in the blueish cloud, but Swati only pursed her perfect lips.

At the temple Shiva made the required obeisances, but it was a ritual of the nervous system alone. Looking about him at the orderly clutter – bowls full of petals and fruit, niches crammed with statuettes of the deities, the altar with its pantheon of prancing gods – it dawned on him how hatefully deranged he now found all the manifestations of his religion. He no longer – if indeed he ever had – believed in the social system that kept the individual Hindu bound into this be-wildering and internally contradictory cosmology. Without regular practice to sustain him and Brahminical disdain to insulate him, the whole tinkling, chanting, incense-burning, food-offering palaver of the festival washed over Shiva. What was it, this Hinduism, with its peasant ornamentation decking out a philosophical tradition of ancient sophistication? Surely only the obsessional activity of a group mind a billion strong? And what of his people, the British Hindus, who knelt hands clasped, eyes wide all around him? What were they, save for the largely silent legions of a mostly covert diaspora? How many tens of thousands of his coreligionists had ended up here, having come in search of good fortune, only to find themselves marooned along the flight path into Heathrow Airport?

Shiva tried to imagine what the Busners' religious festivals might be like. He had hazy memories of Jewish schoolfriends' homes three decades ago, and these he married to the odd bits of information he'd acquired in the intervening period, the half-assimilated facts and deeply maintained demi-convictions which satisfy any literate man that he knows the full truth of something he does not.

While the pandits chanted and their congregation responded, Shiva Mukti, perversely, turned his inner eye not upon moksha, but the Busner family, who were gathered around a long, high table of mirror-shiny mahogany. Busner and a number of adult sons who wore Busner horror masks all sported austere, black-silk skull caps. While an even larger number of grown-up daughters, together with Mrs Busner, had on pompadour wigs as large and red as buses. As Mrs Busner served up food of extreme blandness – watery soup, pulpy noodles – Busner himself read from a tiny scroll which he withdrew from a leather box tied to his upper arm. A giant minora blazed in the centre of the table, its candles guttering in the afflatus of his reverence; slushy, guttural words of Yinglish, which, with their straightforward petitioning of the one-and-only God for greater fees from private patients, and all-round career advancement, were readily comprehensible to Shiva.

In the bowels of the Busners' vast house – which, as conceived of by Shiva, resembled Dracula's castle made over by Ivana Trump – a telephone rang with old-fashioned mechanical vigour. A daughter went to answer it and returned bearing the Bakelite organ in a kidney dish. Busner took the call while nervously rubbing the phylactery strapped to his arm. Yes, yes and yes, he said into the receiver, and then after a pause, No, no and no. Of course I'm sorry – his voice rose – we're all sorry, my family are observing the festival of Yom Kippur this very evening, we are in a most grave state of atonement. I understand . . . thank you.

Busner placed the receiver back in its cradle with exaggerated caution. Raising his glass of ruby-red, sickly sweet wine he toasted the family: The Royal College will be taking no action against me, and as for the GMC, Levy has agreed to put a word in. Praise be to God! The other Busners all cried spontaneously. Praise be indeed, Busner answered them, and draining the last of his wine he hurled the tiny crystal glass at the back of the fireplace – in the grate of which an impressive coal-effect gas fire roared – where it exploded with a loud 'POP!'. Following his lead the rest of the family threw their glasses, white bread rolls, side plates, and whatever else came to hand at the flames. Ach-ach! Oy-oy! Mrs Busner sneezed and cried, holding diamond-ringed fingers to the coiffured sides of her elaborate false hair. Such fun we'll be having tonight, oy!

'Shiva?' Swati laid a henna-tattooed hand on his arm. He'd come to in the Ambika Sweet Centre on Southall High Street without any concrete knowledge of how they'd all got there. Leaving the temple and driving through the tiger-striped London night had the character of a dream. But there was Mohan, standing on tiptoes by the big vitrine of a counter, pointing out a pile of honeyed balls covered in silver leaf to the preposterous proprietor, a huge fat fellow who wore a filthy white kurta and sported a foot-wide, waxed moustache. And there were the uncles clustered around the pan stall in the corner, chatting with the pestle-pounding pan wallah. And right in front of Shiva was his mother, razing a stupa-shaped cone of kulfi to the ground, while his wife was still saying, 'Shiva – are you all right?'

Shiva felt himself islanded, an atoll of self-consciousness in the cacophonous he-said-she-said, multilingual sea of socialising British Asian families. Sawing through the food-smell-thick atmosphere were the serrated chords of a Bollywood musical's soundtrack, the chorybantic excesses of which were being projected over the assembled heads on to a wide, ceiling-mounted screen. Such was his painful self-absorption that every time his wife expressed tender solicitude Shiva was able to convince himself that this was the first time in years she'd done so, so, with self-pity pricking his eyes, he covered her slim filigreed hand with his plain square one and said, 'No, yeah, of course, work, y'know, I'm distracted.'

But nothing could've been further from the truth. Late that night after the last of the rockets had lifted off into suburban space and the final sparkler had spluttered, and Mohan had been wrestled into his bed, and the aunts and uncles and old Mrs Mukti had shuffled off to their rooms, and Swati – with her characteristic yawn that was part sigh and part yelp – had rolled over on to her side and fallen off the precipice of consciousness, Shiva was left perched on the acute crag of his own anxiety, feeling the darkness about the house seething with the spirits of the dead. His father came plodding along the Crescent from the direction of Stanmore Bus Garage. He was wearing his trademark white lungi and tweed jacket, a copy of *The Times* furled around the umbrella tucked under his arm, as if it were a missile with a warhead of ephemera.

Dilip Mukti may have turned his back resolutely on the religion of his forefathers, but he could never entirely escape it. When he was old enough to grasp it his son was amused by the polytheistic cast of his father's rationalism, and infuriated by the seeming hypocrisy which allowed him to consult the astrologers at the same time as he reviled them. 'We live in a heliocentric cosmos, Shiva,' Dilip would tell his son. 'These fools with their ancient bloody nonsense, they not only believe the sun revolves around the earth, they make a damn fine living out of it as well!'

47

Dilip Mukti was an enthusiastic adherent of all scientific theories of social development, Positivism, Marxism, Keynesianism — it mattered to him not one jot where on the orthodox political spectrum these prophets stood. All that was necessary for them to be incorporated into his world view was that they explain human phenomena in terms of physical processes. It was the same for the pure sciences, Darwin, Einstein, Heisenberg, Crick and Watson — these miraculous men had battled with the dark spirits of the irrational, so the reverence he accorded them was sacred in its intensity. While he was alive, a corner of the master bedroom served as a shrine for Dilip's deities. Plaster busts of Marx and Comte, photographs of Friedman and Keynes, volumes of *Das Kapital* and *Origin of Species*. He would even perform his own perverse, secularised pujas, reading aloud key passages while laying newspaper clippings underneath the swollen brow of the German-Jewish philosopher.

Now, in death, Dilip Mukti refused to be frightened away by the fireworks of Diwali, and instead chose to sit on the street sign at the corner, picking fastidiously at his well-manicured nails, while steadily berating Shiva for his professional misconduct. 'Truly, Shiva,' he droned, his nasal, Hindi-inflected voice carrying through the flap window and into his son's wakeful ear, 'this is a bad business, a very bad business indeed. There is no question in my mind but that you are responsible for this man's death. In pursuing this absurd vendetta you have extinguished a life. You were always an impetuous fool and now you've turned out to be a homicidal one as well.

'This man has been telling me of your involvement with him and how you sent him to see this fellow Busner. This man,' he gestured towards the privet hedge at his rear, 'is very aggrieved indeed, and who can blame him?'

'I'm bad, Dr Mukti, real bad.' Rocky crashed through the hedge and stood twitching and jerking next to Shiva's dead dad. 'I knows fine well I was mad an' that, but now I'm dead an' there's no come back like. You oughta be shamed, man. Badly.'

Shiva was shamed badly, shamed and sweaty as Swati moaned and Mohan whimpered and the wintry dawn streaked across the rooftops. But more than shamed he was scared. If Busner was going down he'd take Shiva with him – that much was certain. Shiva considered not going into work, but that would be pointless or worse. To absent himself now could only be construed as an admission of guilt.

There was no further news of Rocky's death that morning; a morning which culminated in Shiva attempting to mould the slippery cognition of a woman whose face looked as if it had been modelled in clay by a forensic pathologist. Nor was there any news of Busner's professional misconduct at lunch, which Shiva ate alone, pretending to read a dog-eared back number of the *BJE*. The blackout continued the following day, most of which Shiva spent trying to divine the truth – or otherwise – of a little girl called Mauretania's assertions that her aunt was sexually abusing her with a hairbrush.

But far from being calmed down, Shiva was convinced that this was only the lull before the storm hit the frail vessel of his foundering career, reducing it to matchwood. Sleep retreated from him and cowered in the corners of the bedroom. Hollow-eyed and shaking, he rode the tube in from Kenton in the mornings as if he were a passenger on a ghost train, accompanied by the shades of his father and Rocky. Rocky, who in death had assumed a fluency and command of English that drove him irresistibly towards poetic trope and descriptive hyperbole. 'De train burrows troo the city like a worm troo a corpse,' he swung low on his strap to mutter in Shiva's ear, 'like a maggot lay its eggs, so de tube lay its commuters in de very 'eart of tings. Now wha 'bout you, Doc Mukti man, you gonna change into a fly? You gonna buzz off or what?'

After three weeks of these guilty visions Shiva was about ready to give into his fear and contact Busner, the Royal College, or even the General Medical Council itself, and blab the truth about the duel the two of them were fighting. But he was saved by his antagonist, who, displaying a flair for timing which left Shiva quite breathless, chose this moment to expertly parry the low blow that had been Rocky, in the form of a letter.

Dear Shiva

I should've written a couple of weeks ago concerning the unfortunate events surrounding the death of your former patient Gerald Neville (Rocky's given name) but I had to attend a conference in Lodz, where I was giving a paper on endemic Slavic misery. Doubtless you've heard what happened. Suspecting that there was a closed head injury – since there could be no other explanation for Rocky's extreme emotional lability and heightened aggression, I had to have him restrained while a sedative was administered, so that it was possible to do a scan. Sadly, it transpired that he was suffering from advanced arterial sclerosis (probably a side effect – although I mean no criticism of your treatment regime – of the large, intramuscular doses of chlorpromazine he'd been receiving), which led in these stressful circumstances to a fatal heart attack.

Shiva, I'm sure that like me you've long since rejected

the institutionalised amorality which passes for professional ethics in orthodox psychiatry. I also feel certain that you, like me, feel every patient's distress as if it were that of a close family member. Please join me, therefore, separated though we are by time and space, in taking a few moments now to shed some tears for Rocky.

Shiva felt like a purpose-bred rat, lugging an enormous tumour around a vivisectionist's cage. He took a few moments to shed some tears on his own behalf, confronted as he was by such awesomely manipulative guile. But there was more:

On a more prosaic note, doubtless the same rumours that have reached me here at Heath concerning your involvement with the patient have – albeit in another form and with different particulars – filtered down to you at St Mungo's, and featured me in the lead role. I'm sure it doesn't need saying that I THINK WE UNDERSTAND EACH OTHER VERY WELL INDEED – Busner hadn't, like some borderline letter-ranting personality, shifted to capitals, they were Shiva's eyes which capitalised – AND THAT THERE'S NO NEED FOR US TO INVOLVE ANY OUTSIDE PARTIES IN OUR THERAPEUTIC RELATIONSHIP.

He knew! And he knew that Shiva knew, and he was saying . . . yes, he was saying that this was now between them alone, that he wouldn't give or expect any quarter, that he was prepared to fight it out. 'Which is why' – the letters telescoped back to lower case – 'I'm sending you another of my patients for your expert opinion.' Shiva now registered a grinding, clicking noise coming from the vestibule, which sounded as if a human-sized insect were feeding on the scrap of carpet tacked across the uneven old parquet.

His name is Mohammed Kabir and he has one of the most concrete and evolved delusional structures that it's been my privilege to witness in over forty years of clinical practice. Elements of Kabir's delusion are commonplace – the paranoia, the stress on a conspiracy derived from ethnicity – but the sheer elaboration of the scenario, including the attention to the details of chronology and location, mark this out as an exceptional case. I DON'T DOUBT – the significant capitals returned – THAT WITH YOUR THEORETICAL ABILITY AND CLINICAL EXPER-TISE YOU WILL BE ABLE TO GET TO THE BOT-TOM OF THIS.

I remain, as ever, your friend and colleague,
Dr Zack Busner.

Shiva slid the letter underneath his Zovirax Cold Sore Ointment blotter and pen set (complete with plastic box compartment for notelets) and picked up the buff folder of medical notes. For a man with an exceptionally ramified delusion they were surprisingly thin. Kabir, who was brought up in the Birmingham suburb of Moseley, hardly seemed to have been ill in his life at all. There were the usual childhood ailments and glandular fever as a young man. Then there was a break of several years during which he'd had no contact with a GP. And then there was this – this ebullition of mental illness. A total catatonic breakdown during which he remained at his parents' house, bedridden and incontinent for two months, followed by a series of disordered wanderings. Kabir had been found hopping and skipping along the hard shoulder of the M25 at South Mimms, armed with a hunting crossbow with which he was trying to shoot out the surveillance cameras. He'd been apprehended on the tow path of the Manchester Ship Canal, where he was terrifying some teenagers by forcing them to listen to a hellfire Koranic sermon. He'd handed out flyers in the Market Square at Harrogate, each one blazoned with the words 'GOVERNMENT PLOT'. Finally he'd fallen into Busner's orbit, another screaming meteorite plummeting through urban inner space.

Shiva peered around the door into the waiting area. Kabir was a tall, fair-skinned man of Pakistani origin – or so Shiva assumed – who sat splay-legged but arms crossed on the most upright and uncomfortable of the available chairs. His head was long, tapering to a sharp chin, which gave it a conical appearance. His ears were the razor-thin fins of this falling rocket. His heavy-lidded brown eyes zigzagged back and forth across the scrap of carpet as if compelled to follow the pattern they found there. The grinding and clicking Shiva had heard was the noise of Kabir's white even teeth as they struggled to impede the ceaseless chatter issuing from his full pink lips. The maniac wore tight blue jeans and a purple bomber jacket cut from some silky synthetic fabric. One of his trainer-shod feet was tapping so vigorously that it appeared – to Shiva – as a white blur.

He stood and listened for a while, catching the occasional word – stake-out, implant, transmitter – interspersed with fragments of Arabic prayers. Then Shiva broke the bad spell by clearing his throat, 'Erm'. In one sickening lunge Kabir was on his feet, his sharp chin stabbing at Shiva. For a second Shiva thought, this is it, this is how it ends, with Busner's unsubtle assassin, but the tall quivering man made no move towards him apart from extending his hand, which Shiva took. It felt like holding a fleshy, recently struck tuning fork. 'I hope you can help me, Doctor,' Kabir said in a refined voice. 'I don't see how I can be mad, although everyone assures me that I am.'

In the niche Shiva seated Kabir, took up his biro and pad, and began to note down the delusion.

The following day Elmley came by and Shiva took him for lunch in the canteen. 'Busner sent me another patient,' he told his friend over battered cod and broken chips.

'Oh yes.' Elmley tried to look worthy of being a confidant. 'What's this one like?'

'I think I can say with some justice that I've truly earned my bones –'

'Made.' Elmley abandoned confidant for nitpicker. 'The expression is "made my bones".'

'Whatever.' Shiva waved his fork airily. 'Expressions aren't what concern me, it's facts, and the fact is that while this man Kabir presented with all the classic symptoms of a chronic cyclothymic condition, he in fact has nothing of the sort.'

'Really?' Elmley knew better than to ask for a clarification of terms – this would emerge.

'Yeah. He was high as a kite, talking nine to the dozen, told me he couldn't help this because of the transmitter they'd implanted in his brain. But despite this he was able to give me a sustained, coherent account of what had caused his disorder.'

'Which was?'

'After a brilliant school career he gained a place at Cambridge when only seventeen. While studying philosophy and physiology he was approached by a recruiter from MI6. A second-generation immigrant, with all the insecurities that go along with it, Kabir was flattered by this attention and responded to their overtures. So much so that he was eventually inducted into the Service, and during his long vac he underwent a training course at their HQ which ended with him being awarded a commission.'

'But why,' Elmley objected, 'why did they want this guy?'

'Please, David, remember this is a delusion according to Busner and several other doctors. Anyway, after he graduated he was persuaded by these spooks to take up a graduate research post in Tel Aviv. Israel! I ask you, a British Muslim kid studying in Israel! Still, this is what he says happened, by day he got on with confusing rats or whatever, and by night he infiltrated one of the many groups of militant Israeli Arabs, a group with connections to Hamas extremists.'

'Do you want the end of my cod?' Elmley prodded at it with his fork. 'I can't be doing with it.'

'No, I don't want your fucking cod. Tell me' – Shiva glared at him – 'is none of this grabbing you at all, do you not find this story remotely interesting?'

'Well . . . yes, I do, it's only that you've told me plenty of your patients' delusions before.'

'This one is special. Frightened out of his mind, this poor kid is pushed by his controllers to penetrate these groups deeper and deeper. He's taken to clandestine gatherings deep in the Occupied Territories, where men in keffiyehs brandish Kalashnikovs and swear death to all Jews and American imperialists. He's made to swear terrible oaths and agree to participate in terrorist attacks. Then, the inevitable happens –'

'The Palestinians discover he's a British agent?'

'No, no, worse than that, he's being brought back across the line of control one night when he's captured by the Israelis. Far from supporting the story he gives to his inter-rogators, British intelligence deny all knowledge of him, and he's left to fend for himself in the hideous bowels of the Mossad torture cells.'

'Steady on –'

'Steady on nothing, David. If you don't believe such places exist you're living in a playground world where the biggest danger you face is knee socks that won't stay up! No, they torture him, these thugs, and, of course, eventually they break him, he confesses to everything they suggest and he's sentenced by a kangaroo court to centuries in jail.'

Shiva paused, partly for effect and partly so that he could exercise his paranoia. Elmley looked in the wake of Shiva's wary eyes as they scrutinised the whey faces of junior doctors who were flirting with canteen workers wearing nylon snoods. Elmley wondered if Shiva ever thought nowadays of his first marriage. If only he hadn't bowed to his parents' pressure and David had – mysteriously, impossibly – been in the right place at the right time, then perhaps he would be sharing a bed with the ineffably beautiful Swati? He imagined that her heavenly body made no impression on the marital mattress at all, and that when she arose it was as if a desiccated dandelion head had lifted off in a spring breeze . . .

'Are you listening to me?'

'Yeah-yeah.'

'I'm saying that not content with torturing the man and committing him to almost certain death in their foul gulag, the Israelis then leave him to be grossly assaulted by hardened criminals.'

'C'mon, Shiva, you're really going too far now, anyone listening to this would think you were an anti-Semite!'

'It's a delusion, David, remember that, a fucking delusion. So, he's buggered remorselessly and Kabir begins to get ill, very ill, so ill that it looks as if he's going to die. Then, at long last, Her Majesty's poodles do come sniffing around. Apparently it's one thing to abandon one of their own to torture and disgrace, but to let him die would cause all sorts of inconvenience – the family are getting suspicious and they're on the verge of going to the press. One minute Kabir is in the depths of an Israeli prison, the next he's being stretchered on board a British Airways flight out of Ben Gurion Airport, hours later he's back at home in Birmingham. The government, naturally, deny everything, he receives no official acknowledgement of what's happened, no follow-up treatment, and certainly no compensation. And that, my dear David, is what the National Health was presented with. That was what Busner got walking into his consulting room. So, what d'you think he does?'

'Well, I mean, I'm not . . . but I s'pose . . .'

'C'mon, David, you haven't listened to me bang on about psychiatry all these years without learning something.'

'Well, I s'pose he diagnoses him as schizoid and puts him on medication of some kind.'

'Exactly! Exactly – that's exactly what the swine does, and that's what every other shrink who's been in contact with the poor man has done. Not one of them has stopped to consider the validity of his story, not one has bothered to do a proper physical examination, not one has troubled to get in touch with the family and find out their version of things. Busner, with all his posturing over the years about the existential-phenomenological approach to mental disorders, is the very worst, the most pernicious and self-serving of hypocrites, but the rest of the so-called healers who've had contact with this man are almost as bad –'

'But you have.' Elmley prompted the inevitable bout of self-congratulation, eager to get it over with so he could choose between apple crumble and a small, cellophane-wrapped plate of cheese and biscuits.

'I most certainly have, oh yes indeed I have. I examined Kabir, I did his bloods, I called his family and spoke to them, I even fought my way through the bureaucracy of the Foreign and Commonwealth Office – what a euphemism! – and you know what I found out?'

'What?'

'It's true! It's fucking true – all of it!'

'All of it?'

'Well, when I say all of it – as much as I could find out. MI6 are hardly likely to admit the whole extent of their disgusting behaviour to the consultant psychiatrist at St Mungo's. But the facts are there for the finding – all Busner and those other charlatans had to do was pick up a phone. Mohammed Kabir has a British Army commission, and although he was circumspect with his parents, they still had a pretty good idea what sort of work he was doing. As for his mania, that was so readily explicable that Busner's failure to spot it is tantamount to malpractice – the man has syphilis, full-blown bloody syphilis!'

David Elmley took his time in responding to this tirade. It wasn't that he didn't necessarily believe Shiva, or that he was unimpressed by his detective work, but the self-righteous – almost fanatical – vehemence was difficult to take. From his – admittedly lay – perspective, it seemed as if Dr Mukti was manifesting all the symptoms that he attributed to these patients; and, as with them, Elmley suspected the cause to be quite other to the obvious one. 'Um, Shiva,' he cautioned, 'are you suggesting that this Kabir fellow was infected with syphilis by the Israeli prisoners? What about the transmitter thing, you said he told you he has a transmitter implanted in his brain. What's that about?'

'I'm not making any claim about the Israelis – I've got no proof; nor have I had it directly confirmed by the secret services that Kabir was working for them, they'd hardly be secret if they had. But look at it this way, suppose you'd been through what he has? And suppose you ended up as he has, wouldn't the idea that your tormentors had planted a transmitter in your brain be entirely reasonable – rational even?'

'So what're you gonna do?'

'What am I going to do? Why treat him, of course. Moffat can look after the venereal infection, I'll see if I can ameliorate the dementia; although frankly I think our chances of bringing him back are pretty small. Then there's the question of compensation to be considered.'

'Compensation?'

'Why certainly, after all someone has to be made to pay for this.'

When he said this Shiva was thinking of the Ministry of Defence, but when he returned to his niche and lodged himself – like a lifelike carving of a worried deity – in its plaster confines, his sense of triumph and clarity of purpose began to waver, distort and then transmogrify into the most monstrous of suppositions. Surely it was the crudest of tactical thinking to presume that his enemy's enemy was his friend? At the very least – knowing full well that the man had syphilis – Busner had sent him Kabir as a way of wrong-footing Shiva's diagnostics, and at the very worst – exactly as Shiva himself had intended with the unfortunate Rocky – Busner was trying to assassinate him, employing the psychotic as a remote out-of-control weapon, a dumb bomb, an unmanned bio-mechanical drone.

Or was he being ridiculous? Granted, Busner's treatment of Juniper, the Creosote Man, had also been neglectful, but even after the infection on his back cleared up Shiva's own diagnosis had hardly been borne out. Once Juniper's medication was tapered off, lo and behold! The church warden turned out to be seriously disturbed after all. True, he wasn't in as extreme a condition as when he'd initially presented, but he remained convinced that it was his mission to bring creosote to an untreated – and decaying – world. After three weeks on Moffat's ward, Shiva had to arrange for Juniper's transfer to a mental hospital near his Buckinghamshire home, and so far as he knew it was there that he still languished.

Now there was Kabir, another case that might have either a medical or a psychiatric aetiology, but although Shiva felt certain that his senior colleague was toying with him, gloating over his discomfort, he also knew that to show any sign of the confusion he felt – let alone to acknowledge what was going on between them – would only be to invite disaster. No, he'd write back to Busner in the correct manner – with clarity and calmness – betraying none of the anxiety that plagued him.

Part Three

Dr Zack Busner stood at his office window staring distractedly past the massive trapezoid bulk of the west wing of Heath Hospital towards the green parkland that reared up beyond it. A fine rain was falling, shading in the houses in the surrounding streets and fizzing on their rooftops. Busner's gaze wandered from the window to take in the well-ordered interior of the office itself. An entire wall of neatly shelved books – everything from Aquinas and Adler to Szasz and Zoroaster – three mono-lithic filing cabinets full of case histories and medical records; on the remaining wall space hung the three clay 'imaginary topographies' by Beuys, given to Busner by the grateful artist after he'd treated him for a drug psychosis in the early 1970s.

Yes, order was good, mused Busner, order was productive. In the heady days of his Concept House and the origination of the Quantity Theory of Insanity, Busner had taken entirely the contrary view. Then his life – like his mind – had been characterised by a wilful disregard for all categories, all classifications, all systems. But with advancing age – and the chaos of his home life presenting quite enough of a problem – he'd come to value whatever clarity he could obtain in the murky waters of mental healthcare. 'All there is,' he was fond of lecturing his students, 'is the here and now. That's all we have and we must make of it what we will.'

As if both to support and confute him in this contention,

Busner's unrivalled collection of coprolites, which had once ranged hither and thither over every available surface, now massed in an orderly array on his desktop, surrounding the computer as if it were an alien spacecraft impounded by a platoon of fossilised shit. Meditating on the objective and the definable brought the Great Man back to the matter in hand, the letter he'd received that morning from Shiva Mukti at St Mungo's. There was a ward round beginning in a few minutes, and, while there was no necessity that he join it, Busner rather felt that he ought. Mukti had sent him another patient for an opinion – as he knew full well he would. He'd read the first part of Mukti's letter – concerning Mohammed Kabir – with considerable interest, but why not encounter Mukti's new referral unprepared, like an *espontáneo* leaping into the ring to confront an enraged bull, armed with nothing but his wits and his hastily removed jacket, with which to cow the creature? The idea of this pleased Busner, and a thin smile seamed his full and froggy features, while a plump hand went to the end of his mohair tie and commenced, dexterously, to roll it up, as if it were the tongue of some immensely specialised creature, a psychiatric predator, evolved so as to feed off the bombinating flies of psychosis. He turned as abruptly on his heel as was possible for a man in his late sixties and left the room. Behind him on the desk Shiva Mukti's letter glowed with the intensity of its author's rage:

St Mungo's Hospital
Department of Psychiatry

Dear Zack

I'm writing to you concerning Mohammed Kabir, who you very kindly sent to me for a second opinion. What a richly rewarding case this has turned out to be. I have no desire to criticise your treatment of Kabir, but I have to report that your diagnosis has been superseded following my examination of him. Far from being an advanced case of hypomania, it transpires that Kabir's condition may – in a large part – derive from late-stage syphilis. I discovered this with a routine blood test. Further, while it may have been considerably elaborated, the essence of what Kabir says is true. He has been a serving officer in the Army, and he was engaged, in Israel, in some kind of undercover work.

I have no wish to offend your personal sensibilities, but I've a duty to pursue Kabir's case with the authorities, and to that end I'd like to include your name on any correspondence. I will, of course, keep you informed of any further developments.

It's becoming quite a to-and-fro between us, because I also want to take this opportunity to ask you for another second opinion. You should've received the case notes of a Mr Tadeuz Wadja who's been a patient of mine for the past couple of years. Wadja is a Polish émigré of fifty-seven, who until recently was employed as a health-and-safety officer. Wadja has no symptoms of major psychopathologies, except for a bizarre and pronounced form of echolalia. I say bizarre, because rather than echoing the speech of others, he exactly and entirely repeats himself, while otherwise observing the rules of normal conversation. In a sense it would be wrong to label this man with any pathology at all, since apart from his own discomfort, his family's bafflement and the irritation of strangers, there is no functional impairment. However, Wadja has energetically investigated his own condition and unearthed a copy of your early paper, 'Times Two, Repetition as Iterative Cognition', with predictable results.

In short, he's asked me to send him along to see you, in the hope that with your superior grasp of the psychology of cognitive dysfunction you'll be able to help him. I've only to add that, should Wadja prove neither interesting nor fruitful for you, please don't hesitate to send him straight back again. I know how annoying an annoying patient can be.

I remain yours, etc,

Dr Shiva Mukti.

To call 'Mr Double' as Dr Mukti had dubbed him 'annoying' was a dangerously irresponsible understatement. Mr Double was enraging: five minutes in his company would've had Albert Schweitzer chewing the keyboard of his organ. The man was a psychic leper, bits of whom flaked off on all those he came into contact with. It wasn't the echolalia per se that was to blame, it was the way that Wadja responded to it. He bridled, he jinked, he hesitated – he tried every possible tactic to outwit his own rogue mind. A sample exchange with him might go:

How're you today, Tadeuz?

– OK, OK, I – I guess-guess, tryingt'doalittlemore work on this, have you noticed – tryingt'doalittlemore work on – oh shit – this, have you noticed – oh shit. It hurts, damn it! It hurts like hiccups, damn it! Like hiccupsdamn-damn.

– Have you been taking the pills I prescribed, Tadeuz? I think their sedative effect might help you.

– Took two – took two. Sorry-sorry. Took two – took two. Sorry-sorry. Jesus, I can't stand this – I read in the paper this morning that the Jesus, I can't stand this Home Secretary . . .

And so it went on, with the inevitable histrionics. Shiva had tried cognitive therapy, he'd prescribed a galaxy of pharma-ceuticals, he'd even attempted the fullest, most sympathetic engagement with his patient that he could muster. He'd become involved with Wadja's home circumstances, which were predictably dreadful. There was an obese and angry wife; an obese, fanatically religious mother; and two grown-up children, who, like fat native-born cuckoos, refused to leave their immigrant nest.

Initially, Shiva dared to think that there might be a productive aspect to Wadja's disorder. That just as Busner, his nemesis, had whittled his misshapen patients into the rungs of his career ladder, so Shiva would take Wadja – chemically muzzled – out to fashionable literary salons, where the Pole's uncanny ability to repeat great tranches of his own dialogue would impress highly sexed women poets with its Beckettian absurdity. Later they'd wrap themselves around Shiva, reciting Symbolist stanzas with a mounting rhythm until they came with a great howl. Or so he'd fantasised, because he was soon forced to acknowledge that there was nothing remotely seductive about Wadja, echolalia or not. His appearance didn't help. His great red-and-white cube of a Slavic head, with its iron-filing crest and its façade scaffolded with burst capillaries was set on top of broad shoulders from which dangled frightening mechanical-grabber arms. The idea that this runaway train of a man had ever been responsible for enforcing safety standards was ridiculous, especially when you considered the drunkenness.

Ah, the inebriation, that little detail which Shiva had forgotten to mention in his letter. He hesitated to label Wadja an alcoholic, both for reasons of cultural prejudice – Shiva assumed that all Poles were subject to heavy drinking – and also because, despite the fact that he glugged slivovitz and gargled overproof vodka, it could be explained as an understandable act of self-medication.

Down the pub with his cronies, Mr Double's cut-and-pasted reiteration passed for ordinary intercourse. He felt – as he explained to his therapist – 'liber–liber–ated–ated'. The odd condition that caused him to repeat fragments of speech – the 'uhs', 'ers', 'whats' and 'yuhs'; nonce words 'really', 'actually', 'terribly'; and even phrases 'd'youknowhatImean', 'at the end of the day' – marked him out as simply another of the chaps down in his cups so deep that the walls of the vessel bounced back his cries. But Shiva also knew full well that Wadja was violent when drunk, and that when he lost control it happened suddenly and completely.

Forgotten? Was it altogether credible that Mukti had omitted to mention such an important aspect of his patient's malaise? Wasn't it more likely that he hoped Wadja would be drunk when he turned up at Heath Hospital (a journey taken on Shiva's initiative rather than his own), so drunk that if Busner displayed any irritation – or worse, weakness – Wadja would attack?

David Elmley had taken to probing Shiva Mukti with unsettling regularity about his interactions with Busner, but Shiva confessed nothing to his friend, any more than he admitted it to himself. Instead he waited and he brooded, snapping at his colleagues, yet continuing to prove so exemplary in his dealings with his patients that none of them thought anything of his behaviour save that he was overworked. When the inevitable news came – in the form of a note from Busner's senior registrar, Kevin Whatley – Shiva found himself strangely relieved. So, he thought, as he scanned the sparse communication of Busner's injuries at the hands of the maddened alcho–echolalic – it has truly begun. Busner cannot now deny that this is a duel to the death – any more than I can. I've drawn the first blood, now I must expect the most extreme retaliation.

Shiva armed himself with a hypodermic syringe loaded with enough chlorpromazine to stop a berserker on phencyclidine. He got Maintenance to install an angled mirror on the wall outside the niche, so that he could see who was waiting in the vestibule by glancing up through the transom. As he stalked the warped and gloomy corridors of the old hospital Shiva would periodically revolve on his heel, so as to catch any assailants in the act of launching their attack. He was sure that matters were now so serious that to expect Busner to behave chivalrously and stick to their agreed choice of weapons would be folly. No, the next time the wily Jew struck, he might be wielding a nurse, an auxiliary, or even another psychiatrist. To have a chance of survival Shiva must expect trouble from any quarter at all.

Only days later, when he'd absorbed the full import of Whatley's note, did Shiva stop to consider if things had gone too far. Whatley's description of Busner, spreadeagled on the floor of the ward, while a baying Mr Double tried to stuff pieces of The Riddle into his mouth, was pitiful as well as painful. Two of Busner's ribs were cracked, and the jaw that had uttered a thousand self-satisfied pronouncements had been dislocated. He'd taken indefinite sick leave, but his colleagues assumed it would be permanent.

But what pulled Shiva back from the soft brink of sympathising with the old man were the very feelings that had driven him to this extreme course of action in the first place – now hideously reinforced. What influence could mere sympathy exert in the face of these howling and atavistic imperatives? Shiva, his moustache twirled to savage points, his war elephants in full array, confronted his enemy on the ancient battleground of honour, ambition and hatred. The more he reflected on the way the situation was developing, the more he appreciated its justness. His father had been profoundly wrong to reject his own heritage. What possible sway could the febrile, girlish theories of the nineteenth century exert over Brahmins from a virile tradition that had lasted for five thousand years or more? Theories that were – Shiva could not forbear from noting – the intellectual needlework of those supremely effete casuists, the Jews.

Zack Busner lay on the chaise longue in the small dressing room adjoining the master bedroom of his house on Redington Road, Hampstead. But really, considering his bulk and length, chaise courte would've been a better name for it. And as for master bedroom – Busner bitterly ruminated – why not mistress? He was bloody uncomfortable, his hairless white shanks stuck out over the end, their calves hung with bunches of untreated varicose veins. His fingers – crackling with arthritis – clutched at the wad of blankets and tried to position it more comfortably about his shivering form. I'm running a bloody fever, he realised miserably, although whether it was a function of the beating he'd received from Mukti's patient or an unrelated malady he was unable to say.

In the next room he could hear the reason for his exile, the thudding of cases and suit bags being pulled out from cupboards and wardrobes, the sharp swishes of silk dresses being overlaid by silk blouses, and the rattle of face paints being loaded into a make-up bag. Charlotte – the second Mrs Busner – was going on one of her 'little trips'. It had – Busner worried the emotional sore – been a profound mistake remarrying. He couldn't unwish the children he'd had with

Charlie, but if he could by some paradigm shift have managed to delete her from his life, he rather feared he might've done so. With what he now, too late, saw as yet more evidence of his unresolved Oedipal issues, he'd been foolish enough to imagine that by coupling with a woman twenty years his junior he'd acquire another lease of life. Charlie had been so bright and vivacious when Zack met her at that conference in Finland (entitled 'Endless Wastes and Limited Affect' if he remembered it rightly). Vivacious as well as seemingly caring. Busner had been nearing sixty and was worn out with work, marital wrangling and the interminable end-game of rearing adolescents. Charlie had offered her torso to him – complete with capacious shoulders.

How could he have foreseen that it would all end up like this? With him – now knocking on seventy! – sick and ill and condemned to thrash about on a dwarf couch because his unfaithful wife was off to see her Italian lover? Oh yes, she still had sufficient shame to dress it up as a work trip, and to style Massimo as just a fellow shrink with whom she was collaborating on a research project. But what kind of research could possibly require this ever expanding wardrobe? Only perhaps a comparative study aimed at assessing the impact of La Perla underwear – when worn by a statuesque forty-year-old English blonde – on two male psychiatrists, one half the age of the other.

Busner tossed and turned some more. No wonder it's impossible to get comfortable, he silently groaned, what with these great horns I'm sporting. And the consideration of this led him back once more to the arrogance and folly that had landed him on his back. To play at being a psychotherapeutic *espontáneo*, at my age and with my experience! Daring to examine a new patient without having adequately absorbed the notes – or even read them at all! No, Zack couldn't blame the debacle on anyone but himself.

Charlie swept into the room, her Junoesque form sheathed in costly tailoring and giving off the heady aroma of rapidly dispersing ambergris. She's covered in whales' intestines, Zack chuckled inwardly, and this thought did a little to dispel the pain of her blithe betrayal. 'Here's the schedule, Zack.' She rattled a piece of paper. 'Anna will get the children up and make sure they get off to school. All you have to do is cover for two hours in the afternoon when they're dropped back. You can manage that at least, can't you?'

'Well . . . ye-yes, b-but . . .' he spluttered.

'Come on now, Zack, they are your kids.'

'I know that, but can't you see the state I'm in, Charlie, I can barely speak because of this bloody jaw.'

'And whose fault is that?' she snapped. 'You shouldn't even be practising at your age, let alone trying to treat severely ill patients with no preparation.'

'But it's my métier, Charlie – it's what I do!'

'What you do now, Zack, is look after the children while I'm gone. Two hours a day and the nights – not too much to ask, I think.' She bestowed a kiss on his sweating brow so cursory that it felt only as if a fly had alighted there for a split-second, then she barrelled out of the door.

He could hear her yomping down the staircase, clacking across the hall and opening the heavy front door. A waiting cabbie was called to and in due course he manifested himself in the dressing room, Charlie's luggage arranged around his thick trunk like unseasonal leather fruit. 'Orlright, old feller,' said the cabbie, as he dragged a macho swathe of cigarette smoke and old-car smell through the residue of Charlie's perfume. But Zack Busner didn't reply: he turned his face to

70

the wall, sighed, and shut his large and furry ears to the clamour of his abandonment.

A week of childcare in his condition! At his age! It didn't warrant thinking about. Not that he didn't love Alex and Cressida, but their bickering and bouncing, and their breaking of whatever norms he tried to establish utterly exhausted him. When he was force-feeding the twins their supper, or trying to stop them watching too much television, or removing one's clenched fist from the other's yanked hair, he tried to recall what it had been like with his first batch of children, how he'd coped with them. Of course attitudes had been a lot laxer then. When the two boys were very small, the whole family had lived alongside the patients at Zack's Concept House in Willesden. Not that the residents were called 'patients' in those heady days, let alone 'clients', a euphemism Zack frankly despised. Nor were they treated as such, no matter how flamboyant or flagrant their behaviour. No, they all rubbed along together, patients, therapists, adults and children. There must've been ordinary domestic tasks, the milk-ordering, homework-supervising, bum-wiping basics, but Zack couldn't for the life of him remember how it had all got done.

It wasn't that he'd abrogated such responsibilities – far from it. He'd always prided himself on taking up his share of the burden, but somehow the atemporal nowness of domesticity – which was not unlike, he'd often had cause to remark, the freeform encounters of dynamic, interpersonal psychotherapy – wasn't conducive to any firm chronology. Was it David, his eldest, who'd chipped his tooth falling down the garden stairs, or was it Bruno? Had Bruno also been the bed-wetter? And when was it exactly that the two of them had been allowed to wear long trousers? Why was it that he had a distinct memory

71

of the two of them, their top lips already shadowed, and their bare legs not bare at all, but those of privately educated fauns?

Even now, as he laboriously concocted bowls of cereal and read aloud children's books which had become classics during his own parenting lifetime, Busner tried to reactivate the wonder he'd felt as a young father, watching those two billion neurones self-assemble into sentience, and the semblance of this on porcine little countenances, their snouts flanked by two downwards-curving tusks of snot.

But that evening, lopsidedly revolving the open-plan kitchen, his dressing-gown cord snagging on the fashionable fittings as he struggled to prepare the twins' supper with arthritic fingers, while his injured jaw ached and his fevered brow dripped, Zack Busner couldn't achieve any contact with his children's minds, let alone some exalted intimacy. In the current – and to his mind loathsome – idiom, he simply wasn't there for them.

Instead he was with his young colleague Shiva Mukti. These Indian families – it bore down on him – were so closely entwined and mutually supportive. Far from finding himself isolated like this, he would doubtless – were he Mukti – be surrounded by sandalwood-scented, sari-clad womenfolk, all vying with each other to ease the weight of his responsibilities, to serve and generally mollycoddle him.

As he sat, hunched up in his study and listening to the sickeningly mushy sound of old gums dealing with dahl in the next room – how could something so soft be so grating? – Shiva Mukti was plagued by visions of the repose his nemesis was doubtless enjoying. Visions which were rendered hideously concrete since he'd taken to smoking a joint in the evening. Shiva had done his fair share of drug experimentation when he was a medical student, a dab of speed for revision purposes, the odd beta-blocker to ensure calm during oral exams. As a junior doctor he had even skin-popped the tail-end of a shot of diamorphine which he was giving to some poor, old, pain-addled soul. However, he'd never truly taken to intoxication of any kind – saving speed and sex – until now. He'd had the hashish for months – it was given to him by Rocky in a lucid moment of self-preservation. Rather than throwing it away, Shiva chucked the nugget in his desk drawer and forgot all about it.

For a week now, each night after supper, he'd take up his station by the bins in the back of the garage. Looking out over the fenced-off pens of the suburban gardens, each with its bare-branched tree and nude trellis, he performed his elegiac ceremony. The harsh smoke rasped his sensitive membranes, while he offered up his profoundest apologies to the soul of the departed schizophrenic and in return was granted long moments of peace.

But once back inside, the kitchen lino reared up at Shiva and the strip lights strobed down on him. The aunts and uncles chattered as if they were the sacred monkeys of his grandfather's temple, mysteriously transported halfway around the world. So Shiva retreated to his study, and there shut up among the box files he tormented himself, night after night, with imaginings of his rival's peaceful convalescence.

Dr Zack Busner was staying at an exclusive sanitarium high in the Austrian Tyrol. While he lay in state on a divan swollen with satin-tasselled cushions, dimpled frauleins deftly de-crusted his cucumber sandwiches and fawning doctoral students played court. Wadja's attack – far from being a painful and disturbing violation – was a fresh opportunity for Busner to spin out his flimsy thread of theoretical speculation. 'Who fully grasps the interrelation between malaises?' Shiva could hear Busner address his adoring audience in his trademark oracular style. 'Was my assailant's peculiar echolalia an attempt to confront his alcoholism? Perhaps by repeating himself verbatim Wadja was enacting his obsessive-compulsive disorder? Or was the reverse the case, and Wadja, far from being a violent alcoholic, is rather drinking to medicate his own unipolar depression? It would follow that the repetition was an alarm being constantly sounded to wake him from incipient catatonia . . .'

Under the elastic influence of Rocky's rubbery old dope, Shiva's Busner scenarios expanded and their content became so plausible to him that he began to find credence in the false Busner's theorising. Shiva even jotted down his ideas with half a mind to examining them further at some point in the future.

Then, inevitably, the hash started mashing up his mind and Rocky's shade came hammering for admission to the house. The big dread shinned up the drainpipe and poked his head in through the tiny flap window of the bathroom. Sensing his presence as he took an uncomfortable late-night piss, Shiva looked up to be confronted by the grey-black face. Rocky's sad, slack mouth opened and the boring beseeching began. 'Got any jobs you want doing an' that, Doc? Small jobs, tiny jobs, there's no job too small for me. I'll clean your nails for ten pence, yes I will, clean 'em till they shine like new half-moons, yes I can . . .' And Shiva had to stare into the sad dead eyes then shut the window with great deliberation, rearrange his clothing and flush away the wasted life.

David Elmley sat in his flat in Tooting. It was on the ground floor of a 1930s block called Mimosa Court that stood twenty metres back from the High Road. Its foundation was fringed with broken glass and dirty grass, while four storeys up its flat roof supported the monochrome sky. Spiralling about Mimosa Court were the two strands of South London's genetic code, the endlessly recombined sequence of halal butcher's, international call centre and convenience store. While behind the horizontally leaded windows its inhabitants led their oblique lives.

To begin with Elmley had rented a room in the flat from a fellow student who had the tenancy. There were four of them in those days, each creating his or her little world in one of the cubic rooms which opened off the narrow hall. The cramped kitchen was in a continual ferment of experimental cooking, with pots of pulses bubbling on the grease-painted cooker and strange fruit drinks being concocted in the huge blender. Elmley could remember the carefully drawn-up rota – complete with coloured Dynotape strips for each flatmate – that was the focus of many an emotional confrontation. At the time these harsh accusations of wilful neglect and frozen postures of martyrdom felt like a descent into barbarism, but looking back Elmley recognised them as only the necessary flexing of young characters seizing up into the atrophy of adulthood.

Gone were the dusty pot plants and uncomfortable futon-and-pallet beds, gone were the battered and beloved collections of LPs, gone were the posters advertising art exhibitions in European capitals, and gone as well were the be-jeaned students who used to kneel on the worn carpet to roll their joints, stick their tongues in each other's pimple-fringed mouths, or play Go. One by one they'd moved on to be replaced by older versions of themselves. The tenancy devolved to Elmley, and when his business was doing well enough he stopped sharing. In the early 1990s he exercised his right to buy the flat from the Council.

It was the failure of his marriage to Michiko that pushed Elmley into this permanence. That he should've mistaken a business arrangement for a loving relationship was no surprise to Shiva Mukti, who understood that Elmley's effervescent and groundless enthusiasm made him see the basis of every union as fungible. Convenience or conviction, either one could be taken in lieu of the other.

Over the years Elmley did the place up tastefully but austerely. The walls were white, the original parquet flooring was stained black. Furniture and fittings were kept to the bare minimum and were mostly pieces contemporary with the building. While he was creating this environment Elmley took pleasure in it, but now it felt chilly and empty, its echt Modernism self-parodic.

After Michiko left Elmley convinced himself that he'd make a tolerable life for himself as a bachelor. He'd have his work and his flat, his cultural pursuits and his hobbies. He would travel. Far from being one of those single men who couldn't relate to children, he'd maintain close and loving relationships with his friends' offspring. How the put-upon parents would envy him. And when the kids grew older they'd find in Uncle David precisely the kind of trusted – and never condescending – friend, who can make all the difference when it comes to negotiating the choppy hormonal passage between child- and adulthood.

Unfortunately there weren't the friends needed to breed the children required for Elmley's ideal. He could've hung on to them – he thought – but the getting of friends was a trial. Forming a new relationship required spontaneity, a quality that Elmley possessed only in those flights of fancy when he proclaimed himself on the verge of taking up this, doing that, or buying the other.

Instead he remained stuck with Shiva Mukti. Shiva Mukti with whom he'd wandered the delapidated shopping parades and steel-cluttered playgrounds of Kenton. Shiva Mukti, who'd allowed him the leftovers – the odd grope or tooth-clashing snog – that fell from his own groaning board. Shiva Mukti, who he'd never really liked, but was stranded with on a makeshift raft of uneasy amity, the two of them sitting across from one another in the staff canteen at St Mungo's, both chewing over the increasingly institutional character of their relationship.

Godfather wasn't a polytheistic position, but Elmley tried to build up something special with Mohan. To begin with he'd zealously remembered birthdays, but Mohan was absorbed into the Mukti household and hardly acknowledged them. Then, as the years of married life had passed, Shiva seemed less and less inclined to break down the partitions between work, family, and what little social life he had. Elmley was confined to the work canteen and seldom invited back to the domestic one.

He would've loved it if the Muktis had come to see him in Tooting. He'd often thought of how he'd entertain them and the pride with which he'd display all the ordered intimacy of his happily solitary life. Elmley knew there was something not quite right about this, that it was the impulse of a grown-up boy needing to show off his toys. It didn't matter though, because even Shiva hardly ever bothered to make the long southerly voyage, and when he did it was only so he could sit eyeballing the floor in the living room and complaining about his lot. Recently Shiva had been accompanied on these late-night journeys by Rocky's hash. As they both puffed and Shiva fulminated, roasting in the hot coals of his fervid imagination every slight directed at him by Zack Busner, so his friend's brain fried in its bone pan. For want of anything better to think about, David Elmley found himself considering the feud as if it were personal to him, and with which – no matter how he tried to avoid it – he was closely involved. He discovered that it now made sense to him. His life had been a succession of failed connections; only in his profession did he find 180 degrees of predictability. Plainly it was up to him to solder together these sundered men, or else twist them apart irrevocably.

In this moment of hash-leavened perception it also struck David Elmley – with all the force of a religious conversion – that although he understood he must play an active role in the war between truth and falsehood, sanity and madness, good and evil, he didn't know which psychiatrist was which of these, or even whose side he was on.

There could only be one way forward, he concluded as he climbed back into his Elmley suit of jeans and checked shirt, and assumed the required expression of attentiveness. He would go and see Busner, he would wittingly become one of the man's assassins, then he would know what to do. Either carry his mission through to a grisly and near-fratricidal conclusion, or else once and for all rid the world of the inventor of The Riddle.

Charlotte returned from Venice looking as pleased with herself as a rapacious doge. Busner went back to work. At least his colleagues were pleased to see him. They tried to persuade him to take things easy, confine himself to less taxing teaching duties and preparing his forthcoming lecture at the Royal Society of Ephemera. But Busner felt that he must remount the bucking bronco of doctoring. With a peaceful old age out of the question, and his elixir of life being glugged down by Massimo, it was best that he get on with what he knew best. He sensed that if he faltered now it could be the end.

A patient called David Elmley was referred to him by a GP in Fitzrovia '. . . shows signs of near-acute depression, somatic disorders etc, also suicidal ideation. I would've sent him to St Mungo's but he says there could be conflicts with the staff there of a personal nature. He may need a course of psychotherapy or even short-term inpatient treatment.' Lantern-jawed, jug-eared, sparse-haired, Elmley had a thigh-slapping manner that was almost offensively inappropriate.

'I'm an architectural ironmonger,' he told Busner. 'I run a small business with my partner, I'm responsible for the hinges . . . and now . . . heh-heh, now I'm afraid it's me who's become unhinged . . .' He paused so that Busner could regurgitate a morsel of chuckling, but far from obliging the fleshy-faced psychiatrist only sat behind his oddly adorned desk, skinny ankles exposed by the inaction of his crossed legs, and apparently completely absorbed in contemplating the bright-purple socks he was wearing.

They sat like this for a full five minutes, the unhinged hinge designer and the mental locksmith. To begin with Elmley was profoundly uneasy, but gradually the force of Busner's impassivity began to impose itself on him. He became calm and began to consider all the forlorn by-ways and desultory cul-de-sacs that had brought him to this suburban breakdown.

Eventually, remembering that he had a powerful ulterior motive for being in this particular consulting room, he spoke. 'I suppose, Dr Busner, that before you can help me you'll need to know a little bit about my history.'

There was another long and profound silence; like an ankle-high relic, the sock received further devoted scrutiny.

Then Busner cleared his throat with a loud 'Erumph!' and replied, 'Not necessarily.'

That had been a week ago. Now Elmley sat and stared through the window at precise slices of Tooting and sky while fingering the plastic canister of pills in his pocket. All the way back from North London, as he pedalled his midget-wheeled bike past the parade of shops that linked Vauxhall Cross, Stockwell, Clapham, Balham and finally Tooting itself, peace had descended upon him. As kebab-joint sign after kebab-joint sign loomed up out of the gloom to take on the appearance of a severed human thigh with bone protruding, so David Elmley had grasped more securely that he had freely chosen to do that to which he was compelled.

A couple of days after that Elmley was back in the canteen at St Mungo's sitting in his usual position. Was the tightness he felt in his belly caused by the antidepressants Busner had prescribed for him or their side effects? Or was it the anxious anticipation – no matter how misguided – of betrayal? It was hard to tell – ever since he'd gone in search of help Elmley felt as if he'd entered a hall of mirrors, but when he looked into them he saw not his own face but the crazy masks of people at once familiar and strange to him. Had it been Busner who, like a spymaster, had 'turned' Elmley, or was it he himself who'd volunteered his services as a double agent? Whichever was the case, he now sat cutting his Cornish pasty into a series of cross-sections – as if preparing it for an anatomy class in which the function of diced potato in the life of the organism was to be explained – and stealing the occasional glance at his friend-cum-enemy across the table.

There didn't seem anything untoward about Shiva: he was eating his cheese sandwich with characteristic nibbles of his front teeth, while one blocky hand toyed nervously with a cruet, spinning it round and round on its base by its knurled sides. But if Elmley looked away and then looked back quickly, Shiva's lips curled into murderous, distended red flaps, bared to reveal fangs. He sprouted two additional pairs of arms, and in each of his four free hands he held a severed head. The cruet became a skull which he brought to his mouth brimming with blood. Elmley had to shake his head to dispel the terrifying vision and Shiva said, 'Everything all right?', to which he grunted non-committally and made a dismissive gesture.

Part Four

In the impressively large but slightly shabby lecture room of the Royal Society of Ephemera the atmosphere was subdued yet engaged. A medium-sized gathering of like-minded professionals and well-informed lay people sat here and there on the leather-covered seats. Through the tall narrow windows, from which velvet drapes had been pulled back, there was a view of the Mall and beyond it St James's Park. It was a clear evening and a very cold one. Frost dusted the tarmac, the trees and the grass like icing sugar, so that when a car crunched past it couldn't help but look shiny, tiny and decorative. Under these conditions Central London appeared about as magical as it ever did, save for when companies of centaurs trotted down Constitution Hill, or winged serpents thronged the sky above Trafalgar Square.

Zack Busner stood at the lectern summing up what had been a most wide-ranging lecture. Indeed, so eclectic had it been that the majority of his listeners, despite their own credentials, would've been at a complete loss if called upon to summarise it. He had set out the arguments of others and provided his own rebuttals; he had told several amusing anecdotes and exhibited a prodigious display of theoretical impedimenta; he had illustrated the lecture with a number of odd artefacts laid out on a baize-covered table and his assistant had projected a selection of curious slides. So well-pitched was the overall tone of the presentation that at any given time a sufficient proportion of Busner's audience was able to feel that pleasant state of intellectual arousal which passes for understanding. So it was that the lecture was judged an unqualified success.

There was, however, one member of the audience who didn't share in this communion, one head that didn't nod on cue, one mind that refused to accept the primacy – even for a few moments – of this psychological pargeting over the more durable – and believable – interior that it had constructed for itself. Shiva Mukti was hunkered down so low in his slope-backed armchair that from the lectern all that was visible of him was the perfectly centred crown of his lustrous dark hair. His lips moved, but his words were addressed to himself, introjecting a stream of remarks which were inaudible even to his immediate neighbours – glosses on Busner's remarks, disparaging observations and bitter imprecations. Shiva marked off the fingers of his left hand with vowels, and the fingers of his right with consonants, then he twisted them into painful, fleshy acrostics. His brown eyes, from deep inside their purple tunnels of fatigue and anxiety, hunted the lecture room, tracking down the members of the conspiracy ranged against him, who had gathered here – in this most august of institutions – to receive the latest briefing from their overlord.

After Busner had concluded and there'd been a smattering of applause, the audience rose and moving awkwardly between the chairs they formed small groups around small groups of canapés and trays laden with glasses of sweet and sour wine. These men and women displayed all the skill they'd accumulated from hundreds of such gatherings. The way they deferred to one another, the way they adopted poses both critical and disinterested, the way they listed to afford the passage of waitresses bearing trays, all of it suggested an unforced intimacy born of long professional association.

To Shiva this was nothing but smoke, fiendishly concocted cover for their nefarious activities. He shrank behind a Doric column, the sausage roll in his hand throttled to within a tenth of an inch of its original girth. The dust from the long maroon drapes and the burgundy carpet tickled his sensitive nose, while the companionable hubbub assailed his lank-lobed ears with wave after wave of encryption that was indecipherable on the spot, but which he felt confident he'd be able to crack at his leisure, if only he could manage to take in as much as possible.

He noted that each of the little groups had at its centre a Jew. Levy from the Institute of Psychoanalysis over by the projection screen, Berners from the Maudsley under the bust of Robert Burton, Weissbraun, Director of the Gruton Clinic, behind a baize-covered table, and of course Busner himself, still positioned by the lectern and receiving the attention of a small crowd of acolytes. And, as Shiva observed this sinister master of the Kabbalah directing his golems to commit more outrages, the full character of the conspiracy impacted on him. This was no mere Semitic mutual advancement pact, oh no. Just as Busner was intent on annihilating Mukti using psychotics as assassins, so the Praesidium of the Elders of Psycho-Zion was bent on controlling all of society, employing not only hapless isolated drones, but whole clusters of neurotic bomblets, which would lie on the firm ground of sanity for months – years even – before going off in the face of someone who handled them by chance. No, theirs was a campaign of carpet bombing the culture with manufactured mental malaises. The whole modern obsession with the disorders of the psyche was of their engineering, and was deployed everywhere you cared to look – in the advice pages of women's magazines, on daytime television, in the academic press and the self-help sections of high-street bookshops. The severely mentally ill – now released back into the community – were only these monsters' fedayeen, suicidal bombers, each primed to detonate in a crowded mall, sending shock waves crashing through the happy shoppers.

In this moment of unmasking Shiva Mukti found himself unmasked. He saw Busner turn from the group he'd been holding spellbound – a smooth man in a furry suit, a cadaverous woman with hepatitic skin, another woman, grotesquely tall, with pendulous, dirigible breasts – and beckon Shiva to join them, a broad smile playing on his froggy lips, Busner's manner was hammy, doubly contrived like an actor playing an actor. Shiva backed away several metres and collided with an ugly bronze of Alkan, the great founding father of the Implied Method of Psychoanalysis. He yelped, turned on his heel and rushed out of the room.

'Shiva Mukti,' Busner explained to his queer interlocutors, 'as skittish as a foal. Of course, I've had my eye on him for quite some time now.' And the four of them tittered knowingly.

Zack Busner was perplexed, no, genuinely flummoxed. He couldn't see how this young woman who sat before him – paper-white where her skin was exposed and dusty-black where it was covered by dusty-black clothes – managed to remain upright. Outside the room, in the sunlit limbo of a Tuesday mid-morning on the psychiatric ward at Heath Hospital, a trio of old women patients – who had mysteriously ended up lodged in the crannies of the Department, like last autumn's furled and desiccated leaves – mumbled and clucked to themselves as they threaded outsize wooden beads on to lengths of leather thong.

Busner had made more than a cursory examination of . . . he looked back at her notes on his desk . . . Liz Good, asking a female nurse to be present while he did so. You could never be too careful where hysterics were concerned, and he knew this to his cost. Lacan may have viewed the female hysteric as a cultural icon, but so far as Zack Busner was concerned they were a dangerous liability at worst, and at best a righteous pain in the arse.

Liz Good's arse had looked like the plucked scut of a chicken once she'd peeled off her dusty-black, skin-tight clothing. Her goose-bump flesh was bisected by her ill-advised and profoundly unalluring black satin-look thong; a piece of apparel which – Busner felt – stood in the same relation to underwear as marginalia did to a text, and which he had neither the strength nor the inclination to ask her to remove. It was like an exoskeleton, this thong, a caricature pelvis drawn on to the outside of her emaciated body. She professed – artlessly and blithely – to have no idea what was the matter with her, only admitting to the extreme lethargy and faintness which had brought her into A & E.

Busner reacquainted her with the facts the duty doctor and various nurses had already made a lean meal of. 'Your haemoglobin level is six, Ms Good, six! A healthy level would be between twelve and fourteen. I'm not surprised that you've been feeling very tired and that you fainted this morning – by all rights you should be dead! Do you understand me – dead!'

Feeding her white limbs back into her black, patchouli-scented clothing, like a snake reassuming its skin, Liz Good had paused to give him a wan smile, freighted with a curious mixture of contempt and self-deprecation. Busner was flummoxed.

He leafed through the notes again, but there was nothing there save for the test results and a few scribbled remarks. In answer to the standard questions Liz Good had given no information whatsoever. She denied having a fixed abode, a GP, or any next of kin. She had no occupation, history of illness, or religion. She had admitted to an age – twenty-eight – and a gender, but, judging by the dismissive manner she employed with Busner, these had been granted only under duress.

'I repeat, Ms Good, there is only one conceivable way that you could've arrived here with such a low haemoglobin level, and that's due to major blood loss within the past week or so. Now, Georgina and I have thoroughly examined you and we can find no evidence of any injury or trauma. If there's nothing that you can tell us then it's extremely difficult to know how we should proceed.'

'I'm not mad,' she said in a small resolute voice, as she picked at the split ends of her dusty black pelt.

'I'm not suggesting that you are,' he replied in his best public tones – but his internal address system squawked: YOU'RE ABSOLUTELY BLOODY INSANE! 'Listen,' he continued. 'I'm not certain of a course of treatment but for now I'm going to give you a bed on the ward so that you can recuperate after the blood transfusions we need to give you. There's also a young colleague of mine at St Mungo's – you know the hospital?' He probed her further, hoping to elicit responses that would indicate her grip on reality.

'The big Gothicy place near Warren Street.'

'That's the one. Well, this doctor, Shiva Mukti, I think he might be able to help you, so I'd like him to come up here and take a look at you.'

She shrugged, the points of her shoulders rising up like a yoke of willed self-destruction. Her heavily chewed fingers yanked down the hem of her rollneck pullover, so that her naked mole-rat features burrowed back into the consulting room. 'Take Ms Good into the treatment room, please, Georgina,' Busner said to the nurse, 'and beg, steal or borrow the necessary bloods. I think it would be best if we did these transfusions right away.'

When she'd shuffled out, with Georgina supporting her famine-sharpened elbow as if it were a shard of bone china, Busner turned to the window. Through long practice he was able to shut out the distressing mooing and baying that came from the Bedlam beyond his door. And when Georgina came back fifteen minutes later to tell him that Liz Good had absconded, he only gave an indifferent shrug. It was almost as if – Georgina thought later, as she sat in the cafeteria tonguing the grooves of crinkle-cut chips – the old man had expected her to do a flit. Although why this should've been the case she didn't take the trouble to speculate.

Dr Shiva Mukti, returned to the many bosoms and multi-tudinous arms of his family, had a moment of clarity. If not exactly going mad, he was – he conceded – suffering from an aggravated case of stress. On the night after Busner's address to the Royal Society of Ephemera he'd found himself unable to sleep. He felt as if he were lacking vital, emotional Factor 8, which would clot his feelings, stop the awful blubbering and keening haemorrhaging away. He woke first Mohan and then Swati. She put the bedside lamp on, which cast sixty watts of yellowish uncertainty, then the overhead light which can-celled them out with a hundred of complete certainty. Shiva was having a breakdown. Mohan saw his father standing at the bedroom window and inveighing against the sacred monkeys he saw climbing all over the trellises in the back garden. 'You saved our Lord Ram,' the psychiatrist shouted. 'Why the hell can't you do the same for me!'

Swati hustled Mohan off to sleep in her mother-in-law's room, and from a locked drawer in Shiva's desk retrieved a couple of the sedatives she knew he kept there. Sweeping back into their bedroom, her nightdress and dressing gown flaring about her like the unearthly emanations of a goddess, she put the beaker in his hand and when his mouth popped open in surprise she popped the pills inside it. He swallowed them like a lambkin.

The next morning Swati called the senior administrator at St Mungo's and explained that her husband wasn't well. Then she took Shiva to their own doctor and sat with him through the consultation required for getting a sick note. This was – at Swati's instigation – marked ambiguously 'chronic exhaustion syndrome'. Then she took him back home and set him to preparing food with her in the kitchen, an activity he'd never been known to engage in before. Throughout all of this Shiva remained curiously docile and biddable. He kept his cool even when she got out his address book and plonked it down beside where he was de-seeding some okra. 'I think you should talk to someone, Shiva,' Swati said. 'There must be an old friend who's now a therapist and who you could trust. You've got to talk to someone, you can't go on like this. Your behaviour is disturbing Mohan, he's wetting the bed. His teacher told me he's been bullying one of the younger children, he's moody and withdrawn. He never sees you, Shiva, you never do any of the things with him that a normal father does with his children –'

'B –' He pursed his lips to protest, but she silenced him with a look of such emotional complexity – love, anger, compassion and revulsion – that he merely dipped his head to accede.

Shiva made an appointment to see Gunnar Grunbein, with whom he'd been friendly enough at medical school. Grunbein had several things to recommend him besides paper qualifications. He'd trained as an analyst under Adam Harley, one of Busner's staunchest critics. Also, the fact that Grunbein was German made him an unlikely member of the crypto-psycho-Semitic conspiracy, which in his manic phases Shiva saw running the world.

Grunbein lived nearby. His consulting room was tacked on to the side of his frighteningly dull house in Dollis Hill. He called it a consulting room, and had even tricked it out to be one, complete with regulation ottoman, Persian miniature, and vestibular waiting room, but there was no disguising the fact that it was a garage conversion. An oily taint remained within the off-white walls, despite the presence of a large, robotic air conditioner.

In keeping with the history of his consulting room, Gunnar Grunbein took a mechanical approach to soul-doctoring. Not for him the ethereal conjuring of the orthodox schools, nor did he subscribe to the touchy-feeliness of interpersonality. No, if you went to Grunbein you were paying to have your psyche stripped down to its core components then meticulously reassembled. Oily ego, bevelled superego, vulcanised id, all were given a rub with the rag of his sensibility before being replaced in the engine compartment of identity.

'I normally find it sufficient,' he was fond of saying, 'to show the analysand the contents of his mind and then let him get on with the business of running his life.' Of course, such a technique had all the therapeutic success of any other established method. His clients found Grunbein a better or worse therapist depending on whether or not they liked him, and stayed or moved on accordingly. As for those with serious problems, they remained long enough to be told they were resisting his methods, or weren't being honest about themselves, before drifting away to the care of suffering relatives, or the bald horror of the streets. Grunbein remained in his garage, where his black-leather office chair sat in a small depression chipped out of the concrete floor. It was as if he were residing in an inspection pit from which he could direct his steely gaze upwards into the cluttered innards of his clients.

I can't've seen Gunnar for at least seventeen years, thought Shiva as he swung his legs up on to the ramp of the ottoman. At med school Grunbein had been a slim, elfin-faced figure, but now he was a heavy-set, balding and irrefutably middle-aged man. They chatted for a while about colleagues, spouses and children. Grunbein admitted to having three of the latter, and Shiva – who'd peered into a front room of awesome asperity on his way up the garden path – found himself chilled at the idea of kids being raised in this frigid atmosphere. Set beside this cold haven the Muktis' home appeared in a kindlier light. The old bronze statuettes of prancing, squatting and cavorting deities, the dusty wall hangings of faded silk, the black-and-white photographs of Muktis travelling on the branch line up to Mussoorie, their uniform, black-framed spectacles like the eye sockets of startled forest creatures. Even the kitchen-cum-canteen, with its gummy old folk slurping their food, was preferable to this.

In the garage Grunbein unclipped his psycho-socket set and began to wrench away at the bolts securing Shiva's consciousness to his subconscious. And perhaps precisely because Grunbein was so unemotional – while retaining a face-to-face directness with his addled client – Shiva found himself able to talk and talk. Talk of how his father's ghost still haunted him, hanging around the street corner begging for the pinda, the ball of rice and sesame seeds he needed to bail him out of limbo, and which his son's negligence had denied him. Talk of his marriage, which, in a peculiar reversal, seemed increasingly arranged so that Swati became more and more of a stranger to him. Talk of his son Mohan, who Shiva had so few dealings with that when the boy gave fantastical explanations for his wrongdoing – he'd spread jam on the walls because of a duel with a giant fly which lived behind the skirting board – Shiva automatically diagnosed him as schizophrenic and began considering what medication would be suitable for a six-year-old. Finally, he talked of his work, and was just getting to the revelation of the cabal and Busner's role in it when Grunbein chimed in, 'I'm afraid that's all we've got time for today, Shiva.'

'What?'

'That's exactly fifty minutes, Shiva. We'll need to resume this conversation at another time. I have slots free on Thursday and Friday.'

'But I was getting to the important stuff.'

'It's all important, Shiva. What you've been saying has great significance, it's given me plenty to think about.'

Unbidden, the image came to Shiva of Gunnar Grunbein pondering his problems in the bath, casually considering Shiva's neuroses as he lifted his Teutonic balls and soaped his smooth perineum. It was as he'd always suspected: being in therapy meant paying for the slender reassurance of another's minor consideration.

'Look.' He tried to impress his own objectivity on Grunbein by staring at the psychoanalyst as if he were a plank. 'There's a situation, a developing situation. I didn't come to you for commiseration or advice, there are peo –'

'There's someone waiting, Shiva – he's a person too. Whatever it is will have to wait, now, Thursday or Friday?' Grunbein had extracted an appointments diary from beneath his chair and sat, pen poised, looking exactly like a receptionist at Kwikshrink plc.

'Oh, Thursday, I s'pose.'

'Good, eleven o'clock sharp, that's settled.' He plopped the book shut. 'And one more thing, Shiva.'

'What?'

'I wondered – and I'd like you to think about this – I wondered why it was exactly that you became a psychiatrist in the first place?'

In the waiting booth Shiva tummy-rubbed with a striking figure, two metres of black cashmere overcoat, topped by the perfumed and precisely curled black beard of an Assyrian god-king. Its owner regarded him through black eyes that were motionless in their blue-brown sockets. They didn't exchange words.

Swati was waiting outside, her elegant fingers in their lacy mitts of henna tapping on the wheel of the people carrier. To underline their change in status, she stayed where she was and drove them home to Kenton. Shiva sat and fulminated about how unprofessional Grunbein had been; surely his clients should have time to get out of the garage and off the forecourt before the next clapped-out banger was wheeled in? Un-professional and insensitive, so insensitive that his behaviour – along with his extreme anal retention – was redolent of pathology. Shiva decided to take a look in the *DSM-IV* when he reached home, although he was almost certain he knew already which personality disorder Gunnar Grunbein had.

For the rest of that week, at Swati's firm insistence, Shiva did his best to integrate himself into the life of the home. Swati had been watching and learning all these years, almost as if she knew this day would come. Now it was time to use the therapeutic knowledge she'd gleaned from her husband on her husband. She did so with zeal. The days unfolded with absolute clarity, tasks were allocated for the patient and if he did them adequately he was rewarded, but if he neglected to apply himself he was suitably penalised. Double okra.

Shiva took Mohan to school and for the first time spoke to his teachers, Shiva did the household accounts and presented Swati with the figures, Shiva cleared out the garden shed and took the rubbish to the dump. In the afternoon Shiva collected Mohan from school and when they got home they did reading practice together. Their reward was a video game. But, although he couldn't speak of it to his nurse, Swati, Shiva found the games session extremely disturbing. The television screen began to bulge as the pixelated figures chased and zapped one another, then it ruptured completely. The green tendrils of the jungle scenario Mohan favoured spread so that they interleaved with the multiple limbs of the table-top bronzes.

Careful not to betray any sign of fear to his young son, Shiva watched, awed, as Kalki, Sarasvati and Ganga leapt into the fray and did battle with extreme mesomorphs dressed in camouflaged singlets and sporting the rigid coxcombs of post-apocalyptic punks. Mohan chuckled, trilled and then spasmed as his riffling fingers sent lighting bolts through the crumbling walls of abandoned temples. His father felt like screaming as the punks tried to climb up his trouser legs. The sessions were limited to one hour, but to Shiva they seemed like manvan-taras, 4,320,000 years of demented combat.

Suppertimes at the Muktis' were seldom talkative affairs.

The slushy twirl of fingers in rice and dahl, only interrupted by a gummy request for a dish to be passed or a drink poured. Shiva didn't even know if his mother and the aunts and uncles had been told by Swati what ailed him, but they made no comment on his absence from work. After they'd eaten and Mohan had been put to bed, they all sat in the overstuffed sitting room, watching television indiscriminately – cop shows, dramas, comedies, news bulletins – with only the occasional scandalised mutter from one of the old people breaking the reverential silence. The adulterous actors, portentous news-readers and choleric law-enforcement officers seemed to Shiva to be doing the living for the Muktis, who were themselves elevated to heaven, becoming old gods and goddesses, draped in colourful cotton, who oversaw with vedic cynicism the antics of these mortals on the earth below. Feeble creatures whose illusory significance might be snuffed out at any moment by a divine finger on the remote control.

When at last the old folk had dispersed and he and Swati went to their own bed, Shiva's dreams began. He had no difficulty in getting to sleep – temazepam saw to that – but oblivion was unavailable. As his head neared the smooth pillow it became a chute down which he slid into the tumultuous pit of his own dissolution. Here he ended up a skinny-shanked boy once more, his fiercely pressed grey school shorts flapping in the hot wind of hell, while deathly juggernauts plunged towards him, their radiator grilles bared in ugly steel grimaces. And as they howled past Shiva tried to grab the pathetic teddy bears that were lashed to them, their foam-rubber wombs prolapsing through their brushed-nylon fur. But despite his infant body there was still no way back to his youth. The juggernauts disappeared in a hail of grit and Shiva was left with the painful realisation that all that enthusiastic coupling had been merely frantic cuddling with teddy-bear women. The reality was death. The truth was nothing. Then the dreams proper commenced.

First came the landscapes of his childhood, so distant that they had the appearance of other people's nostalgia for a time and place unknown to Shiva. In this encrypted terrain a distant hill served only to emphasise the utter flatness of the dun-grey fields. The air was as warm and sickly as sweet brown chai, and the very soil itself looked lived in, as if each and every handful of dust had been cupped and then trickled between careworn fingers. A railway line sliced through the plain like a dull iron scalpel, and beside it welled up a bloody mauve convolvulus of flowers, while suturing each undifferentiated section of trackside to the next was a single strand of telephone wire, knotted at regular intervals by perching, sleek-tailed drongos.

Then this vision would shimmer and decode itself into the prosaic hummocks and hillocks of middle England. The tidy farms and model homes Shiva had stared at through the window of the family car, as old Dilip Mukti piloted them from one wayside picnic to the next, subduing the realm with a series of Formica-topped table forts, each garrisoned by women in saris doling out chapatis from Tupperware boxes.

Shiva had only been back to Uttar Pradesh once in his adult life, a trip taken in a misguided spirit of enquiry. The train bringing him from Delhi wheezed across mile after mile of the Ganges plain, before coughing him up – another dollop of human sputum – into a lethal spittoon of intercommunal violence. The train was halted in a remote labyrinth of mud bricks, compressed cow dung and neon which called itself a town. In dusty darkness a mass of people thronged the maidan, feverishly trying to pick sides so that one could annihilate the other.

Poked and stabbed by the sharp knees and sharper elbows of the stampeding host, his eardrums perforated by its screeching, Shiva had somehow managed to commandeer a tuk-tuk, and paid the bhang-blasted driver to get him out of town. He reached a wayside halt, a tumbledown caravanserai, where he slept for three nights on a sagging charpoy, and spent three days hearing worse and worse news, as murder and rapine flared across the flatlands.

Eventually, Thomas Cook's traveller's cheques secured him a seat in a minibus which trundled north towards Nepal. The eight passengers were locked in by the driver, an excitable Sikh who steered with his knees, leaving his pudgy hands free to caress the barrel of an enormous old Enfield revolver, which he propped in his groin like a steel lingam.

Sitting opposite Shiva as the minibus jolted over the interminable ruts was an Australian hippy, whose sole garment was a Victorian nightdress. Shiva supposed he thought this a reasonable approximation of traditional Indian clothing. For mile after mile the hippy read from Shakespeare's sonnets, ignoring the flies that explored his thick, dirty-blond tresses. Ever afterwards Shiva felt nauseous when he heard the words 'Shall I compare thee to a summer's day . . .'.

But the most singular occupant of the bus was a tiny boy in blue shorts and an Aertex shirt, who sat calmly between his diminutive parents. All three of them were immaculately groomed, and no matter how hot, smelly or fly-blown the bus became, they never perspired or showed the slightest visible sign of discomfort. For three long days and three long nights the little boy played with a toy car, a toy cow and a toy harmonica. As Shiva watched he carefully balanced the three objects atop his flattened thighs, trying car on top of cow on top of harmonica, then harmonica on top of cow on top of car. Over and over again, as if he were investigating the workability of new Hindu cosmologies.

At a village where they stopped long rows of thin men shat openly and fatalistically by the road in a ditch full of broken bricks. A few yards away a battered tarpaulin protected a couple of food stalls from the sun's savage stroke. A slab-sided giant, naked save for a gingham loin-cloth, made jalebi by extruding an endless turd of dough from a paper cone into a brimming pan of sizzling oil. Shiva, together with a crowd of boys, gawped as the giant deftly fashioned fried snack after fried snack, sugaring them with a swipe of one hand as they lay smoking on a greasy sheet of newsprint, which crawled with the ancient beetle script of Sanskrit. The heat drilled at his temples, striking off splinters of bony brain. A man behind another warped stall was doling out sweet lassi from a zinc tub, lifting up his ladle then pouring the white spume into metal beakers. When the lassi man grinned – which was frequently – his betel-stained lips parted to reveal a stalactite of tooth which dangled from the roof of his mouth. Shiva saw icebergs in the milky sea. He knew they'd been made using unpurified water, but surely one beaker wouldn't do any harm? He had to stop the madman who was trepanning him with heat.

Three months later, two stone lighter and a quarter of a world away, Shiva lay on an examination couch in the Hospital for Tropical Diseases, just another dysentery case back from the subcontinent who couldn't believe how crude a colonoscopy was. The doctor – an irritable man with an impressive overbite – had Shiva assume a bicycling posture on his side, then inserted a steel tube into his anus. Then he put his eye to the other end.

'What can you see?' Shiva asked, since the doctor seemed disinclined to offer any opinion beyond effortful grunts and annoyed clucks.

'Nothing much,' he replied. 'Only some rather rabbity-looking faeces.'

'Well, whaddya expect if you look down a tube you've shoved up my arse?' Shiva retorted, but this was lost on the tropical-disease specialist, who merely withdrew the tube with an audible 'plop' and told him to get dressed.

Shiva's dreams possessed a realism long since absent from his waking life. They terrified him. As he thrashed and moaned, a slim and elegant physician observed him. For years Shiva had used all the diagnostic tools at his disposal on his wife, shoe-horning her into this or that dysfunctional slipper, but there was nothing wrong with Swati at all. Her refusal to couple with sufficient enthusiasm, her lackadaisical absorption into the boarding household, her efficient piety – none of these were symptoms of a neurosis or a behavioural disorder. No, Swati Mukti became aware of her husband's instability soon after marrying him. She waited before risking a pregnancy, contraception needn't be that sneaky, because Shiva was so profoundly self-absorbed. Once she was pregnant with Mohan she was already regretting it. Shiva's rages, his mood swings, his odd beliefs – all of it drove her to read his professional manuals. Swati Mukti had concluded that, if not actually schizophrenic, then Shiva did at least have a border-line personality type.

There could be no question of any more children. Watching Mohan grow up and trying to outguess the emergence of whatever psychological problems he might develop would be labour enough. There was this task and there was waiting for her husband to fall, hovering behind him with a chair as if he were a slapstick drunk. Shiva thought Swati didn't love him, but the truth was that hers was love of complexity and depth that he was quite unequipped to perceive. Swati was there to stop him falling, not because he was a loving husband and a dutiful father – he was neither – but as part repayment of the debt owed to him by the mentally ill he himself had tried to help. So, Swati Mukti, erect in her quilted bed jacket, with its peacock motif embroidered on the left breast, oversaw her tormented husband and waited for morning. There could be no question of him continuing to see Grunbein on such an informal basis: hospitalisation would be the next step.

Whimpering and grinding his teeth, Shiva swung open the gate and entered another of the fields on his funny farm. He herded the cow into the hoof-cratered corner by the water trough, then slipped his trousers off so he could mount her. His first wife Sandra bucked and mooed beneath him. Despite the tumult of upheaving flesh Shiva still noticed – with lofty, Brahminical pity – the sprinkling of livid spots on the inside of her anal cleft. Sandra's conical fingers, which resembled jeweller's ring trees, dug into an earthen bolster, and her high-pitched bellows rent the rapidly compressing atmosphere.

'What's all this about, Shiva?' cried Zack Busner, pushing open the door with one of his hands, while the second snapped on the light, the third adjusted his spectacles and the fourth rolled and unrolled the hairy tongue of his mohair tie. 'I can't see that indulging in erotic reveries about your former wife is going to take you anywhere much – not in career terms at any rate.' Sandra had seen Busner's blood-stained teeth, and mewling, pulled herself out from under Shiva, then shuffled into the far corner of the dingy little student bedsit. The sand of total inhibition trickled into Shiva's mouth. Busner came over to the squashy single bed and sat down on its disarranged sheets. He put one arm around Shiva's shoulders and continued. 'Untrammelled female passion, its destructive and consuming aspects . . .' Another pair of hands fiddled with the folds of his white coat, which parted to reveal a burgeoning bulge in his corduroy trousers. 'But surely, Shiva, this characterisation of the Jew is a bit of a cliché?'

'C-can you be a Jew and a g-god?'

'Ye-es,' Busner drawled. 'I am – as you observe – Zakibusna, your consort, but that doesn't stop you from projecting the most outrageous imaginings on to me, hmm?'

Shiva struggled to answer this accusation, but all that emerged from his mouth were parched burbles. It didn't matter anyway, because Zakibusna wasn't listening, she'd expertly flipped her spectacles cord over Shiva's head and was now tightening it around his neck. Shiva felt the blood vessels burst in his face, as if it were fleshy bubble-wrap being popped by an evil child. Eventually all was subsumed by a red darkness.

Swati left Shiva to sleep in, but when she returned from the school run she found him already up and dressed in suit and tie. 'You're due to see Dr Grunbein this morning,' she said. 'Why are you all dressed up like that?'

'I'm not bothering with that fraud again,' he replied. 'I'm far better qualified than he is and I've decided that I'm going back to work. I've recovered.'

'Don't be idiotic, Shiva.' She laid a hand on his shoulder. 'You were delirious in your sleep last night – you can't go into the hospital.'

'Can' – he shrugged off her hand – 'and will, and don't try . . .' He picked up his briefcase and waltzed towards the front door. 'Stopping me!'

Part Five

He set off at a good pace around the placid curve of Kenton Park Crescent and then down Kenton Park Road to the Kenton Road. From the junction it was half a mile's stroll to Kenton tube station. Kenton, Kenton, Kenton – for the balance of Shiva's life these two syllables had meant home, routine, the tight mental brace of the mundane. Ken-ton. Ken, ton. Divided from each other what did they imply? A ton of Kens, or – in the Scots vernacular – a knowledge of weight? Or were they only sounds, 'ken' and 'ton', as full of import – for Shiva – as Mandarin words, the meaning of which might veer wildly if pitch or tone were slightly altered. 'Ken-ton' in Mandarin, Shiva thought, might mean something complex and poetic, such as: That feeling you have walking to the tube station having decided that very morning not to succumb to a mental breakdown, but instead to vanquish your enemies.

I need a cuddle, Shiva realised. Why can't I go into that scrappy front garden and knock on the peeling paint of that front door, and fall into the arms of the overweight and overwhelmed woman who answers it? At once, the thought of the Bakerloo Line to Oxford Circus, then the Central Line to Tottenham Court Road, became frighteningly alien. The journey would be interminable, the brute power of the metropolis would be scored into every electric-blue check of the tube carriage's seats. Swati was right – he wasn't up to it. He was ill, he should turn back, see Grunbein later in the day, try and get some clarity. What was it that Gunnar had asked him to do for his psychotherapeutic homework? Think about a question – but what was it? Yes, that was it, why had Shiva wanted to be a psychiatrist in the first place?

To please his father, he thought. During Shiva's early adolescence, when they'd been closest, Dilip Mukti took his son into his own intellectual confidence, and took him as well on the long, meandering public-transport journeys which became the outward expression of their intimacy. Father and son fleeing in order to get near to one another. Sleepy off-peak overground trains muttering over the rails to Berkhamsted, Chertsey and Amersham; Green Line buses tunnelling through the deep-cut lanes of the Kentish Weald; and always the tube and the London buses, royal roads, open to his father whenever he waved his staff pass. On these vague voyages Dilip Mukti would talk and Shiva would listen. Staring out over the backs of trackside houses – each one a strip of garden, a blob of shed, a wink of greenhouse, a child caught in the instant of catching a ball – Dilip would tell his son of his own childhood in the hissing and deadly snake pit of high-caste Indian religious politics. The names – Vivekananda, Ramakrishna – meant little to the boy, and the sects his father described – the Aryo and Bramo Samaj – seemed to have no conceivable relevance to Shiva's own world of cliques and cricket teams, canoeing on the Welsh Harp Reservoir and canoodling at school discos.

Nor did the central dilemma of his father's life – whether he should continue in the family tradition or break decisively with it – find any answering echo in his son's sensibility. Dilip Mukti would have Shiva believe that at his age all that had preoccupied him was whether the truth could be reconciled with archaic religious practices, or better served by embracing modern realities. But all Shiva was fixated upon was the ugliness of the hard-core porn passed around in the boys' toilets at school. Could it be that the girls he viewed through the pastel-hued lenses of romance had the same gaping wounds underneath their Bandaid-sized skirts?

Dilip Mukti had a way of talking about himself that omitted the personal pronoun. 'What to do? Where to go? It was one thing to rebel, understand, quite another to know what that rebellion was for. To go to England? Many had gone before for economic reasons, but to go for the philosophy? Why?' Years later Shiva understood that this was simply a function of speaking in a second language, but at the time his father's recollections had an oracular quality, as if they were on a par with the Ramayana.

Dilip Mukti may have tried to strike off the chains of caste, class, culture and nation, but he couldn't abandon the search for jnana, the way of knowledge. In the shaggy-faced thinkers of the European Enlightenment, Shiva's father had discovered another form of smirti – what is remembered – and so he laboured to remember it, and to create his own oral tradition by passing it down to his son.

Those interminable journeys! Traversing and re-traversing the conurbation, while his dad spoke of Darwin, Mill, Marx and even Freud, an Everyman Library volume of the relevant thinker like a sandwich on his lap, opened out to reveal its filling of knowledge. Why had Shiva become a doctor? Why, to please his father, and why a psychiatrist? To please his father still more. Surely this was what Dilip Mukti had been calling upon him to do for all those miles of tarmac and steel? To use the highest faculties of reason to map out the irrational, segregate and then annihilate it? The monkeys would be caged, the elephants put to work, the tigers shot and the snakes handled. The entire, ever-inchoate, shape-shifting bestiary of Hindu belief would be fit meat for his heir's career as a psychological vivisectionist.

But by the time Shiva came to train his father had reverted almost entirely to type. His trousers had been slit up the seams and rearranged into a lungi. He'd even abandoned his gardening, claiming that the soil was infertile and used up. But Shiva knew that his father feared its defilement now that he was approaching the end of his lifetime. Feared that all of his contact with John Innes potting soil might prejudice his chance of reaching enlightenment of a different order. So, like Oedipus, despite his very best intentions, Shiva found himself committing an act of parricide. With Dilip putting back on the pious garb of their forefathers, Shiva's white coat became an arrogant and offensive bit of character armour.

In the final years of his life — despite Shiva's marriage to Swati — Dilip often alluded to the shame of his son's first forlorn liaison with 'the English girl'. Dilip seemed to believe that it was this impulsive act that had decisively altered the status of the whole Mukti clan, and not his own, heavily ruminated decision to leave India and seek his truth in the West. When the old man's will was read, it transpired that the task of taking his ashes back to Varanasi, so that they might be scattered in the waters of Mother Ganga, had been allocated to his brother-in-law Jayesh. Shiva was left behind in Kenton, having been mysteriously reincarnated in his father's discarded self-image.

'Why, Dad?' Shiva asked aloud outside the florist's next to the station. 'Why couldn't you love me like a father should love a son? After all, I was your only child.' But Dilip's shade, for so long present at the periphery of Shiva's darkening vision, was now nowhere to be seen. Shiva bought his ticket, got on the train, and dry-heaved the whole way into town.

Whatever worry they may have felt at the hospital to see Dr Mukti back so soon was cancelled out by the need there was for his services. It hardly mattered to his hard-pressed colleagues if Shiva Mukti was sane or not, all that concerned them was that he shoulder his share of an overwhelming case load. Cases like Darlene Davis, a young woman who'd been discovered that very morning by one of the porters, collapsed in a dead faint by the hopper full of clinical waste which was next to the entrance of A & E. 'She's got a haemoglobin level of six – six!' mouthed Shiva's secretary as he took Davis's notes from her and ducked back inside his niche.

Darlene Davis suited St Mungo's only too well. With her skin-tight black clothes and dusty-black, Struwwelpeter hair, she fused all Gothic revivals together in one gloomy incarnation. Her skin was so white, her eyes so sunken, and her mouth so lipstick-livid that had he a coffin to hand Shiva would've tucked her up in it without hesitating. She sat, rocking on her pelvis, tied up in the bondage of her own limbs, while he roamed about posing questions. How had she come to lose so much blood? Had she any idea what was wrong with her? Who was her GP? To begin with she behaved like many prisoners of the mental-health wars, refusing anything but her name and sexual rank. It was only when Shiva began a conversation with himself – 'I've always lived with my family or with friends, but I wonder what it would be like to live alone' – that Davis joined in.

'I don't live by myself.' She sounded proud of this. 'I live with a group of . . . err . . . I s'pose you'd call them creative like people.'

'And what do you call them?'

'Artists.'

'I see, and where is this artistic community situated?'

'In London.'

'I realised that.'

'And Paris.'

'Paris, well, that's nice.'

'I dunno about nice, but it's fucking cool. Most of the time we hang out here, but when we feel like it we up and fuck off like, get on the ferry or whatever, take the vans and go over. We got another squat opposite this weird park, the Butte Chaumont, d'you know it?'

'Not as such.'

'Didn't think so.' Davis hugged herself tighter with self-satisfaction. 'It's this big like limestone bowl that's been carved out of a hill. All that's left of the rock is this big like pinnacle thing in the middle, with a bridge going over to it. Digger says the Surrealists called it the Bridge of Suicides and this poet bloke, Aragorn –'

'Aragon.'

'Whatever. This poet bloke said that people who'd only gone out to do some like shopping found themselves driven like . . . to like . . . throw themselves off it.'

'Who's Digger?'

'He's a bloke.'

'An artist?'

'A bloke.'

It went on like this, with her evasions and nonce words forming the dots and dashes of a telegram, that conveyed to Shiva the news that important command centres in Darlene's mind had been overrun by delusional thinking. When he brought her back to the matter of her physical condition she became surly. 'I dunno.'

'But you must know – you must've lost at least a litre of blood to have a haemoglobin level this low . . .' Shiva walked behind her and looked hard at her scrawny neck. 'Tell me, Darlene – you needn't feel ashamed about this, it's a not uncommon thing – but have you been cutting yourself?'

'No.'

'Have you had an accident in the last week?'

'No.'

'A miscarriage?'

'No – don't be fucking stupid! Look, I know what I need, blood, so why don't you give it to me?'

'It's not that simple, Darlene – you'll have to have a physical examination first.'

'Well go on then.' She uncoiled herself and began pulling off the stretchy black clothes, revealing tuberous white limbs as speedily as if they'd been yanked from the earth.

'Hold on, hold on,' Shiva blurted. 'I'll get a female colleague.'

Shiva left the niche. In the waiting area a thirtyish man sat reading a glossy magazine. Even as he swept past, Shiva noted the contrast between the shiny faces on its cover and his pasty one. The man's big nose was pitted with old acne scars and a sideburn of pus joined his spiky, part-bleached hair to his unshaven cheek. He glared at Shiva, who at once intuited that there was a connection between him and Darlene.

Shiva leant over the receptionist's desk and whispered to her, 'Call Security and have them station someone in the corridor. I have a potentially dangerous patient in my office and I don't want her leaving the hospital under any circumstances. Also' – his voice dropped – 'call Sharon, would you. I need her to do a physical for me.'

When the staff nurse arrived five minutes later she found Darlene shivering in a hospital gown, while Shiva Mukti sat at his desk noting down numbers from the phone directory. 'Could you give Ms Davis here a complete physical examination, please Sharon? Look for any traumas or breaks in the skin, no matter how small – this young woman has mislaid a large amount of her own blood.' He smiled facetiously. 'I've got to do some telephoning.' He left them to it.

Sharon asked Darlene to take off the hospital robe. Underneath she was naked save for a satiny black thong, which on her cadaverous body stood in the same relation to sexual allure as a greasepaint moustache does to real hair. Sharon was struck by how fine Darlene's body hair was – with such an advanced case of anorexia she'd have expected a coarse profusion. She went over each goose-bumpy portion of Darlene carefully and conscientiously, but could find no rupture in her translucent skin, certainly nothing that would've allowed for the amateur extraction of a litre of blood. She knew she ought to ask Darlene to take off her thong, and do a vaginal and rectal examination, but there were limits.

Meanwhile, in an office along the corridor, Dr Mukti was getting results with his ring-round. He hadn't believed 'Darlene Davis' was the patient's real name for a second, and the more he thought about it the more convinced he became that this wasn't the first time that this young woman had cropped up in the A & E department of a London hospital with a haemoglobin level of six. First he checked with A & E downstairs, and asked them if anyone answering to Darlene's description had presented in the past year. He drew a blank. But then, when he cast his telephonic net further afield, he began to get results. A woman of twenty-eight, in a similar condition to Darlene and also refusing any cooperation, had obtained a transfusion at the Whittington six months previously. Another young woman had done the same thing at the Middlesex two months before that, and in the early summer of the preceding year a Darlene-alike had been seen at St Thomas's, but absconded when she was referred to the duty psychiatrist. Shiva's last call was to the A & E department at Heath Hospital. Yes, they too had seen a woman of twenty-eight, white, and with a haemoglobin level of six. Yes, she'd been sent up to see Dr Busner, but had also run away before receiving any treatment.

A rivulet of chilly sweat trickled down Shiva's ribcage. Busner. The fat Judensau suckling on the blood of this girl. The conclusion was inescapable: whatever she said she was being systematically deprived of her blood. Busner was both more diabolic and more Machiavellian than Shiva had ever dared to suppose. He'd been 'running' Darlene around the city for over a year, having seized on the insane young woman as the perfect weapon in his duel with Shiva.

Shiva replaced the receiver on its cradle with a trembling hand. He inched to the door of the office and peered into the corridor. Dhiran, the plump Nigerian security guard, was wandering up and down. Dhiran lent an almost frantic languor to the business of paid-for vigilance, but he was at least big and there. Shiva ducked back inside — other connections were being soldered in his molten head. Was the spiky-haired man her minder? Or was he one of Busner's as well? Whichever the case Shiva had to move fast.

Back to the rough wall, Shiva rasped his way along the corridor. Yes, the man was still there and he looked up, giving the psychiatrist a piercing stare of comprehension. Shiva shuddered. Would this man actually attack him if he detained

Darlene? He looked insane enough to try anything, even in the midst of St Mungo's morning bustle.

Shiva turned back to the main corridor and beckoned to Dhiran. 'C'm'ere,' he called. The plump Nigerian shuffled obligingly over. 'Keep an eye on things.'

'Will do.'

Summoning himself, Shiva confronted the threat head-on. He went over and sat down beside the man. 'Are you a friend of Darlene's?'

'Who?' He looked bemused.

'The young woman in my office.'

'Oh yeah, she called me and said she was here, that's why I came by, I thought I'd take her home when you've done the necessary.'

'The necessary?'

'The treatment, given her the treatment like.'

'Listen, Mr . . .?'

'Digger.'

'Right, Digger, OK, listen carefully. I suspect that this young woman has been losing blood on a regular basis, large quantities of blood, in fact. I don't, as yet, know why, but I'm determined to find out. Is there anything you can tell me?'

'There's all sorts of things I can tell you.' Digger laid the magazine down on the chair next to him and adopted a professorial pose, legs crossed, hands cupped on knee. 'Things about forces, impulses, laws and events, but it won't help you much, not given all this fucking rigmarole.' He spoke without malice as if addressing a foolish child.

'Rigmarole?'

'Your butcher's coat, your cattle prod, your anti-psychotic breeding super mental bugs – all that rigmarole, y'know like.'

'I see.' Shiva grasped his lapels and leant back in his chair.

'You're referring to my status as a psychiatrist.' Despite the crackling tension in the air he was enjoying himself. There was some dreadful complicity between this scabby man and the mysterious anaemic.

'Yeah, soul doctor blues man, sold out to pharmocorporate shit, man. Yeah.'

'Tell me.' Shiva hunched forward so that he could look directly into Digger's eyes – the pupils were no more than pinpricks. 'Do you live with Darlene?'

'Live with her, lay with her, milk her, mix her, drink her, whassit t'you?'

'So you're one of this group of . . . artists then?'

'You might call us that.'

'And you live between London and Paris?' To Shiva this sounded like absurd drinks-party banter.

'Between Babylon and Kush, between the earth and the sky. Yeah, we catch the falling star and it cuts our hands to pieces, like.'

'Stereotypic schizophreniform ideation,' Shiva muttered involuntarily.

'Whassat?' Digger snapped.

'Nothing, nothing,' Shiva flannelled. 'Nothing that need concern you, but what you should be worried about is your friend's condition, and more importantly how she got into it. Listen to me, Digger, I've every reason to believe you may be involved in Darlene's loss of blood, given that you spend so much time with her. This could be a criminal matter, so if there's anything you want to tell me now I think you should, before the police get involved.'

But Digger only glared at Shiva with his jet-brooch eyes, before declaring, 'No-thing.'

Inside the niche Darlene was back in the chair, a rigid pole tenting her hospital gown. 'I can't find anything,' Sharon said as Shiva came in.

'No trauma, no bruising, no rupture, no puncture marks even?'

'Like I say, nothing.'

'And you examined her thoroughly, including a vaginal and rectal?'

Sharon coloured. 'Well no, I didn't think . . .'

'Didn't think what?' he blustered. 'Well, no matter, we'll have to do that now. Would you mind slipping back out of that gown, Ms Davis, yes, and the thong as well, please.'

The gown fell from her coat-hanger shoulders and she stood like a veined shard of dirty marble, sickeningly exposed in the sunlight that streamed through the window. She was so weak she had to steady herself on the back of the chair in order to step out of the scrap of nylon. Once it was gone she looked still worse. The thong had been a rip-cord, and now the sheer awfulness of her condition billowed about her.

'Good, thank you, now, Sharon, could you help Ms Davis up on to the couch?'

The nurse held the shard gingerly, as if afraid it might cut her, and together they made halting progress over the parquet. Once the young woman was laid out, Shiva, having drawn on rubber gloves, closed in on her. And there it was in the raw groove of her groin. There was no need to do a vaginal or rectal examination, because there it was. Half an inch long, livid in the middle, yellow and black at the edges. There it was – the unmistakable wound left by a catheter.

'I got it all out of her in the end.'

'What, the blood?'

'Aren't you listening to me at all?' Shiva leaned right over the table, thrusting his animated face into Elmley's stony one.

'No, no, I was listening, I just wasn't clear about what exactly it was you'd got out of her. I mean, the whole tale is about blood, isn't it?' There was definitely something wrong with Elmley. His usual doggy enthusiasm had slipped its leash – even a friend as uncaring and unloving as Shiva could see this. Come to think of it, Shiva couldn't remember seeing him for quite some time, at least two or three weeks before his own brief absence. Now Elmley had the abstracted yet mindless air of someone on medication. There was that, and there was also a seediness about him, a shabbiness even, that Shiva couldn't remember noticing before.

'Do you want to know then?'

'Oh yes, I'm agog.' Elmley did his best to look agog, letting his mouth gape open and allowing his gaze – which had been buzzing about the canteen – to alight on Shiva.

'Once I'd confronted her with the evidence – the admissions to other hospitals under assumed names, the catheter scar in her groin – she 'fessed up. It's a blood-letting cult!'

'Are you serious?'

'Absolutely, it's a satanist blood-letting cult, and she's the fucking brood mare, or rather the blood bank. All the circumstantial stuff she told me is true. She's part of this group that moves between squats in London and Paris, but they aren't artists, unless, that is, you think devil-worship is a kind of creativity. Anyway, every couple of months they take two or three pints out of the poor girl, and mix it up with earth and semen and whatever else, then daub it all over the show, making pentagrams, I suppose. It was strange.' Shiva paused, searching for the right words. 'But she was only too willing to tell me all about it – almost as if she was primed to.'

'So what did you do then?'

'Meaning what?'

'With the girl – the young woman?'

'What do you bloody think I did? I slapped a section on her faster than you can say ECT, she's as mad as a bag of fucking snakes. No, I've got her number, Dave. All those other quacks let her get away, but not me. She's been put straight on to the locked ward – she'll get her transfusions there. We'll fatten her up and then we'll get to the bottom of this cult nonsense.'

'I would've thought . . . I would've thought . . .' Elmley intoned, while he turned a plastic spoon crowned with a ruff of aerated cream this way and that. 'I would've thought . . .'

'But I'm too bloody catatonic to have any thoughts,' Shiva put in. 'What is it with you today? If I didn't know you better I'd say you were stoned.'

'I never smoke dope at work – you know that.'

'Yeah-yeah, you might have an industrial accident, like design a hinge that opened the wrong way.'

'Strictly speaking' – Elmley's tone was flat but his eyes burned with anger – 'that isn't possible.'

'Strictly speaking, what were you going to say before we veered off into this redundant little appendix?'

'Only that' – at last the tiny spoonful of trifle made it into Elmley's mouth – 'I would've thought the boyfriend represented your best chance of finding out more.'

'You're right.' Shiva looked a little abashed. 'I did think of that, not only because of finding out more, but he and the rest of these freaks should be facing criminal charges. But that fat fucking Nigerian we've got doing security couldn't hang on to his own bloody trousers if he wasn't wearing a belt. He let the boyfriend walk out. Still, if we hang on to her I expect he'll turn up again, I mean she's the bait, he's the –'

Shiva stopped abruptly. While he'd been talking he compulsively fed chicken nuggets into his mouth and chewed them up as he spat out his ire. Now he sat frozen, his mouth agape, a stray thread of flesh dangling from his lower lip. Elmley – ever the human hinge – turned 180 degrees in his seat to see what his friend was staring at. White-faced, spiky-haired, unshaven, thirtyish, the man stared belligerently back. 'It's him,' Shiva muttered, 'it's the bloody boyfriend.'

Elmley registered an abrupt shift in the normally foetid and comfortable atmosphere of the canteen. He was on a windswept, rain-raked moor, darkness was falling and he was alone. The man got up from where he was sitting and walked over to them, knocking against a table of physiotherapists, such was his haste. Elmley was surprised they didn't remonstrate with him. The man sat down at Shiva and Elmley's table.

'I'm Digger.' He thrust his chin at Elmley as if on the point of delving into his face with its sharp edge. 'What's this one been saying then?'

'N-nothing.' It wasn't so much Digger's air of barely suppressed violence which put Elmley on guard, it was more the anxiety he felt lest he miss a vital cue. For clearly Digger was here at the behest of the man who controlled both of them, and was going to deliver some long-awaited instructions to Elmley.

Shiva, however, was unaffected. 'I've been telling Dave here about your walking blood bank. I'd ask you what her real name was if it weren't for the fact that I'm pretty sure Digger isn't even yours.'

'Course not, it's a fucking nickname, innit.'

'Is it?'

'Yeah.'

'Well, Mr Enigmatic, you've got a bloody nerve coming in here – this is a staff canteen.'

'I wasn't eating anything, I wanted to find you.'

'Oh really.' Shiva cast about the table, as if looking for a lit cigarette or a tumbler of whisky to prop up his tough-guy act. 'And why's that then?'

Digger stood up and reversed his chair. Then he sat down again, riding it like a plastic horse. He hitched up the sleeves of his combat jacket to expose hairless forearms rendered puny by the heavy black curlicues of modern primitive tattooing. 'That's better,' he announced, and Elmley wondered if this was the signal. 'Look,' Digger continued, 'now you've got her banged up it's all up with us, isn't it.'

'Is it?' Shiva sneered. 'I shouldn't have thought you'd have much difficulty getting another poor, mentally unstable person to act as your zombie.'

'You don't – you don't understand.' To both Shiva and Elmley's amazement tears were rolling down Digger's cheeks, his shoulders heaved with emotion. 'You've gotta love 'em, it won't work if you don't love 'em. It's all about love – the whole ritual, you've gotta know that much.'

Shiva had been on the point of telling Elmley to restrain Digger – or try to – while he went to phone the police, but this revelation caught him off guard. 'I'd like to know more.' Shiva steepled his fingers. 'It does sound fascinating.'

Digger collected himself and took a slug of Elmley's Coke, confirming the bond between them. 'It is fascinating and important. If you're interested I'd like to show you – both of you.'

'What, the blood-letting ritual?'

'No, obviously I can't do that, it's secret – private anyway – but I can show you where we do it, then you'd understand, intelligent man like you. You want to go?'

Shiva looked at Elmley who nodded once, his long face

moving with slow and weighty emphasis. 'All right,' Shiva said.

What a coup, Shiva thought to himself as he followed Digger's retreating form along the corridor and down the two flights of stairs to the street. On my first day back this walks right in through my door and announces itself, a bona fide example of psychotic confabulation embracing an entire group of people! This will definitely make the most remarkable case history that I've ever written up. The possibility of a lead paper in the *BJE* had momentarily driven all thoughts of Busner and his cabal from Shiva's mind.

When they reached the main entrance Digger motioned Shiva and Elmley to join him in a huddle. 'It isn't safe for you two to be seen with me,' he said, 'and I mustn't be seen by anyone – they watch us all the time.'

'What d'you mean?' Shiva asked, but Elmley remained silent – he knew.

'Our cult is only a sub-cult; there's one above it and another above that. For all I know there may be still more cults which oversee that one, but none of this matters now, as far as we're concerned the important thing is that I'm watched all the time to make sure that I don't reveal any of my knowledge. So, when we leave, I'll go first, then you follow.' He pointed at Elmley. 'Leaving at least a hundred yards between us. Then you bring up the rear' – he indicated Shiva – 'leaving the same gap between you and him. I'll make sure I walk slow enough for you to keep on my tail. Got it?' The other two nodded and Digger stepped out into the street.

Hearing the metallic air-groan of a jet braking overhead, Shiva looked up into dark-blue sky. The heat and the semi-nudity of the passers-by and the tables set up on the pavement outside the restaurants all brought home to him that it was summer. Suddenly summer. It hadn't been this season when he got on the train in Kenton that morning, had it? But if not, which one? When he took the trouble to look back over the past few months, Shiva realised that the change of seasons had completely failed to impinge on him since as long ago as Diwali. That's being preoccupied, he concluded, that's being overworked. He stripped off his suit jacket and draped it over his shoulder, he loosened the knot of his tie and yanked it down, he unbuttoned his collar. When he looked to see where Elmley had got to the architectural ironmonger's back was disappearing around the corner into Charlotte Street. Shiva hurried to catch up with him.

The trio, strung out like beads on the drool of an idiot, worked their way north through Fitzrovia. Damnably clever, David Elmley thought – the whole set-up had been brilliantly contrived so as to appeal to Shiva's vanity. Busner's hand had been hidden from Shiva by his own arrogant conviction that he was solving a great psychiatric mystery, as he padded through the mental miasma of Central London like a latter-day Sherlock Holmes. Elmley fingered the steel lozenge in his jacket pocket, his thumb on the ridged catch slid the blade in and out. A Stanley knife might not be the most effective of weapons, but he was confident that when the time came he'd be able to wield it with a free hand. Digger would make sure that Shiva held still, or indeed vice versa.

Office girls sat on benches eating beansprout salads from transparent containers; beside them were sausage-meat men stuffed into greasy clothing. Shiva thought about the timeless problem of what people should do with their elbows. Shiva thought about the Neasden Temple, what was that? Its pinnacles rising up in the drizzle above the surrounding roofs, it looked like nothing so much as a mausoleum sinking into a morass of muck. Shiva thought of the painted figure of the Red Indian chief which stood outside the Lone Star Diner in the Gloucester Road. Twenty years ago he'd assumed that it couldn't last — its paint was already chipped and its themed shtick already hackneyed. But it was still there while countless mighty blocks of concrete, steel and glass had been levelled to the ground. And still next to it was the restaurant's pathetic window display, a flaking plaster cactus, a dusty tumbleweed made of wire, a painted backdrop of adobe wall. Shiva wondered, if I were to insinuate myself into this mock-up of Apache country, would I feel any more Indian than I do now? Which is the same as to say, would I feel Indian at all?

Dave Elmley saw the Jews on the tops of the buildings skipping from ventilation shaft to water tank, their long black coats flapping. More frummers drove slowly past in their Volvos, their skull locks swinging in the warm breeze. To head north like this, into the very heart of their territory, taking the fight to them. It was hardly what they'd expect — they might even feel a tremor of fear.

By the time Shiva reached the junction of Grafton Way and turned right into Tottenham Court Road, Digger had already crossed the Euston Road and was heading up Hampstead Road at speed. While Elmley was in the middle of the intersection, caught up in a mêlée of ongoing roadworks, and apparently in conversation with a huddle of yet-to-be-installed traffic lights.

Shiva could see an ambulance pulled up outside the entrance to the University College Hospital's A & E department. It was a garish vehicle, its red-and-orange chevrons go-sicker stripes. The green-and-white checks on its rear doors were inset with a stylised caduceus in a blue asterisk. Shiva thought, you'd have to be mad to willingly enter such a jazzy van, in which case – he snickered knowingly – you might not be mad at all.

Up Hampstead Road and then over on to Stanhope Street where Rocky had lived. Who, Shiva wondered, inherited the Rock? Up Park Village East and then over the railway line. Along Mornington Terrace then across the junction with Parkway and on to Oval Road. Shiva had read once that when Regent's Park Terrace was built it stood alone in open country, a row of houses like a giant piece of Lego, waiting for a new piece of city to be attached. In the stinking heat of the summer afternoon the houses looked cool and inviting. From what he could see of their dark hallways hung with old prints, Shiva theorised that each one was occupied by a different family of upper-middle-class bien pensants. No doubt at this precise moment they were discussing elegant – yet workable – solutions to the very problems that plagued him. The tea they drank was fragrant and refreshing. China not Indian. Milk? I don't think so. In the mid-distance the hunched figure of Digger passed the Old Piano Factory and turned the corner into Jamestown Road. Shiva began to skip.

Twenty minutes later Shiva was standing in the doorway of a launderette on the corner of Queen's Crescent and Grafton Road. The smells of broiling fabric flapped in his face, and the chinking, thrumming sound of the machines filled his ears. Two doors along Elmley loitered by an off-licence. He'd got hold of a quarter-bottle of Scotch which he was swigging quite openly. With his dishevelled air and pale, worried face, the hinge-maker was playing his part of afternoon layabout with considerable brio. Looking across the junction, Shiva saw Digger use a succession of large keys to unlock a steel door that had been put up – presumably by the Council – to prevent the likes of him entering this large four-storey house.

Digger disappeared inside the house and Shiva let his attention fly between the blocks of flats on Mansfield Road, vault over the swelling green belly of Parliament Hill and then rise up into the sky. Digger resurfaced in the dark rectangular pool of the door and motioned to them, his hand grabbing at the air. First Elmley and then Shiva stepped out across the pavement and into the road. He was so awash with adrenalin that every step Shiva took felt like an anatomy lesson. His muscles lengthened and contracted with fluid ease, his cartilage absorbed the impact of his leather soles with the tarmac, his nerves up-loaded every twinge and glitch of his being-in-the-world. At the same time, irrelevant memories came to him with complete clarity: a schoolboy from a quarter-century ago, squatting down to sweep up a strew of fallen potato crisps from the playground, laughing when he finds them mixed up with autumn leaves, and then putting them all indiscriminately back into the packet.

When Shiva got inside the door he found Digger and Elmley standing very close together. They made room for him grudgingly, and then Digger went through the laborious operation of shutting the steel door, locking it, then closing the front door and locking it as well. 'You can't be too careful,' he whispered. 'We've been under surveillance for weeks.'

'By the police?' Elmley whispered back.

'No,' Digger hissed, 'by the other lot.' But instead of elaborating on this he indicated that they should follow him and they embarked on a peculiar tour of the derelict house.

In each of the rooms they entered Digger gave a little spiel, as if he were an outlaw estate agent persuading them to take on the purloined space. 'This is Pedro's room.' His gesture

encompassed the boarded-up windows, torn-out light fittings, a ripped-out sink which lay on its side in the middle of
the floor. 'It's fourteen by eighteen feet, roughly, and the
ceiling is twelve feet high. The original mouldings are intact,
but Pedro has taken a few pot shots at the ceiling rose with his
air gun.'

Pencil beams of sunlight pierced the two-by-fours nailed
across the bay window, and Shiva followed their tracer paths
to where they impacted on the floor and walls. Indistinct
pieces of trash wriggled in and out of view, a flute of copper
tubing bent to charm some springs which were uncoiling
from a slashed armchair. On the far wall there hung an
extremely badly executed oil painting of an ugly middle-
aged woman. The eyes had been crudely hacked out and
replaced with bits of old orange peel.

The adrenalin surge was still propelling Shiva along. Time
had slowed down to such a degree that he could spend long
extruded moments listening to the wheeze of Elmley's lungs,
or the rasp of Digger's fingernail as he scratched his jaw.
'Where is Pedro?' he asked, and his voice sounded amazingly
deep and full-bodied.

'At work,' Digger snapped in reply, as if this was obvious.

On they went, Digger stepping into each room and intoning
its dimensions, the name of its occupant, then drawing their
attention to what he thought were notable features. In the
second room there was a teetering pile of old mattresses covered
with a lumpy-porridge: foam-rubber chaff mixed up with spilt
wood glue. 'Andy's thing,' Digger explained. 'It's in progress.'
The contrast between the sharp light from the chinks in the
wooden cladding and the deep wells of darkness filled Shiva's
eyes with after-images, but even so, by the time they reached
the first floor he began noticing the evidence.

On small sets of shelves, in defunct fridges, and propped on top of doorways were small earthenware bowls and crudely moulded clay statues. All of them were stained rust-red. The old iron smell of dried blood permeated the house, and mixed with the homelier odours of stale sweat, evaporated alcohol and blown-away dope smoke to create a heady aroma of once and future misrule. 'The master bedroom,' Digger said, 'an impressive eighteen by twenty-two feet, twelve-foot ceiling, custom paint job. Melissa strings her rags up here, calls them her moon mice, yeah.'

His eyes adjusting to the light, Shiva saw that the pink room was criss-crossed by myriad clotheslines, and that these were hung with hundreds – thousands even – of old tampons. Obliquely lit, the dipping rows of dried-blood-encrusted cotton wool looked altogether unearthly, beautiful even. Shiva couldn't prevent himself from saying something which sounded intolerably prosaic. 'She must've been living here a long time in order to collect so many . . . moon mice?'

'I didn't say they were all hers personally.' Digger's brow was furrowed. Again, he seemed to think Shiva should not only appreciate the art work – if that's what it was – but understand it as well. Elmley was leaning against the wall outside on the landing, from which ancient wallpaper peeled away in damp ribbons. The sweat stood out on his high brow, his own wet Anaglypta.

'Are you OK?' Shiva placed a hand on his friend's arm. Elmley jerked away and his hand withdrew from his jacket pocket, the middle finger dripping with blood.

'Cool,' said Digger.

They mounted the tumbledown stairs – treads kicked in, banisters kicked out – and Digger called upon them to admire the giant collage on the wall of cartoon posters, drinks advertisements and old playbills. Objects had been glued on to the bumpy surface, including milk cartons, used tea bags, and a desiccated little bundle which, Shiva realised – as he made his way gingerly past – was the corpse of a mouse. There was a clatter of wings overhead and he looked up to see a tangle of gutter-rooted vegetation pushing through a broken window. Pigeon shit ill-starred the glassy peaks.

'Eleven feet by seven, ten-foot ceiling. A hutch, yeah, for a cowed little hamster serf, yeah?'

The wallpaper was striped in here, the floorboards bare except for remote islands of lino left behind when the rest was torn up. A small wire rack, which Shiva recognised as the kind once used for storing 45 rpm records, stood on top of an old piece of plasterboard. Three matching women's court shoes – two right and a left – were lined up along the skirting board. A picnic basket lay murdered, its head bashed in by the counter-weight from a sash window. On the windowsill itself stood three toy soldiers, their rifles levelled at an ancient crust of toast. Nearby was the slim, naked torso of a much larger plastic doll, its nipple-less breasts shiny in the sunlight. The toys presented a disturbing disjunction in scale, suggesting the possibility – by analogy – that the squat might once have been tenanted by giants, or dwarfs, or both. Shiva became aware of the insistent 'coo-coo-coo-coo' of roosting pigeons, the stress falling again and again on the final 'coo'.

'Shall we move on?' said Digger.

On the final flight of stairs leading to the attic the clay models and dishes began massing into disorderly platoons of misshapen men. The bloodstains on the walls connected up into a full paint job. The three men paused awkwardly, first Digger, then Shiva, then Elmley, as Digger fished out his keys and unlocked the door. Stepping inside he ushered them after him. 'Zack's room,' he announced, then continued, 'now –'

It was the sign he'd been waiting for. Elmley spun round and grabbed Shiva by the shoulders. Bloody hell, he's strong, Shiva thought, as he was hurled in Digger's direction. It must be all that cycling. Digger, having no option if he wished to avoid being knocked over, caught Shiva in his arms. Elmley's Stanley knife was already out of his pocket. He darted forward and sliced one way and then back, deep and hard across Shiva's windpipe.

Falling to the floor took five minutes. At first Shiva assumed that the pink droplets spraying over the sloping walls and splattering on the dormer window were part of another artistic effort, but then he understood that this was his own blood airbrushing the outlines of a disgraceful mural. Some 1970s rock-album cover, Shiva guessed, refracted through the stoned eye of a dreadful painter. The mural took up three of the irregular walls, great swathes of blue, purple and mauve banishing both planes and angles with the superimposition of a desert landscape. Three pyramids clustered like discarded cardboard boxes beside a thicket of wonky palms. A caravan of camels wended over the dunes with a refractory inability to conform with even elementary perspective, the lead camel being far larger than the one bringing up the rear.

David Elmley grappled with Digger, making the slow and leaden movements of someone putting a theoretical knowledge of violence into practice. So leisurely was their combat that Shiva thought Digger might not be there at all, and that his old friend was doing a jig with his own Stanley knife. Elmley passed the blade back and forth in front of his equine muzzle while uttering peculiar brays and snorts. But whatever the truth about this one-sided fight, it wasn't long into Shiva's second minute of falling that Digger fell too, and although he couldn't forbear from hating Elmley, Shiva was still glad he'd managed to vanquish the cultist.

Shiva Mukti spent his third minute of falling reading the slogan scrawled over the desert sky. The meaning of the characters bore no apparent relation to the work, and its rusty colour, together with the way the ascenders and descenders trailed off into splashes and smears, suggested it had been applied some time after the desert scene. It read: 'I caught a falling star and it cut my hands to pieces.'

I caught a falling star and it cut my hands to pieces. It had a certain naive Symbolist verve to it, Shiva thought, and in this context an almost piquant horror. Elmley had backed his lanky form into a far corner beneath the steeply sloping wall. He was folded up like a cowering house spider, and with shaking hands he fed pills into his moaning mouth. Fed and gobbled and crunched, so that a chalky froth gathered on his lips, then fell in globs on to his dimpled chin. Even from four-fifths of the way to the floor, Shiva could make out the slogan on the pill pot: 'Do not exceed the stated dosage,' and this too had a certain naive Symbolist verve.

In the last minute before he reached the floor, Dr Mukti had plenty of time to appreciate exactly what he was falling into. It was the very centre not of the blood-daubed penta-gram he'd expected, but a carefully delineated Star of David. The two interlocking triangles were traced on the floorboards with thin lines of white chalk. 'Coo-coo, coo-coo,' commented the roosting pigeons. Through the skylight Dr Mukti saw a plane heading up into the cerulean aether, like a heavy car being driven up a crystal hill. Then he hit and lay slopping about in his own blood, a weak and overqualified seal.

Dr Mukti thought it would be appropriate at this point in the proceedings if all the dramatis personae had been able to join him and Elmley in the attic of the squat. Swati, obviously, as composed as ever in a beautiful, gold-trimmed sari; Mohan, perhaps, although he conceded the situation might have a negative impact on the child; his mother, the aunts and uncles, filing silently in through the door, then lining up to form a grave, Graeco-Indian chorus; his colleagues from St Mungo's carrying Gunnar Grunbein in his leather office chair; and of course the patients that had shuttled back and forth between Heath Hospital and St Mungo's, some of them perhaps walking past this very house. Those animate weapons, once used then discarded, which now, by rights, should be allowed to witness the coup de grâce. The English teacher with hypoglycaemia, Creosote Man, poor Rocky spouting his cereal-packet poetry, Mr Double, Mohammed Kabir – they should all be here. He desired the Kumla Devi of his own life, a mass gathering on the bank of this gushing river of his own blood. But of course, the only sadhu he was permitted was Dr Zack Busner.

He came in through the door looking altogether ordinary, playing the part of himself with affecting ease. He was dressed in his habitual grey-flannel trousers, his green mohair tie was askew and one tail of his Viyella shirt poked out below the hem of his tweed jacket, a particularly unthreatening little detail which Dr Mukti noticed when Dr Busner turned to shut the door and bolt it.

'What,' Shiva bubbled, his voice sounding like a toddler half-gargling with its drink, 'no aspect of a frightening Hindu deity today, Dr Busner? No multiple arms, no necklace of skulls, no bloodstained teeth?'

'I rather thought,' Dr Busner said mildly, 'that at this late stage we might as well dispense with all of that.' He strolled over and placed his foot in the middle of Shiva's chest. 'To the victor,' he said conversationally, 'the spoils.'

'There is one thing . . .' Shiva gurgled. '. . . I'd like to know . . .'

'Yes?' The fat fingers rolled and unrolled the green tongue of tie, the prominent nose dipped.

'Why? Or rather, why me?'

'Well, you remember when we first met?' Dr Busner removed his foot and bent down laboriously so as to bring his full and froggy features up close to Shiva's face.

'Yes . . .' The darkness at the edges of the attic was massing and lumping. It had already swallowed up Elmley's recumbent figure, and now it sent exploratory tentacles into the Star of David. '. . . it was at that conference on affective disorders.'

'That's the one. Well, I introduced myself as your neighbour up at Heath Hospital. Do you remember that?'

'Yes.'

'And you looked at me rather disdainfully and said, "I know." Do you remember that too?' Dr Busner's head was cowled now with a dark hood.

Busner said nothing more, only looked at Shiva, his expression at once pitying and devoid of pity.

It dawned on Shiva that that was it. 'That . . .' he managed to spit out, 'was it? That was what all this was about? The whole business between us, all those ill people so cruelly used, the entire . . . fiendish plot . . . my life . . . Elmley's . . . that was all because of that . . . that snub?'

Busner took his time answering, and the dark cowl tightened, eclipsing his moon face until only his slack old crater of a mouth, grey and uninviting, remained in the diminishing spotlight of Shiva's consciousness. The mouth opened and closed, and as if from a long way off Shiva heard the final words of his nemesis: 'Isn't that enough?'

161

He slipped into the flat just as the old man stooped to lift the paper from the mat. The boy couldn't believe his luck – here he was being chased by a vicious bastard, his lungs bursting, his heart hammering, his knees aching with the impact of flight up flights of stairs, and his pants damp with the acrid trickle of fear, when this door opened. The old man emerged and sanctuary was visible, a sunlit room dusty and composed. The boy waited for a few seconds. The old man having picked up the paper shuffled a few steps into the corridor and peered in the other direction towards the lift lobby. It was all the opportunity the boy needed – he nipped in through the flat door, skidded across the tiny vestibule, leapt into the bedroom and went to ground, quiveringly still like a rabbit.

Would the old man have noticed? Or worse, would any of his pursuers have seen any part of him enter the flat, a flap of shell suit or a flicker of bleached hair? They might not come after him at once. No, they wouldn't. Once they knew where he was they could afford to wait as long as they wanted, until darkness if necessary. Not that they needed to worry about creating a disturbance, the block was nearly empty now, with most of the former residents long since rehoused. The problem families – problem for themselves mostly – had been packed off to another block exactly the same, which stood defiantly on the other side of the city, challenging everyone and anything because it was a renegade made concrete and gigantic. As for the rest of the residents from this block, almost anyone in good standing with the Council found that they were entitled to rehousing. Sanctuary was a tan-brick three-bedroom semi on one of the kidney-shaped islets of suburbia that had risen up out of the waste ground left behind when the block's identical siblings were demolished. Each of the new dwellings came gift-wrapped, a wooden fence enclosing a few square metres of lawn – ample space for bulbous, plastic toddler toys, a water feature or a conservatory.

So this block was almost empty. Only a few diehards were left, who wouldn't let go, who positively liked the place. Mostly they were elderly, old enough to have moved into the block when it was first stacked up – prefabricated section by prefabricated section – forty years before. Then they'd been the parents of young families, now they were retired. Then they'd moaned about having to leave the grid of small streets they'd grown up in, now they felt the same about leaving the block where they'd spent the greater part of their lives. Unsurprisingly, it was those who'd complained most vociferously about being rehoused in the block in the first place who now inveighed against quitting it. You'll never get me up – you'll never bring me down. A four-decade-long mood change.

And there were also the eccentrics, the collectors of miscellaneous jumble, and the curators who mounted bizarre, sparsely attended exhibitions of artefacts they'd looted from abandoned flats. There were even pigeon fanciers who indulged their feathered lovers to the fullest by allowing them to tenant the balcony and even move into the other rooms. Here the birds spread their substance over torn drapes, frayed carpets and scuffed lino, to create caves of guano in this artificial cliff face.

Now the block had only a third of its a hundred and seventy flats occupied at all, a hundred or so residents where once there had been a thousand. The boy knew this – he knew the block. He also understood that his pursuers knew it just as well. When the population had leaked away – leaving only puddles and smears of humanity – in came the malefactors, such as Twisted Gut and his crew. They moved into blocks like this one and set up their rackets, cooking up crack cocaine, fencing stolen goods, even – on especially grim occasions, the birthday parties of Lucifer himself – taking captives into the abandoned flats, either the girlfriends of their rivals, or these rivals themselves. Blood-soaked mattresses in gory twilights.

Twisted Gut looked as if he'd attended a devilish party and come away with a most unusual going-home present, scalded flesh which dangled like a rumpled bib from around his neck. There wasn't anything that Twisted Gut wouldn't do to the boy – whose name was Carl – when he caught up with him. There was nothing speculative about Carl's fate: it would happen. They would get him. It was only – like the fulfilment of any desire – a matter of time.

Why not get away? This city had once been a mighty port, a place of embarkation more than destination. Carl could still jump a ship bound for China or Brazil. Once there he'd take a foreign wife and learn the language like any other canny escaped convict. He'd come back in thirty-five years and open a restaurant, not in the old neighbourhood but one near by, where the story of what had almost happened to him was murky myth rather than dangerous rumour. Why not? Because Carl was transfixed, stunned by the enormity of his own transgression. He was rooted to the spot like a kid who's smashed a greenhouse, and remains there, petrified, as if a shard of glass was pinioning him to the well-mulched earth.

It was like a dance they'd spontaneously choreographed together, the old man's slow bend, the young one's quick lunge. Carl got his hiding place and the old man got a free newspaper full of adverts for exhaust-fitting centres, tanning salons, carpet warehouses, all the amenities. Adverts that were a no-man's-land surrounding tiny contested redoubts of editorial, write-ups of street parties, school gymnastics competitions and local crimes. The old-age pensioner raped, the young single mother robbed, the disabled man belaboured with his own crutches. Mass crimes committed against particular people. Carl was responsible for some of the crimes reported in the *Advertiser*. He may not have had the nous to plan them, or have been evil enough to start them, but he definitely didn't stop them going off. He'd grabbed hair, stashed valuables, heard the nauseating munch of stone eating flesh. Carl could read well enough, but he chose not to look at his own notices. He knew what had happened – he'd been there.

The old man picked the free newspaper up off the mat – an offcut of Axminster, neatly gaffer-taped to the line – although there was hardly any point. He too could read, but the ads weren't aimed at him. In his prime he'd read quite astonishing quantities, areas of print measurable as if they were floor-coverings. Fifty square feet of novels, thirty of poetry, eighty of history, and many hundreds of newspapers every year. Now he needed not only the spectacles with their fish-eye lenses, but also a convex piece of transparent acrylic, which he laid over an entire page, rendering the legs of the letters hairy with magnification. Even so it was a slow business, this ancient decipherment of modern texts. Yes, it was hard labour, this reading, but it couldn't be baulked. The old man came of an era and a class when self-improvement was reckoned more important than any other pursuit. He couldn't have stopped reading now even if he'd wanted. So, he read what was to hand, the free sheet or, on the rare occasions when he made it to the base of the block, the assortment of less local news-papers to be had in the corner shop. His home help brought him large-print books as well. He was a thoughtful man, the home help, but almost illiterate, so the same titles would arrive again and again. Dermot – that was the old man's name – knew some of them by heart. The implausible gunfights at hokey corrals had become his creed; the gunfighters lived, then died, and then were resurrected by rereading.

Dermot shut the front door, and using his stick and a series of handles that were screwed to the walls he made his way back to his chair. The handles he'd installed to assist his wife in the last two years of her effortful, deliberate progress towards the grave. The chair – which was nothing special in the way of furniture – sat facing the window, its worn nap registering the passage of clouds across the encompassing sky.

Carl stood behind the door in the adjoining bedroom. Sweat gummed up his T-shirt, gluing it to the inside of his nylon top. He shook with fear. He waited for the door to the flat to be kicked in, for Twisted Gut and the others to find him. He waited for the old man to come through and discover him, or to sense his presence and call the police. The flat was small – two rooms and the kitchenette which faced on to the balcony. It was so small that surely a hard heartbeat or laboured breath could be clearly heard? Carl began to hate his host, hate him for the betrayal he knew would soon come.

He stood, wedged behind the plywood bedroom door, and took in the clutter of several lifetimes, which had been tipped into this concrete drawer, then jammed into a two-hundred-foot-high filing cabinet. What a load of crap. How could anyone waste what little space they had by stacking two wardrobes horizontally? Big, heavy old things, with mirrored doors and their own internal sets of drawers. They were shoved up against the right-hand wall, while against the left was a row of armchairs, as grim and overstuffed as unwelcome elderly relatives watching the dancing at a wedding. One was covered in green plush velveteen, the next in greasy brown leatherette, while the third along had foam rubber bursting from its wounded shoulders. A fourth canted painfully, one short leg broken beneath its sagging arse.

Carl stopped his inventory, double-taking on the fact that he was able to do this at all while so imperilled. He stopped and strained to listen to the odd scraping, whistling, rushing noise of a bag of rubbish passing by his ear, its sound muted into an odd musicality by the twelve inches of intervening concrete. How long had it been since he'd bolted into the flat? Could he be – by some mundane miracle – safe?

Next door in the living room, the old man, Dermot, sat and looked out over the city. It was an oblong – this city. An oblong full of rectangles, stacked neatly in the right angle between the sea to the west and the river straight ahead of him to the south. Early on wet mornings – and there were many of these – from where Dermot sat in vigil, the slate roofs of the houses seemed to shine. The light obliterated the grooves between them so that they looked like individual slates, stacked neatly on end by a tidy labouring god.

Was this the same god as the one who lived in the lunar-module cathedral, the building which sat squarely in the centre of the city and the middle of Dermot's view? Or was it the other one, the god who rented the next-door cathedral? A gloomy building – part boarded-up cinema, part electricity substation – which was at the end of the giant lane. Right to left: the minarets of the old shipping offices on the quayside, the dirty white stalk of the radio station, the sickly brown bulk of the hospital – with its own tapering chimney stack for the burning of pus-filled dressings – then, at last, the two out-houses of the gods.

Dermot didn't believe any more in the god who was said to pilot the lunar module. He hadn't believed in him since his wife died in the sickly brown hospital. Those last two years he'd nursed her, Evelyn had looked out each day from their cliff face, across the intervening canyon – choked with the lives of so many more – to the cliff face where they both knew she would die. It was simply a matter of when her breath would falter, her blood thin too drastically, her heart pitter but no longer patter, as to when the transport would be required. When Evelyn was bedridden and dying the city turned its massive cold back on Dermot. Once it had been soulful, but now its bricks and its mortar were less an expression of its inhabitants' spirit than a ready-assembled factory for the processing of their bodies.

When he was growing up Dermot had been instructed in the nature of the lunar-module god. He was a jolly fellow right enough, in his white dress, always dancing with the kiddies and covering them with the odour of his sanctity. But he was stern as well, capable of inflicting awful punishments on those who refused to accept his way of going about things. As he grew older Dermot came to appreciate that everything was permitted by the jolly stern god so long as you watched out for his avenging stick. A stick like a steel beam that could beat you into pulp, a stick like a davit on one of the cranes down at the docks. Dermot accepted this because it seemed vital as well as true of human – if not godly – nature. There had to be a totting up. Columns of good and evil.

The last twenty years had been in the reddest of bad. Dermot thought his faith was all gone when his son died, but this turned out to be only the first part of his fall into despond. He grabbed for his marriage and hung on to it – painfully, precipitately – until Evelyn came away and he fell with her. What got you through when your face rasped past the rough concrete? It was God's white dress that acted as a parachute; the other stuff – the doing good so that good would be done by you – that meant nothing, that was a strawberry-flavoured supplement. When he realised this in its hateful entirety Dermot hit the stony ground of scepticism, and the cathedral – which he'd thought well intentioned if unlovely – became the miss-hit shuttlecock, the loudhailer for shouting at the ground, the split yoghurt pot. But mostly it was the lunar module, because it had gone up at the same time as those foolish men. They walked on the moon – while it landed on this dead and faithless planet.

In the bedroom Carl relaxed enough to feel the fullness of the pain in his bladder and the ache in his knees. He remained rigidly to attention, lest the smallest scratch of nylon on the plaster-pimpled wall alert the old man. Terror continued to trickle from his chest into his legs. Twisted Gut and his gang would bide their time, then they'd turn him over. They'd wait for aeons until the exact syzygy of boot and groin and brick signified revenge. Revenge, the only dish which for Twisted Gut wasn't the fastest of food.

But this stuff, Jesus, this stuff! These wardrobes, tables and chairs, these skeins of dusty curtains, these stacked mirrors and leaning towers of furry books, these burnt-out bar heaters and fused electric kettles. There were Hoovers so old-fashioned that Carl thought them bodged up from hairdryers and trouser legs. There were still other devices that he couldn't even identify; two metallic jugs set beneath spigots which jutted from a central chamber with a clock-face on it. Could the old man be a retired inventor? A Dr What as well as a Mr Who?

The bedroom was what, nine feet by fifteen and maybe nine feet high? Carl had once worked in a builder's yard and he knew his basic arithmetic. So, this space, these one thousand, two hundred and fifteen cubic feet, held how many others of hard old wood, soft dank foam, springy horsehair, flaking silver nitrate and damp chipboard? Over all of it the old man's smell lay as heavily as the dust.

Dermot had taken the furniture over. His own parents' when they ascended to wherever and he and Evelyn came up into the block. Then his daughter-in-law's sticks when his son died, and finally his own daughter's when she decided to move away from the city. At one time the family had occupied three flats in the block. Dermot wasn't fool enough to think that these had been happy times, but they'd been times nonetheless.

Time had at least passed, paced by the irregular succession of life's events, rather than standing almost still as it did now, the days revolving, each like the last, as he wound downhill towards the inevitable and complete motionlessness. When a tenant left a flat for the last time the maintenance men came in and 'soft-stripped' it. Then it became a void flat. Dermot had decided to resist being voided, and so he soft-stuffed his home.

Fifteen assorted sofa cushions, bed pillows – some in polythene, some loose – two sets of nesting tables, hexagonal and rectangular, a high chair, three upended mattresses, one of them double, on top of it a thatch of women's clothing. To

Carl's ignorant eye some of it looked good, the rest shabby, but all of it was ludicrously out of date. A carriage clock, a plant stand, two muddy oil paintings, a tea chest full of china, another full of pots and pans. Carl could tell that they hadn't merely been slung in here – these five hundred-odd cubic feet of decommissioned furnishings – they'd been carefully stacked and skilfully arranged.

Every week when the *Advertiser* came, Dermot would use the classifieds to price the stuff in the bedroom. This way he found out how far his stock had fallen. Three sets of full-length curtains together with nets. Blue. £5. Tel. 678 9115 eves. After that he'd have a cup of tea and a cup of strawberry-flavoured dietary supplement. He had five of each every day – the supplements saved the bother of having to cook or even make a sandwich. He did take some solids, two slices of bread with his soup in the evening, but the soup itself came in sachets like the supplement. Dermot liked sachets, he thought of them as oblongs full of life. Five regular top-ups through-out the eighteen hours of his day. One trip to the kettle every three hours, followed twenty minutes later by one to the toilet – if he made it. If not, the heart-rendingly lonely affair of stripping off sodden trousers and underwear, sponging himself down, depositing the soiled stuff in the bag and searching out the clean. Why, he inveighed on these occasions, why had she left him alone to endure this? This hadn't been part of the deal, this widowhood, this awkward and faltering existence.

Throughout the short nights he lay on a sofa bed which he unfolded beside his chair. The days were placid by comparison with those few short hours of age-tossed sleep, his feet too cold, his head too hot, his arthritic hip joints telegraphing pain all over the place, making his bones hum and vibrate, as if he were an iron bedstead struck with a crowbar. The days at least had clarity, whereas the nights had little definition. Were they normally or infernally dark? Sodium- or sulphur-orange?

Carl heard Dermot go shuffling through to the kitchenette for his noon cups. He heard the click and bubble of the electric jug, the click of the old man's dentures, the bubble of his lungs. The liquid noises agitated the boy's distended bladder. There was no other way out – he'd have to piss. He couldn't wait for the old man to nap so he could use the toilet. No, he was going to have to piss right here.

Carl cast about for a suitable vessel in among the welter of stuff. All he needed was a vase or a pot and he'd be sorted. But there was nothing big enough, and even the small jugs and saucepans were so jumbled up that if he moved one the others would chink and clatter. Carl was going to have to do it where he stood. Still, he reckoned, given the stench in the flat, the old man wouldn't smell it. He turned to the wall as if it were a welcoming splashback and yanking at the elasticated waist of his trousers eased himself out. He would, he decided, piss in a series of neat concentric circles, the better to minimise the noise. The letting go was so intense that Carl lurched and nylon snagged loud on Artex.

Carl choked off the flow between his thumb and index finger. The blue swallow tattooed on the fleshy webbing was drenched. He waited for the inevitable bubble and click as the old man made his way through from the next room. He braced himself for the scream, the shout or the gasp . . . but there was nothing, nothing save the soft slap of paper on paper. Hunched over, Carl shuffled around the door and into the vestibule. There was a barometer on one wall, a calendar on the other. A telephone table leant next to the front door. Stormy. Fair. Changeable. Prediction. Definition. Communication. No exit. He peeked into the living room and saw the old man's head – shiny on top, mottled behind – poking up above the back of an armchair facing the window. It was so vulnerable, like an egg demanding to be cracked, or a golf ball longing to be driven over the city centre, rising up high over the river, the next finger of urbanity, and even the estuary beyond that, until it plummeted back to the ground, hopping and skipping to a standstill on the apron of green fields that mounted towards the misty horizon.

The old man's head was absolutely still for long minutes, until it trembled and there was another soft slap. Drunk with danger, Carl knocked with his street-scraped knuckles on the white paint of the doorjamb; the head didn't so much as waver. Carl advanced a half-step into the room. Now he could see the old man's collapsed cheek, and his ear, a lumpy chunk of cartilage chewed upon by time, and set on the side table by his chair there was the flesh-coloured plastic rind of a hearing aid. The boy guffawed, whip-cracked two fingers, turned, barged into the bathroom, and releasing his other hand he sprayed urine like a dog.

In the afternoons Dermot read the large-print books. He had no preferences. Anything his home help flung his way was fit meat for consumption – he was too old now to be poisoned. Too old and too proud, up here on the twentieth floor surveying the city's deconstruction. At one time he would've seen tens – scores even – of other blocks, but now he was alone and the block was alone as well, the only one left standing, like a drunk leaning against the cloudy bar of the sky, while all its mates had collapsed to the ground having drained their fill of the human spirit.

Dermot read books not caring what they were about. The characters were strangers to him, exactly as the people in the street below were strangers. The passage of time makes fiction of everything, he thought. When his family first moved into the block, taking up residence in a three-bedroom flat on the twelfth floor, Dermot had recognised every third face that passed him on the surrounding streets, and if he didn't know the name attached to it he knew its mother's, father's or cousin's. The process whereby a street had been sucked up then stored in the new concrete silos – the two-up-two-downs disassembled then reassembled two hundred feet up in the air – had placed people even more securely in a grid of relationship. Oh there's so-and-so who used to live at the end of such-and-such; and there's her, who was always carrying on; and those kids who kept breaking into the haulage yard at the back of the works, even their lot got a flat in here, now they're up and down the lifts all day causing the same bloody mayhem.

Carl came out of the toilet and hovered in the vestibule, his hand on the latch. If he was going to go he might as well go now; after all he couldn't possibly stay. And yet . . . and yet . . . out there was everything worth avoiding, the fine mesh of badness he'd been entangled in for years. Why not stay in here, why not? They'd take him by the scruff of his neck and throw him on top of the garages at the end of the close, then they'd drag him off again. They'd pick the broken glass out of his cheeks and shove the splinters in his eyes. One would hold his legs open while the next took a goal kick.

What was there outside the block for Carl? Only a beating and a torturing and maybe even a killing. It happened. If he survived at all his only prize would be free entry back into the kickmill of aggression. Oh yes, there was a girl too, a girl with savage plaits and a sunbed tan; a girl unusually pretty, a girl foul-mouthed but fanciable. And that was the trouble, because this girl, Dawn, was only using Carl as a stepping stone to cross over the final river of restraint. He knew only too well where she'd next place her shiny shoe: on one of the henchmen, or even Twisted Gut himself.

Carl thought about it. Now he was banged up in the old man's flat he had time for considering these things in a way he never did during his daily circuit of drugging, drubbing and shagging. Wasn't this whole business – a dispute over the takings from a pawnshop robbery down in the city centre – really about Dawn? Hadn't Twisted Gut given him the nod so that he'd have an excuse to get Carl out of the way? It didn't do to dwell on it, but what the hell else was there for him to do? Think about the others who might miss him, discovering a Carl-shaped space in their lives?

Carl knew he was in flat 161, or maybe 162. He knew this block well enough because his mother was a tenant in the one on the other side of the city. Tenant – mad to call her that. She had no rent book, she undertook no communal activities, she was a brass, pure and simple. A prossie. She roosted on a dirty ledge, high up in this other concrete escarpment, together with a shiftless flock of her own kind. Girls well into their forties with smack habits to feed. Girls who received filthy-minded boy visitors at all hours of the day and night – twisted desires distort time. Girls who bagged up the used condoms at the end of the twenty-four and chucked them on top of one of the already overflowing wheelie bins. A rubber bag full of half-humans gets you a paper wrap that will halve your humanity. Neat that.

Yeah, Carl knew this other block, but he only went by to get the occasional hand-out, or exchange a few unpleasantries with her. She was dead to him, the dirty cow, taking on all comers, even the immigrant geezers who'd flowed into the block as if they were a dirty tributary of the dirty river itself. Even them. In the spare bedroom Carl felt the metallic bile rise up into his mouth. You might've thought that having known nothing else he'd be used to this, but he wasn't.

Dermot remembered going to a pawnshop with his mother so that she could redeem a brooch. It was a dark, clinking place, with the cheap gold set in worn old wood. He would've been what, four or maybe five? It was before the war. On that day his mother had been happy, but she made certain Dermot knew that there were others less fortunate. She told him that every ring in the window for sale was a tale of woe, a ductile band of happiness that had been shaped easily into sorrow. Throughout his life, whenever he'd walked past a pawnshop in the city, Dermot had heard the unredeemed pledges whimpering from behind the glass.

Yes, they'd all known each other, the people of the block. There had been coach trips and whist drives, and during the long summer evenings the shirt-sleeved men and the cotton-frocked women would stand out on the apron of paving stones at the foot of their collective home to smoke and talk. It had been a good community, or so they thought. But now Dermot understood that all it had truly been was an eye of neighbourliness in a storm of civic disintegration. When they'd gone up into the block the children were eleven and nine. Families with smaller kids were confined to the first four floors. Even so, Dermot thought of his children as being raised in the block, raised up to adulthood. When he'd arrived he was in his prime, vigorous and optimistic. He knew enough – and was vain enough – to believe that other wives besides his own found him attractive.

Their flat on the twelfth floor faced the opposite way to this one, towards the park and the suburbs. He remembered sitting at the window – the same oblong screen as this one, but showing a period film – and watching as a young woman he'd dallied with came pushing her pram along the cinder track beside the bowling green. He recalled being able to see every movement of her heavy breasts and the pendulum of her caramel hank of hair as it swung between her shoulder blades. He remembered being entirely bound up in it, this tight bundle of emotions, fear and lust and remorse. A drama played out on the paving stage in front of the block, that constant and immovable prop, always present in every scene, its shadow so long and dark that it regularly eclipsed hundreds – thousands even – of lives.

Then he'd thought that no mere passage of time could possibly diminish what he was going through, but how wrong he'd been. Dermot had confessed to the lunar-module god, and the astronaut in the white-surplice space suit told him to put his own mission in order. Dermot did so, as entranced by the breaking off of the affair as he had been by commencing it. He renounced it all, the unfamiliar white limbs casting familiar shadows against the rose-patterned wallpaper.

Evelyn, he thought, had never known. When Dermot eventually let go of the lunar-module god, he felt that it no longer mattered at all. He watched God's spacecraft tumble end over end before being burnt up in the incense-laden atmosphere of that alien planet; faith in the future. Their son's death had hurt them both so much, scoured out the stuff of them – what could a few long-gone afternoons mean now? They'd only been intermissions, ice-cream advertisements to remind him – now that he no longer had a sweet tooth – that once he had.

The afternoon wore on. In the spare bedroom, in among the unnaturally inherited furniture – from son to father – Carl hunkered down on his rubber heels. In case the old wanker came into the room he stayed penned behind the open door, only peering out from time to time to see where the milky eye of the sun had got to, as, filmed over by cloudy cataracts, it bleared its way across the sky. He marked the passage of time by sounds he'd never bothered to pay attention to before; not that they were at all subtle, it was just that in Carl's life, up until this moment, there'd been no call for subtlety whatsoever.

He heard the police cars' sirens and, rather than wondering if they were coming for him, he savoured their puniness. They were like the drills of feeble dentists, squealing and revving as they struggled to drill the immoral caries out of the decaying city. When the school across the way was let out and Carl heard the chimes of an ice-cream van, he was able to compare the two noises. To his surprise the ice-cream van sounded more threatening than the police cars, calling children to come and enjoy a lolly truncheon or a pair of wafer cuffs.

At dusk the wind got up and boomed against the window. Carl watched as a pigeon who thought it was a hawk twisted and then fell past. He'd long since moved from squatting to kneeling, but even so the numbness of his calves and feet felt like death. He envisioned them white, bloodless, cloven like pigs' trotters in a butcher's window. He eased himself upright, but they couldn't support his weight and he pitched forward into the room banging his head on a chair leg. Carl moaned, a loud and guttural sound.

The old man, Dermot, chose that moment to come into the bedroom. He set down, his soft slipper within inches of Carl's ear. The boy lay still, feeling knitting needles rattle and chink in his hollow legs. He twisted and peered up into the owlish eyes of the old man. They were looking directly into his, yet the old man gave no sign that he'd noticed Carl at all. He merely shuffled round a hundred and eighty degrees, brought the rubber tip of his stick down precisely on the lobe of Carl's left ear, then retracted it and shuffled away. Carl was too shocked to cry out; besides, he'd had another revelation: either the old man was senile or he was near blind, because he'd failed to see Carl now and perhaps he never would.

Night fell. The sky leached the darkness out of the land, leaving behind cubes of light floating in a choppy sea of masonry. Dermot had his two night-time cuppas and then, as he slumbered in his chair, Carl had his. He padded across the back wall of the living room and into the kitchenette. He tickled the faucet into life and filled the kettle with a limp trickle. When the automatic click was coming Carl moved to muffle it with a tea towel. He made himself a cup of the strawberry-flavoured dietary supplement; he'd been in the thieving game long enough to know that you always took what there was most of. He slurped his supper standing by the door to the balcony, listening to the low susurrus of the old man slumbering in the next room, the sough of the ventilation system, the moan of the wind.

It was, Carl noted, painfully tidy in the old man's kitchenette, every prong, plate and packet fiercely aligned. It was painfully tidy – but horribly dirty. Seasons of strawberry snowfalls had dropped into the crevices between cooker and fridge, fridge and worktop. What dirt and mud the old man dredged in from his infrequent forays into the outside world had all washed up here forming a brown moraine on the dun, marble-patterned lino. In front of the sink waterfall had eroded this lino, exposing its thread-veined structure.

Had he the ability to read it, Carl would've understood that this was the same old story of the old. Dermot did the best he could to keep the small space clear, then the home help came and rubbed it all out. Carl stood and supped then gnawed a couple of pieces of bread. There was a spice rack screwed into the wall beside the cooker, and on top of this there was a line of pill pots, the old man's medication. From shape, hunch and words recognised the boy saw some things of use. He neatly twisted off the child-proof caps and took two of one and one of the other, necking all three with a final swig of the strawberry gloop. Then, spreadeagled against the wall, he made his way back to the bedroom. Carl had decided to stay the night.

While Dermot went haltingly through his bedtime routine – wedding sagging flesh to wrinkled pyjamas – he thought of the thousands of bedtimes that had joined up his married life. He recalled what it was like always to be under the eyes of another, eyes full of resentment or suspicion, but never cold and seldom indifferent. Now the moist orbs of his family had been replaced by the cold lenses of the CCTV system, which was meant to protect the dwindling population of the block from any harm. Dermot never believed that this was an effective deterrent. What was needed was a gaze that antici-pated trouble rather than registering when it had already occurred. The gaze of a lunar-module god who came down to earth, or a wife at bedtime, who checked jealously for the marks left behind by another and tell-tale modesty.

Mostly Evelyn's gaze had that lukewarm acceptance of one parent for the other's physical presence. For the first few months after his wife had died Dermot's daughter had returned to the city. She stayed with friends who lived on the other side of the river, out where the city fringed the countryside. Every day she came over to see him on the ferry which honked its way between the high-stone embankments.

Dermot could sense Susan's warm gaze approaching, welling with liquid daughterly concern. But he was wise enough to appreciate that this wasn't an inexhaustible commodity, that she was doing her duty by him, that soon she would feel both exasperated and claustrophobic. Then she'd have to leave. Certainly, she could never stay the night in the block itself; to do so would've been to shut her up in a maddening box.

Since then gazes had been in short supply, and the occasional glance was Dermot's lot. The home help peered at him, checking for vital signs as if they were the tread on tyres. The doctor in the pale-brick pavilion that had recently been erected at the base of the block peered at him with some curiosity, and Dermot knew what he saw. A man in his mid-seventies, a native of a city renowned for its smoking and drinking, a man who'd spent his working life bowed down by hard manual work, the strain of repetitive tasks. Yes, the doctor peered at Dermot and marvelled that although twisted by arthritis he was still a vigorous enough plant.

Most of Dermot's contemporaries were gone the way of Evelyn – to the hospital; a building so huge that it constituted a natural feature, its flanks changing colour as the sun rose, traversed the sky, and then set. Gone the way of Evelyn from the hospital to the cemeteries, necropolises which lay out where the urban jigsaw began to fall apart, and no one troubled any longer to look at the lid of the box.

The Asian man in the corner shop looked at Dermot with some compassion – this he knew – but it was so circumscribed by his sensible awareness that he could do no more for the old man than serve him his newspapers, his dietary supplement and his teabags with polite efficiency.

These were the only eyes that caught his waning image in their fleshy cameras, yet Dermot wasn't bitter. He couldn't blame them for his own vision had become strange. The years of staring down at the bug life below meant that when he occasionally descended they all seemed grotesquely large, their pink mandibles snaffling chips and saveloys in the café, their hairy antennae agitating in the betting shop, their shiny carapaces slick with rain as they scuttled along the street. Despite this, all he wished for was to be intimately observed once more. Even to be stared at with hatred or contempt would suit him – for these were strong and intrusive emotions. As long as there was someone there at bedtime to do the staring, to peer round the door and watch as he flipped open the sofa bed with a practised wrist; to watch as he took his unease on the tumultuous surface, the sheets that weren't changed from one week to the next, only further dishevelled by his dark thrashings.

As for his hearing, well, the same doctor had insisted on the aid. A foul thing of flesh-coloured plastic which Dermot disdained. He took a sip of dusty water and, settling down into the bank of duck down and foam, allowed himself a wry smile at the recollection of what Evelyn had said about his deafness: You can hear things perfectly well when it suits you.

In the night the two of them dreamed their dreams of leaving. Dermot saw the block transformed, massively enhanced so that it was broader, stronger and higher. Its TV aerials and its lift wheelhouse pierced the cloud cover, while the widened balconies foamed with trees, shrubs and flowers. From where he sat, close to the summit of this man-made peak, Dermot could see way into the next country and even the lands beyond. Picking up an ornate brass telescope he found by the side of his chair, he used it to observe people walking in the streets of distant cities as clearly as if they were in the room with him. He soon discovered that if he noticed

153

anything untoward – any bad or mean-spirited behaviour – he'd only to purse his lips or raise a finger in admonition for it to cease immediately.

Carl found rest, at last, in the bottom wardrobe. He'd considered sleeping out in the carpeted open, in the dry gulch between outcroppings of furniture, but decided against it. After all, if Twisted Gut and his posse got in that would be the end of him, staked out in the desert. So he went for the wardrobe, a solid coffin of walnut and mahogany, turned on its side with a mirrored flap for a door. When he crawled in and let it fall Carl feared he would suffocate, so he propped it open with an elbow of coat-hanger which he'd extracted from a jangly skeleton of them in the corner.

Carl crammed himself into the lagging of old suits and overcoats. The decaying naphthalene of mothballs assaulted his nostrils. Yet uncomfortable as he was Carl still slept – the old man's sleeping pills saw to that. They clutched his bony shoulders with their powdery fingers and dragged him down into sleep.

In sleep the sun sank again and again, plunging behind the finger of land beyond the river, sinking into another river of molten lava. The city-centre buildings were thrown into the sharpest relief and their dirty faces shone. Time merged in the city of Carl's birth as the far past and the distant future mated to parent an enchanted realm: domes, castles, space ports, pleasure gardens and open-air stadia where knights strapped into jet packs jousted for the sexual favour of genetically enhanced damsels with conical breasts and conical hats. The cries from the tourney were musical notes strung on staves of jet-engine howl. In the royal box Carl rolled and shifted, banging his shoulders against the sides as he tried to eat his own knees. A listener would've heard only muffled flutters and hollow thumps, the death throes of a giant moth.

In Dermot's tower the tenants weren't content with their allocated living space. They required more. Taciturn men with roll-ups poised on their pursed lips, their flat caps pulled down over their eyes, their sleeves rolled up tight and their trousers cinched with thick leather belts. There were thousands of them pushing wardrobes out on to the balconies, where they became the unlikely foundation for crazy extensions. Sheds were nailed to the wardrobes, then greenhouses and conservatories were riveted to the sheds. Like crenellated davits the long arms of these temporary structures thrust out into the dark sky.

At dawn, on waking, it struck Dermot again — exactly as it had struck him the first time, with well-coordinated force — how richly ironic it was that his body — so warped and peeling, so damp and decaying — should nonetheless appear likely to survive the destruction of this soaring spire of steel, concrete, asbestos and masonry. In the early morning — as if this were the primary fact with which he needed to be reacquainted on waking, more fundamental than breathing, thinking, or walking — Dermot felt the block as a parental presence at once stern and yielding, hugging him with its reinforced arms, protecting him with its reassuring bulk, keeping watch on the hostile world through its hundreds of oblong eyes. The block even smelt like a parent, a heady aroma of intense familiarity — at once attractive and repellent.

Soon after he'd limped back to the sofa bed, stripped the covers, folded it up for the day and assumed his usual position, Dermot's vulnerable head became the focus of another's attention, as haltingly, on the balls of his feet, Carl took the walk through inner space to the toilet. Fucking freaky, he thought – if I hadn't heard his tread and the toilet flush, I'd've sworn the old feller hadn't moved since last night.

How quickly can a routine be established? When two aggressive and frightened creatures are confined in the same space together, very quickly indeed. Especially when one of them is not at all sure what the intentions of the other are. The first full day he spent in flat 161 Carl conformed so entirely to the old man's routines, that by the end of it he felt as if he too had been in residence for decades. When the old man coughed Carl took the opportunity to clear his throat, when the old man drank his tea and slop, Carl seized the occasion to drink his own, when the old man went to the toilet, Carl followed in his wake. The old man was his pacemaker, helping him to race to the next small event. In between these Carl took up a station to the right of the window in the bedroom. Here, if he squatted down, he was hidden by a stack of old kitchen chairs, and if he stood he could look at the city.

As Carl shadowed the old man a peculiar thing happened. He started to learn what it was like to live with someone else, to cooperate and to tolerate the quiet yet jarring noise of intimacy. In contemplating the city, the young man learnt patience. He was receiving an education.

Oil tankers stood off from the container port at the mouth of the estuary while smaller merchant vessels headed upriver, their keels tearing its brown drape of water. Carl learnt to distinguish between the two. He watched the ebb and flow of the newly established households at the foot of the block. Blue wheelie bins jostled at the garden gates, then lined up on the pavement to regurgitate their contents into the filthy mouths of the garbage trucks. Then they turned around and jostled back inside. The wet laundry slapped on the lines and then lay there until with a shiver it was dry. The outsize poultry shed of the neighbourhood primary school sucked in the uniformed chicks then disgorged them, sucked them in and disgorged them again. Carl watched tiny figures – legs grey, tops blue – race their own dark shadows across the green playing field. An old woman held the hand of a toddler as it marched importantly along a wall. And all the while the traffic on the dual carriageway processed, each car maintaining a rigid distance from the one in front, so many little rubber-wheeled carriages running on invisible tracks.

As the hours passed and then the days Carl became detached. He stared at the terrain of paint flake and pigeon dropping on the narrow ledge outside the bedroom window until it grew into a world he reverenced. The play of shifting weather and light over the city held him entranced. Sunk deep in those concrete canyons he'd never minded what went on above. The day was simply wet or dry, the sun on or off. But now each squall or sunny spell provoked a significant mood change in him. Over it all the clouds boiled and coagulated, the very stuff that dreams are made of. Either they piled up into bodies, landscapes, animals and gods, or else they were pulped by the wind and smeared all over the sky.

Clouds, Dermot thought, his fingertips smudging the inky weave on his newspaper rug, clouds can be anything. Is that why we think we can be anyone and do everything? In the very early morning the sky had been a painful lemon-blue, an ice-cream-headache void crying out to be furnished with the mortal con trails and deathly billows of a great dogfight, hundreds of fighters and bombers plaiting the vaporous head of a Gorgon. Then the waves of cumulus rolled in from the sea, and Dermot – from a remote and seldom visited cellar of his memory – dragged forth a recollection of visiting a seance with his mother.

It would've been in the mid-1930s, but people still felt themselves to be living in the annexe immediately adjoining the charnel house of the First War. Dermot grimaced – they hadn't known that Death's new establishment would soon be taking bookings. His mother, sad, pinched, prematurely old in fashions that made everyone look prematurely old – in which case perhaps she wasn't at all? – had taken him down to town, to a darkened hall belonging to a spiritualist church. There, crushed in the middle of a bench lined with similar women – their credulity insulated by wool, muslin and flannel – he'd watched a lady, at first poised, become a groaning thrashing thing, throwing her thick ankles about with such abandon that she exposed her underwear. Then she gave birth through painted lips to a cloudy apparition, which, to the accompaniment of sighs and cries from the audience, took on the appearance of whatever it was they wanted to see. Even aged five or six, Dermot suspected that this was an extrusion of filmy fabric. Yet for him as well this was magical enough, and when they walked home, his mother unable to contain her guilty excitement – uncharacteristically loquacious, swearing him to silence then urging him to sound the trump in the same breath – he didn't feel the need to challenge her version of events. The Red Indian chief she'd seen with her own eyes and the oracular prophecies from beyond the grave. Clouds – whatever they were of – could be anything.

When the kettle's switch snapped, or the bathroom door complained, or even when the paper apron rustled in the old man's lap, Carl's cloud dispersed and he was back, fighting for survival in a hostile wilderness of six hundred square feet.

Adrenalin boiled in his brain; alert yet tranquillised he moved balletically into the tiny hall, sensing with every erect nape hair the other movements in the flat. He consumed the meaty breath of the hot-air duct above the bathroom door, he tuned into the mood music of the fluting draughts, he dabbled by the enclosed water tank which sounded like a pobbling stream shut up in a cupboard. He gazed upon the old man's head with all the homicidal tenderness and murderous reverence of a traditional hunter, whose prey is also his god.

For three days now Dermot had felt the gaze upon him again. He was alive to its changing quality, and in this he became alive to himself once more. At times the gaze caressed him lightly – a mere brush of visual fingertips – at other times it stabbed at him, a sharp look of bloody intent. But mostly the gaze had the lukewarm indifference he yearned for, the wifely acceptance he sought.

Every Wednesday morning at around nine-thirty Dermot's home help arrived, a fat young man called Sean. Carl was reemerging from the wardrobe – having retreated there for a lie-down – when he heard the key in the lock. It was bizarre but true that the scally's new way of life was proving more tiring than ducking and diving on the streets. I'M HERE AGAIN, MISTER O'LEARY, Sean shouted from the front door. IT'S ME – SEAN. I know who it bloody is, the old man replied, who bloody else would it be?

It was hard to say which shocked Carl most, Sean's voice, the old man's, or his very reacquaintance with the fact of speech. Sean's voice signposted DANGER in bellowed capitals, while the old man's tired rattle was a grave disappointment. Without being aware of it, Carl had invested Dermot with all of the attributes that had been lacking in his own benighted father, the most obvious being that he was present at all. The old man was nothing if not there; from this Carl leapt to imagining him kind, wise and competent. A man who, while bowed down by age, still had the ability to command respect just by parting his wrinkled lips and uttering – with a voice at once commanding and compassionate – the single word 'no'.

I'LL DO THE BEDROOM FIRST, MISTER O'LEARY, Sean bellowed as he rattled around for the dustpan and brush in the cupboard next to the bathroom. The rattling was succeeded by a heavy approaching tread. Carl let the wardrobe door to, his muscles seemed to audibly creak, and he wondered why the intruder was oblivious to the high-pitched whine of his nerve endings. The footfalls came to a halt level with Carl's face and the wardrobe on top protested as Sean leant his broad back and generous buttocks against it. Then the home help farted, a long, loud and explosive fart which vibrated against the wood. Then he lit a cigarette.

You're not cleaning in there – the old man's desiccated, distant voice trickled like sand into Carl's ear – you're having a bloody fag, aren't you? RIGHT YOU ARE, MISTER O'LEARY, Sean bawled back at him. RIGHT YOU BLOODY WELL ARE. C'mon, Sean, the old man's voice trickled on, if you're going to sit there having a fag you may as well make yourself useful at the same time. Put on the kettle and come sit in here. Talk to me – y'know I don't see a soul from one day to the next. RIGHT YOU ARE. The nonsensical acknowledgement was repeated, the wardrobe groaned with relief as Sean ceased pressuring it. When he'd left the room Carl propped the door-flap open with the hanger. Whatever the risk he had to know what was going on next door.

Bubble, click, splash, chink, the sigh of an old armchair yielding to a heavy weight. THERE YOU GO, MISTER O'LEARY. Thanks, Sean. I'VE BROUGHT SOME BOOKS, MISTER O'LEARY, I'LL GET THEM FROM MY BAG IN A SEC. That's very decent of you, Sean, very decent. DID YOU LIKE THE LAST LOT THEN? Oh yes, very much. I THOUGHT THEY LOOKED RIGHT UP YOUR ALLEY, MISTER O'LEARY, SO I GOT YOU MORE JUST THE SAME.

What must it be like, Dermot mused, only to be able to judge a book by its cover? What does Sean think when he sees people sitting quietly and reading? I know he understands that there are stories to be unfolded from these layers of paper, but surely the act itself must seem to him a kind of purgatory, sitting and waiting while watching a small screen covered with incomprehensible signs.

.YOUR DIET STUFF IS NEAR RUN THROUGH, MISTER O'LEARY, Sean said after a while. DIDN'T YOU GET DOWN TO THE SHOP ON MONDAY? No, no, I didn't, the old man whispered. To tell you the truth, Sean, I couldn't be bothered. YOU'RE NOT AILING FOR ANYTHING, ARE YOU, MISTER O'LEARY? the home help cried out. YOU KNOW WHAT THEY'RE LIKE DOWN THE SOCIAL. IF YOU DON'T EAT UP ENOUGH THEY'LL HAVE YOU IN THAT SHELTERED HOUSING BEFORE YOU CAN SAY . . . BEFORE YOU CAN SAY . . . He faltered, searching for the cliché. Before you can say euthanasia, the old man put in. WHATEVER YOU SAY, MISTER O'LEARY. SO DO YOU WANT ME TO GO DOWN THE SHOP FOR YOU? I'VE GOT THE TIME THIS MORNING. That'd be great. THE USUAL THEN? Yes, that'd be good, but I'd also like a couple of extra things, Sean, some fruit if you can find it – apples and oranges if they've got them – and a loaf of bread, and some – WHOA! WHAT'S ALL THIS, MISTER O'LEARY. I'M BEGINNING TO THINK YOU MUST'VE BEEN HAVING VISITORS. I THOUGHT THERE WAS A STRANGE FEEL TO THE PLACE WHEN I CAME IN. SOMETHING NOT QUITE RIGHT. Yes, that's it, Sean. The old man was unperturbed. I've got myself a gorgeous young lover, you wouldn't believe how obliging she is, comes up to see me every day, rain or shine. She'll even walk up when the lift's out of order. Amazing catch really, what with my age and my arthritis.

OH C'MON NOW, MISTER O'LEARY, Sean yelled. YOU'RE JOKING WITH ME, SENDING ME UP. I wouldn't do that, Sean. The old man's tone was firm. I need you too much to joke with you. HAVE IT YOUR OWN WAY, MISTER O'LEARY. YOUNG LOVER IT IS, NOW PASS US THAT ASHTRAY AND I'LL GO AND GET YOUR STUFF. I'M ONLY TOO GLAD TO SEE YOU EAT OWT BESIDES THAT STRAW-BERRY DIET MUCK – THAT'S MEANT FOR FAT YOUNG 'UNS LIKE MYSELF, NOT THIN OLD FOLK LIKE YOU.

Carl could picture Sean going out the door of the flat, slopping along the wet floor to the lifts, punching the button, waiting, and when the lift came forcing it down to the ground with his counterweight. With hallucinogenic clarity Carl saw him enter the mini-market and stand swapping sour some-things with the girl behind the counter, and then examine the movement of her hips and buttocks as she went about getting the old man's stuff. After that the fat home help waddled back to the block, buzzed for admission, exchanged cheery nothings with the caretaker who let him in, averted his eyes from those of one of Twisted Gut's gang who loitered in the lobby, took his place in the pock-marked steel casket and was winched back up again.

What was happening to him? Carl couldn't believe the precision with which he'd plotted these movements as, HERE I AM, MISTER O'LEARY, BACK AGAIN. Hello, Sean. SHE HAD BANANAS AND APPLES BUT NO OR-ANGES. Shame, the bananas don't keep too well. NO, I'M NOT SURPRISED – THE HEAT IN HERE. ARE YOU ALL RIGHT FOR YOUR PILLS AND WHATSITS, MISTER O'LEARY? I've all I need. AND YOUR DAUGHTER, HAS SHE BEEN BY RECENT LIKE? OR CALLED? She called a week or so ago. THAT WAS BEFORE I WAS HERE LAST, WASN'T IT? I s'pose so.

Carl heard the preparations for yet another cup of tea, and, while the kettle fulminated in the kitchenette, the home help's heavy tread as he moved about the living room flapping at the few sticks of furniture. Dust is peace, the old man whispered. WHAT'S THAT? Sean shouted. I said dust is peace, the old man repeated, you know you're in a peaceful place when there's a nice soft coating of dust. YOU SAY THAT EVERY TIME I COME, MISTER O'LEARY, Sean guffawed. IF YOU DON'T WANT ME TO DUST YOU'VE ONLY TO SAY SO. Don't bother with the dusting, Sean, there's no need. Sean wheezed and sat down again. IT'S JUST AS WELL, MISTER O'LEARY – MY ASTHMA. There was the sound of two teas being noisily drunk.

In the vestibule, stacking the underemployed cleaning materials, Sean cried out to Dermot, SHALL I LEAVE MY KEY, MISTER O'LEARY? WILL YOU BE WANT-ING IT? No, the old man croaked, you take it with you as usual, Sean. I'LL HAPPILY LEAVE IT IN THE CUP-BOARD HERE, MISTER O'LEARY. YOU KNOW I DON'T LIKE MY CLIENTS TO FEEL UNSAFE. I feel safer knowing that you have a key, Sean. Mine are there, aren't they? RIGHT HERE. Good, then I'll see you next week, Sean. NEXT WEEK IT IS, MISTER O'LEARY. The door was pulled to with a double clunk of great finality.

In the darkness of his wardrobe, like a bemused ghost, Carl wondered why it was that Sean hadn't detected his presence in the flat. He'd sensed something wasn't quite right, but why didn't the fat man smell him? Surely, if he visited the same ones week after week, he knew the smell of his clients' flats? Or was it that the old man's stench – which Carl himself must've become accustomed to – was so overpowering? Queries buzzed and batted about in Carl's skull.

The home help had left his cigarette smell hanging in the close air of the flat. When Sean lit his first Carl gagged with desire. The smoke smelt of everything, of food, sex and drugs, diesel fumes, damp privet and cheap perfume. Carl hadn't realised how much he'd been missing his fags – he hadn't even thought about smoking at all. What was happening to him in this strange refuge? What was he becoming?

Carl considered Sean's visit in more detail and the feelings it aroused in him. Anger – jealousy even. But why did he keep thinking of the home help as fat when he hadn't seen the man? Yet he knew he was fat, because he had a fat voice. A fat voice and cigarette smoke that smelt of everything. If he stayed in the flat much longer Carl suspected he might become altogether changed, become not Carl any more. He'd better get out – Sean had presented him with the means. He'd let himself out that evening, go and see the girl.

The very dangerousness of what he was contemplating made

Carl feel better. That was it, he was getting soft. Anyway, the old man must know Carl was there, he probably always had. He knew Carl was there and he tolerated his presence so long as he stayed out of sight. Fuck it, he'd even made Sean buy extra food, so he must want Carl to stay. Carl thought he understood this well enough. If he felt like this after three days of looking down on the world from the twentieth floor, what must it be like for the old man after years?

In the afternoon, after cuppas, Dermot slowly, painfully, tidied the flat. He did the essential tasks that Sean had expertly avoided – putting bleach down the toilet bowl, bath tub and sink, wiping all-purpose cleaner on the kitchen surfaces, bagging sheets and clothes for the wash. He found a bowl – had it belonged to his son or his daughter? It looked too modern for Evelyn – and arranged the unripe bananas and waxy apples in it. He put the bowl on a table set against the wall to the right of the door.

When at last silence said the old man was no longer in motion, Carl emerged. The vulnerable head was teed up again on the seat back, the newspapers were stacked beside it, the kitchenette was tortured into uncomfortable tidiness. The new items in the flat – fruit, books, bread and butter – had an odd radiance to them, as if they'd been brought back from an alien planet.

Carl stood for a long time looking at the head on the edge of the chair and willing the old man – O'Leary the home help had called him – to turn round, but he didn't. Eventually Carl padded out to the kitchen and buttered himself a piece of bread, taking care to leave everything as near to how he found it. He stood at the bedroom window eating. A mist had blown in off the sea, and together with it came a scattered flock of seagulls. The birds soared up the face of the block.

Carl thought their rigid wings gave them a mechanical look, like feathered model aircraft. He preferred the pigeons.

Over to the west, beside the new container port, Carl could make out the three-bladed wind turbines revolving in the wind. He let the world turn itself upside down and the turbines become the propellers of a city-sized freighter, pushing it out into the ocean of sky. Queasily he felt for the old man's keys in his pocket. They were there.

Dusk took a long time seeping into the sky, and with it mizzle slowly percolated. The close down below became sharply delineated, clean and wet. Carl was fixated by four semis that stood on a garden island surrounded by a moat of glistening tarmac. An umbrella came out of the school and, feet paddling at its rim, it swam around the corners until it washed up on the island. Four men stood looking into the open bonnet of a car, as if it were a dead dog and they were deciding where to bury it. Other men arrived in a van and opened up a hole in the road, they put a waist-high, yellow-plastic barrier around it to protect the city's modesty, and then began performing a gynaecological examination.

When at last the orange pin-pricks had pierced the thickening night, and O'Leary had had his final two cuppas, taken his stuttering leak, then settled himself for the night, Carl made his move. Standing with his hand on the latch he felt poised between everything and nothing, but confused as to which side of the door was which.

One foot across the threshold Carl halted, half-expecting O'Leary to rise up from his sofa bed and implore him not to go. But there was no sound at all save for the clunk and moan of an approaching lift: the block, gulping up its human fodder. Stepping out on to the mat Carl braced himself for the shout of recognition, the slap of their trainers as they came for him.

But still there was nothing. When the lift fell silent Carl bolted across the corridor, heaved the door open and scampered down the stairs. Three flights down he entered the seventeenth floor and took the lift to the ground floor. Its doors parted to reveal an empty chequerboard of linoleum tiles reeking of disinfectant. Through an open doorway Carl could see the nicotine-coloured residents' lounge. Pot plants loitered on low tables, informative leaflets rustled on wall-mounted racks, their leaves caught in an artificial sirocco gritty with the dust of peace. Jaunty pop music leapt from speakers bolted to the ceiling, but there was no one to listen to it, let alone dance. For long seconds Carl was transfixed, the whole weight of the block squatting on his head and shoulders, but then he wrenched himself free and scampered out the door, into the night.

In the long afternoon he'd plotted his route along the backs of the houses, down the trashy alleys and across the patches of waste ground. He moved from one area of darkness to the next one of obscurity, avoiding the pubs, each with its gaggle of door-hanging kids. He bypassed the street lamps and turned his face away from the bus-stop loungers. He reached the border of Twisted Gut's territory and began to breathe more easily. He loosened the hood he'd drawn tight around his head and allowed the night air to play cool on his sweaty face. It felt good. Walking down the long streets lined with thin houses he began to notice things, this faked stone façade, that carriage-lamp-flanked portico. In an upstairs window a girl was having her long mousy hair brushed by her mother. The girl was thirteen or so but her head was tiny, almost deformed. Each stroke of the brush beamed a lustre down at Carl through the gap in the nets. The woman turned to the window as if sensing his presence and Carl moved on. He turned into the next street. Here the houses were three storeys high and every fifth one was boarded up or burnt out. He looked at the decay with fresh eyes. The rotten window-frames, the doors sealed with corrugated iron, the shattered panes, the drains choked with weed.

A lad Carl knew had gone down south and said on his return that the city centres there were like they saw them on TV, shiny, scrubbed, all the buildings properly maintained. Carl knew the lad was stringing him along. All cities were like this one, shattered, battered and burnt out. The cities on TV were cleverly constructed sets, and at the end of the day when the actors who worked on them took off their costumes and put on their shell suits, they went home to streets like these.

Lost in his reverie Carl turned into a main road and looking up saw someone he knew advancing towards him – almost in his face. It was one of Twisted Gut's former lieutenants. Frank, a lad so nasty that when he'd been expelled from the gang he'd escaped with the mildest of drubbings, a bloodied kidney and a blackened face. Luckily Frank had his shaven head lowered. He was hefting a rucksack, a blue-and-white nylon one which matched his tracksuit. Carl flattened his body against some railings and put his hot head behind an arson-melted bin. But if Frank had seen him he made no sign.

Further along the road Carl ducked into an alley beside a bus stop. A grey bus pulled up and he dodged on board as the doors were hissing shut. He sat at the back beneath a lurid orange advert. The advert was for low-cost flights to cheap destinations. For the price of a gram of smack you could be hotly wafted to a sunburnt shore. But then what would Carl do? Only wait a couple of weeks before surrendering himself to the warders at the airport for reincarceration. Under the floodlights of the bus the other prisoners sat shackled to their seats; and the bus like a fat oblong snake hissed its way across the city.

Dawn's family lived in a low-rise block of only three storeys. But there could be no question of Carl buzzing for admission, or even trying her mobile phone. He had to arrive unannounced or there was no guarantee he'd get away again. Carl had feelings for Dawn – but trust wasn't one of them.

He circled the squat building looking for a way in, and eventually, climbing a wooden fence, he dropped down into long grass, nettles and damp cardboard. He knew which was her window, up on the second floor. He went up a drainpipe feeling the plastic rigid and brittle beneath his damp palms. Incey-wincey Spiderman. Holding tight to a bracket he got the toe of one trainer on to the outside sill, and a hand inside the flap window so he could grab the metal frame. He shifted his weight and all at once was looking down into Dawn's room from a twisted, giddy perspective. There she was, in knickers and a T-shirt, lying on the carpet, her plaits more savagely plaited than ever – the hair looked like gloss paint on her round head. She was lying on her stomach, her legs raised with the ankles lazily crossed. A tiny explosion of cotton wool between each furled toe signalled recent nail painting. Dawn was simultaneously leafing through a magazine, chewing gum, smoking, talking on her mobile phone and listening to a CD playing on the boom box positioned close to her free ear. Unseen, Carl was free to observe her plump pink limbs, her cotton-bagged buttocks, her many-studded earlobes – all the feminine otherness of her. This might've been enough for him, and if Carl could've gone back down the way he came up he probably would have. There were also other people to consider: the hard father sprayed with tattoos like a building with graffiti, and the mother, as beaky and sharp as a secretary bird strutting after its prey.

Carl inclined his ear towards the gap in the window and funnelled in the sounds that welled from the bedroom – the girly yammer, the pop piping, the paper slapping. So alive – all of it – after the old man's terminal ward. Carl hungrily sucked on her smoke and scent. She finished her call, put the mobile on the carpet, stubbed out her cigarette. Her buttocks clenched as she stretched to kill the music; in the sudden silence he spoke, Dawn. What – Jesus fuck! She flipped on to her back, one arm went to protect her belly, the other her face. Her eyes groped the darkness without. It's me, Carl, he said, insinuating his stubbly muzzle between metal and glass. What the fuck! What – Let me in, he pleaded. Let me in, Dawnie, I can't hang on out here for ever.

She came to the window, freed the catch and he dropped into the room. It wasn't until he was standing right in front of her, looking into her pale-blue eyes, that he saw the stitched gash on her cheek, the smear of yellow and black bruising above it. Jesus fuck, Dawnie, Carl said. What's this about? He took her sharp little chin in his finger and thumb as if it were a hand mirror within which he could see his own fate, and he queried again, Jesus fuck, Dawnie, what's this about? Nothing, she replied, and then, What d'you care anyways? Where've you been, lover-bloody-boy, the whole fucking town's been looking for you, I dunno how you've got the nerve to show yourself on the street, where've you been?

He drew her to the single bed, which was tucked into a hard bower formed by the flower-patterned wall. In a compartment of the bed's modular headboard clustered con-traceptive pills, cigarettes, a drug wrap, keys, a knife, all the rebellious accessories. They sat knees-v-knees and Carl said, Tell me, Dawnie, was it to do with me? But she wouldn't answer, she only drew his scared mouth to her sullen one with her bitten fingertips.

There was a gnawing quality to this kiss – it was like a rat at a food container. Carl jerked away. Dawn's pretty features – the nose slim and arched, the forehead clear – were shadowed by cloudy emotions. What is it? she said. Oh nothing. He cast his eyes down on to the floor. If you don't want me, I know one who does. She turned away and her T-shirt rode up, exposing coffee-orange skin across which lay the purple-and-yellow welt left by the blow of a heavy belt.

Jesus fuck, Dawnie, Carl said again. Did he do this? Did he?! Say he did . . . say he did and I'll . . . I'll . . . What? She rose, stooped for cigarettes and lighter, strolled insouciantly to the darkened window and stood there looking out, as if she were on the promenade deck of a cruise liner. What will you do, Carl, run away again? Besides, s'pose I like it, s'pose I like what he did? S'pose I like him?

But Carl wouldn't be drawn down this crooked path. He went to her, spun her round by the shoulder. Tell me – jus' tell me, him, was it? She laughed shortly, pushed past him, walked to the door and slid a tiny silvery bolt. Then she went to the bed and extracted the drug wrap. She chopped out two lines of yellowish powder on the headboard. Whizz? She conducted him over to her, using a cored biro for a baton.

They sat side-by-side on the bed rubbing their stinging noses and snuffling, two city rats poisoned with tasty warfarin. Dawn stuck two cigarettes in her mouth and lit the white fangs. She passed one to Carl. Won't your parents come in? Nah, all they're bothered with is that I'm in at all. Besides they've got a few cans going in front of the telly, soon be bye-byes.

She dropped a small hand into the slick folds that gathered in his groin, and squinting through the smoke Carl saw her bruised flesh as an opportunity, not just a threat. When he held her upper arms she forced him on top of her with a neat hormonal throw, and their sex was like judo. They grabbed each other's pyjama clothing and tugged it apart. Their mat was the pancaked duvet. Carl found he could do things to Dawn, but not the ones she wanted. The amphetamine, the tension, the evidence of Twisted Gut – all of it unmanned him. After a while she curled up into a ball, the tough little field mouse in her floral nest. She seemed to sleep.

Maybe, Carl thought, she's doing so much bloody whizz it isn't getting to her . . . But it was getting to him. He sat, he stood, he paced, he leant. He pissed a dribble into the tiny sink mounted in the corner of the bedroom, his dry mouth crinkled about his freeze-dried tongue. Or maybe she isn't asleep at all – she's faking it and waiting for him and this is a set-up?

Carl was frightened to go and frightened to stay. He spent an hour crouched inside the wall closet, her insubstantial dresses and flared jeans dangling over his head and shoulders like a pharaonic headdress. He spent another two hours vibrating in front of the oblong window, his mind scurrying this way and that in its bone cage. When at last the rising sun silvered the roof tiles of the block opposite, he made his move.

Poised on the sill, he turned to face back into the room so he could lower himself by his outstretched arms. Dawn was sitting up in the bed. With her nakedness, her exposed wounds and her expression of beatific hatred, the girl spoke to Carl from outside of this time, this predicament. A cord of betrayal stretched with Carl as he dropped the two storeys into the dewy grass. He hit, rolled, and cursing wished that it might yank him back up again, in through the oblong window, returning him to her perfidious arms. Anything had to be better than this.

This limping, dragging, peg-leg progress along light-shattered streets. This skulking, fearful retreat towards his refuge, the block, which stood proud of the city as if taunting the municipal authorities with the very fact that it was still standing.

There were no buses this early. Carl's route took him between the outhouses of the gods and then up the long straight hill past the hospital. Even at this hour there were still a few vulturine taxis croaking on the rank outside. Death and disease didn't keep office hours.

Carl counted on no one from Twisted Gut's gang having the staying power to wait all night for him. They couldn't have seen him leave the block or they would've caught up with him in the street, or tracked him to Dawn's place and done the business there. No, they were asleep in their mucky beds, licking their bloodied chops, of this much Carl was certain.

He slipped back into the empty lobby. The pop music was still blaring and the doors of all three lifts stood open to welcome him. Carl took Lift A to the seventeenth floor and got out. Sneaking through the door in the direction of the stairs, his hood up, his head down, he didn't notice the mother and child until he was nearly on top of them. He reared back against the wall. She straightened up from the ploughshare of the pushchair and regarded him with the weariness of a peasant called to her labours by natural cycles beyond her control. In the chair sat a toddler who seemed too big to be pushed, or to have its mouth stoppered by a rubber plug. What would happen if the dummy was pulled out, he considered idly. Would the kid spout like a little whale?

Then he recognised the careworn mother, Harriet McCracken – she'd been in his year at school. Carl, she began, what the bloody hell are you doing in here? But he declined to answer, an entire network was connecting up in his mind, Harriet to Pearl, Pearl to Davey, Davey to Dan the Mango, one of the Gut's closest lieutenants. Even if they hadn't been watching the block, hadn't sussed out he was still in here, they'd find out soon enough now. He dodged past her and into the stairwell, and, as he took the red-painted stairs four at a time, he dared to hope her visitation had been exactly that.

He let himself into 161 using the old man's key. O'Leary's head was where it always was, poised like a grizzled egg on the soft cup of the seat-back. Carl was so relieved to be back he almost called out, Mr O'Leary, I'm home. But what was the point of that? The old fellow couldn't hear him anyway. Instead he limped through to the kitchen, purloined a small handful of sleeping pills, chucked them down with tepid water from the faucet, then limped through to his bedroom.

Like a creepy old film, Carl thought, as he lowered himself back into the wardrobe and let the door fall. Surely soon it'll be over? The sun has risen and still the angry villagers haven't come up to the Count's castle brandishing their pitchforks and their scythes. Surely it'll be over soon and I can stroll outside, with only that funny feeling you get when you come out of a cinema in the afternoon to remind me? Soon, in the darkness, Carl slept.

When the gaze was gone Dermot felt abandoned. But when the gaze returned – and he felt it as he woke to the unexpected brightness of a daybreak never more predictable – it had gained a genuine malevolence, a homicidal edge. The gaze was now a sharp point, a burning laser, a death ray.

Carl awoke with a start in the wardrobe and banged his head hard against the hooks. Hang 'em high, he thought, and then, I'm gonna have to kill the old man, I'm gonna have to do O'Leary. I can't run now, not with this ankle. The inevitability of the murder thrummed in his ears, the hot blood rushing to fill a tank of intent. Carl thought Dawn might've waited for an hour after he left her place before she made the call, but he'd no doubt that she had. Then there was the McCracken girl. They'd put two such obvious facts together – even them. They'd come for him and, when the old man let them in, they'd do both of them. But if O'Leary was gone Carl could barricade the door and last out at least another week. They'd lose interest in that time, there were limits.

Yeah, it made sense, get rid of the old man. It was nothing personal really, just one of those things. He'd make it painless, crush some pills into the supplement, then when O'Leary was well and truly under push him down further with a pillow. You'd have to say – given what might go off if Twisted Gut got into the flat – that it'd be an act of mercy on Carl's part. Youthnazia – wasn't that what they called it?

Dermot's sight was sharpest in the early morning. Especially one like this, the sun bright, the clouds gone save for a few greyish smears over the hills to the south. Besides, Dermot conceded, old age was all about the long view. You grew long-sighted, only able to focus accurately on objects a long way off, and you became the same about events in your own life. The four-decade-old indigestible meal sprang to mind with all the swollen, flatulent force that its consumption first entailed. No wonder it felt so right to sit here day in day out up on the twentieth floor. It was a long view.

Sharp or not this lot were impossible to miss. They came up the long straight road which led from the city to the block with all the swagger and efficiency they'd gained from several collective decades of watching war movies. They fanned out, one dropping through the fence on to the wasteland next to the school, one into the park, one into the school playground itself, one along by the health centre. Then they merged again and were swallowed up by the gargantuan gut of the block. Dermot knew where they were headed. He didn't imagine they knew exactly which flat, but they'd figure it out. They were clearly determined.

Carl lay in the wardrobe planning the murder. How would it actually feel? He tried to purge himself of unpleasant memories. When they trapped rats in the builder's yard the other lads had mashed the vermin with sledge hammers and laughed at the twitching mess on the cobbles. But Carl felt sick and skulked away to smoke in the toilets. The key to success would be to move fast and maintain his anger, use it to power himself towards his goal. Wasn't he sufficiently desperate, hadn't he suffered enough? He'd heard of far thicker crimes being justified on far slimmer grounds. He braced his arms and legs against the walls of his mahogany prison and flexed the cramped muscles. Tense and relax, tense and relax, building up the rhythm of rage.

Dermot took a long while to bend and then crouch down. At once abrupt and controlled, he lowered his head towards the floorboards in three distinct stages. It was as if the old man were the block incarnate, and being demolished by carefully detonated explosions.

There was a knock on the wardrobe door. Carl couldn't believe in it, wouldn't accept it.

Dermot knocked on the door again and waited in the peaceful dust of the melancholy bedroom.

Carl pushed open the door and saw the old man's slippers. Involuntarily he pushed the door up more and more, revealing more of the old man, until eventually they were looking directly at one another. We'll have to do something, Dermot said. They've worked out you're still stopping here, but I've got a plan, I can help you.

W-what d'you mean. It wasn't a question, Carl was only calling Dermot's attention to how impossible this direct communication between them was. What could it mean? Had the old man truly known he was here all along? Was this the final set-up?

I mean I'm going to help you. They've staked out the building, they know there's only a few old folks left in here, and they'll come knocking soon enough. Unless we create a diversion, make them think you've gone, they'll find you. They want to beat you up, right? Yeah . . . right . . . it could be worse than that. What's it about then, money, I suppose? Yeah, money. Get up now, get out of the wardrobe, we need to talk.

Carl extracted himself, stretching and bending into the room, a suit of crumpled nylon with a pale human face showing at the collar. He was bigger than O'Leary, younger and stronger, but the old man had decisively wrongfooted him. O'Leary was in control – there was no question about it. What was this, some kind of magic, wisdom maybe?

How much? How much what? Money, how much money? Carl named a figure. Good, we'll split it, get it out. Carl extracted the plastic-wrapped oblong from the seat of his pants. It'd been there for so long he'd forgotten it had an existence separate from his body. It'd become a specialised organ. A money liver or cash kidney. Carl counted out the blood-warm notes into two piles. I'm going to call a cab, Dermot said. I'll get the driver to stop right outside the doors to the block. You'll cover me to the lift, I'll go straight down and out to the cab. Then I'll get the driver to drive slowly past where a couple of them are standing, make sure they can see me, see me taunting them. Then we'll drive off.

And how's that going to help? They're going to think it's you. See those. Dermot pointed at the tunic and trousers which hung limply on Carl's flagpole of a body. Get them off, I'm going to call the cab. But why, why're you doing this, Mister – Dermot, call me Dermot, you owe me that much familiarity. Dermot then, why? Many reasons, boy, many reasons. Some to do with my own son. He got stomped on and killed by a gang like this one. Why else d'you think I let you stay in the first place? But there are other reasons too and some of them are selfish. Hurry up now, get those things off.

Twisted Gut stood on the corner by the Health Centre watching the back of the block. In one hand he held a tiny mobile phone, the hand so big and fleshy, the phone so small and hard that it was a pearl of microcircuitry lost in his scalloped fist. The other hand caressed the rucked-up skin at his collarbone. He waited and he watched. It would happen now, or soon enough, of this he was sure. The phone would tootle inside his fist and he'd set off across the roadway strewn with crushed cans and smashed hubcaps, unbuttoning his cuffs as he went.

A car slowed down to walking pace as it turned the corner

in front of him. Twisted Gut realised three things simultaneously, that it was a minicab, that the hooded figure in the
back was Carl, and that the boy was giving him the finger. He
started towards the door of the car, intending to wrench it
open and spill Carl on to the pavement, but the cab accelerated and he was left cursing, struggling to fit his big digits to
the tiny keys of his tiny phone.

Carl tried out Dermot's chair for size and found that he fitted.
The view was perfect from this vantage, the oblong city sitting
flush in the oblong window. It was a beautiful day and for the
first time in a long while the boy wasn't scared. Dermot had
told Carl he wasn't coming back, that he could have the flat
for as long as he needed it, that it was all his. Carl allowed the
sense of calm, orderly contemplation to descend on him with
its full weight. There was a lot to think about today, but for
now he'd get himself a cup of the strawberry-flavoured
dietary supplement. It was another new taste that Carl had
acquired.

In the financial district the big brown old buildings, which
were five and six storeys high, were cut through by windy
thoroughfares. The city never really bustled any more – it
hadn't done for the last twenty years. The lunchtime hustle –
the hungry convulsion of office workers seeking food – was
what served for bustle. The young women's hips bulging in
their grey skirts, the young men's white shirtsleeves flapped
and their ties were flipped over their shoulders by the wind. In
the outfitter's the shop assistant thought he'd never seen a
queerer customer than the old man who came limping and
scuttling through the door, his tortoise head sticking straight
out from the shell suit's collar. But whatever the assistant's

misgivings the old man was so sure of himself, so at ease, that he did his bidding without a murmur.

I want you to measure me up for a suit, Dermot said, a good three-piece, none of your off-the-peg rubbish. Certainly, sir. And I'll be paying cash, so I'd appreciate it if your people could work fast. Certainly, sir.

Dermot stripped off the boy's shell suit and stood in shirt, trousers and cardigan, waiting for the thin clasp of the tape measure. He could already feel the assistant's calculating eyes upon him, sizing him up. It was a calm gaze, almost wifely in its mixture of pragmatic assessment and muted concern.

THE FIVE-SWING WALK

'It is through children that the soul is cured.'
— Fyodor Dostoevsky

Stephen awoke to find himself lying in a cold damp roadway. His knees were drawn up to his chest, his cramped hands implored the tarmac. His cheek and chin were jammed in a gutter full of sodden, unclean leaves, which had been tossed into a salad with a few handfuls of polystyrene S's, the kind used for bulk packaging. Near by lay the dead body of his six-year-old, Daniel. Stephen levered himself up on one elbow; the driver of the black cab that had struck and killed his son was standing over the child's corpse. Stephen noticed that they were both wearing shorts, Daniel's were denim, the cabbie's khaki. The cabbie was scratching his head in a perplexed way.

'Is he dead?' Stephen asked.

'Oh yeah, 'e's dead.' The cabbie was friendly, if a little solemn. ''e didn't stand a chance, the bonnet hit his bonce like a fucking 'ammer.'

'It doesn't seem right,' Stephen spluttered on the sweet saliva of grief, 'a little boy dying in this filthy place.'

He rose and floated over to where the cabbie stood. He gestured about at the junction, at the freshly cladded council blocks, the tubular garages and workshops slotted into the railway arches, at the traffic lights and the twisted safety railings. Just how twisted could a railing be, Stephen pondered, before it ceased to be one at all?

'No, it doesn't seem right.' The cabbie stroked his mono-jowl. 'You'd far prefer 'im to be all tucked up in a nice fresh bed, yeah, wiv nurses an' doctors an' his mum to look after 'im, yeah?'

'Oh, absolutely.'

'Tell you what —' The cabbie was clearly the kind of man for whom a good turn is a good deal. 'St Mary's isn't too far from 'ere. What d'you say to giving the lad a jolt with the jump leads, and seeing if we can get 'im up and running for twenty minutes? That'll be long enough to take 'im down there an get 'im admitted before 'e snuffs it again.'

They weren't exactly jump leads, they were long thick cables coated with yellow rubber. The plugs were the kind used to link up a portable generator. Stephen was surprised to see — when the cabbie smoothed back his fringe — that Daniel had the requisite three-pin arrangement on his forehead. The cabbie made the connection and walked back to his cab, which stood, engine still stuttering, like a big black hesitation.

'Right,' he called over, 'tell 'im you love 'im.'

'I love you, Daniel,' Stephen said, crouching by his son, taking in for the first time the unnatural angle of the boy's neck, the blood and brain matter puddling beneath his head.

The cabbie gunned the engine, the cables pulsed, Daniel's eyes opened: 'Dad?' he queried.

'It's OK, Daniel,' said Stephen, feeling the vast inexplicability of loss. 'We're going to take you down to the hospital.'

'But I'll still be dead, won't I, Dad.'

'Oh yes, you'll still be dead.'

The cabbie came back and handed Stephen what was either a large pellet or a small canister. It was the same yellow as his jump leads.

'This thing is pretty amazing, mate,' he said. 'If it has any contact wiv water it expands to ten thousand times its own size.'

'Like a seed?'

Stephen looked at the plastic cylinder and felt the all kinds of everything packed up inside it, amazing, bio-mechanical energy. He could feel a tear struggling to detach itself from the well of his eyelid, fighting the tension of this greater surface with its own need to become a moment. Then it was. It rolled down his cheek, dripped on to the cylinder. All hell broke loose.

And resolved itself into an idiotic collage of tissues gummed up with snot, a clock radio, a lamp, a book, the moon face of a toddler confronting him from a few inches away.

'Bissa – bussa,' said the toddler, and then, 'Gweemy.'

Stephen levered himself up on forklift arms. The dream was still exploding in his head, smattering everything he saw with its associations, simultaneously lurid and tedious. Were dreams always this prosaic? he wondered, or had they become so through over-analysis? The collective unconscious now seemed to be expertly arrayed for merchandising, like a vast supermarket, with aisle after aisle of ready-made psychic fare. Still, his kid . . . dead . . . it didn't bear thinking about.

'Currle,' the toddler broke in, butting his arm with a mop of black ringlets.

Stephen snaked an arm around small shoulders and pulled the child up on top of him.

'Hiyah,' he said, pressing his lips into the thicket.

The toddler squirmed in his grasp, butted the underside of his chin, which nipped his tongue between his teeth.

'OK!' Stephen snapped. 'Getting up time!' And he deposited the child back on the floor, followed by his own feet.

A broad little base of squished nappy and brushed-nylon pyjama bottom supported the eighteen-month-old, an expression of stolidity was painted on to the smooth face. Stephen stood, teetering, a pained grimace pasted across his own rough one. Casually yet deliberately, he knocked the small torso sideways with his flaky foot, and it toppled over, curly head clonking on the mat. Too surprised to protest, the child lay there mewling softly. Stephen scrutinised bubbles of saliva forming on perfect pink lips, each one reflecting in its fish eye the bright grids of the bedroom windows. He couldn't say its name, its absurd name. After all, a name was an acknowledgement – and he'd had no part in its naming.

'This bedroom looks like a fucking bathroom!' he cursed, then added, 'while the bathroom looks like a fucking bedroom!'

And they did. She'd put bathroom mats either side of the bed, a festoon of netting by the window had dried starfish and sea horses caught up in its ratty folds, the walls were papered in vertical stripes of blue and white. But there was never any rowing at this regatta, only vigorous rowing.

Stephen stomped into the adjoining bathroom, and here white, lace-fringed pillows were plumped up on small carpeted surfaces; there was a stripped-pine shelf of swollen paperbacks over the bath itself, and the mirror above the sink had a gilt picture frame. Stephen grasped the cool sides of the sink and thought about wrenching it out of the floor. He stared at his face in the mirror. 'No oil painting!' he spat. And it was true, with two days of greying grizzle and the sad anachronism of pimples and wrinkles on the same cheeks, he looked like an ageing slave rather than an old master.

A turd floating in the toilet caught his eye – one of hers.

Smooth, and brown, and lissom – like her. He hitched up an invisible robe and hunkered down over it.

'I shit on your shit!' he angrily proclaimed, while at the same time, in a feat of bizarre moral tendentiousness, he felt satisfied to be saving two gallons of water.

In his mind's eye a video clip of emaciated Third World women was reversed, and they walked jerkily backwards from a distant dusty well to an encampment of battered huts. The toddler came crawling into view.

'I shit on your mother's shit,' Stephen addressed it conversationally, but then, as he strained, he thought, I can't go on behaving like this, these casual kicks, these slipshod remarks. None of it is harmless. But why had she left the kid with him on this of all days?

When he rose to wipe himself, and involuntarily looked back, he saw that his turd had been married with hers, that they were entwined, with a lappet of his shit curled around hers like a comforting arm. Intimacy, it occurred to Stephen, is highly overrated. In the middle of the night she had kicked out at him hard, her heels drumming on his sleep-softened thighs. Kicked him and cursed him, and at the time he'd been inclined to give her the benefit of the doubt – doubting that he was awake at all. Now she was gone.

Over a soft pap of cereal that the toddler made free with, Stephen thought about how he had come to be here, in a tatty kitchenette way across town. Still, two years after the move, he awoke with this sense of disorientation, wanting to go back to the home that was no longer a home, from this, which was no kind of home at all. He looked at the kitchenette, at the sharp flaps of melamine detaching themselves from the surfaces, at the Mesopotamian outline of the electric jug, at the nodular malevolence of a mug tree, and he grasped how all the lines of his life had unruled themselves. He wouldn't – he couldn't – take responsibility for this . . . He wouldn't own these other, bonded lives, this bewildering emotional dovetailing. He felt only a monumental sense of self-pity for his own self-piteousness.

'Zyghar,' said the toddler.

On the radio a weathered voice spoke of cloudiness. Stephen had heard how they held up a grid to the sky and counted the cloud cover in each square. There was such a crude calculation – he understood – as average cloudiness. Squinting up through the tiny flap window, Stephen saw, between tapering walls of London brick, a sky of more than average cloudiness, grey on grey on greyer, shapeless shoals of grey slipping over and under each other. It was always gloomy on these, his days off. Off from what? He remembered yesterday morning, and the ugliness that occurred beside the Sasco year planner when he reminded his boss that he wouldn't be coming in tomorrow. 'But what about –' and 'Didn't you realise –?' and 'Couldn't you have –?' When it was all there already on the board, his days off, meted out in felt-tip strokes. And anyway, Stephen's job, what did it consist of? Save for saying on the phone the valediction 'See you' to people who, in fact, he had never seen.

'H'hooloo,' toodle-ooed his breakfast companion.

Stephen tried to wrench it out of the high chair too fast; chubby legs were caught under the rung and he swung the entire edifice – a tower of metal and plastic, a penthouse of flesh – aloft. Then set everything down, disentangled the feet, tried again. He did a nappy change, wiping the grooves around its genitals with careful uncaring. He taped up the little parcel of excrement with its Velcro tabs. In due course, he mentally carped, this would be added to tens of thousands of others, and deposited in a landfill in the East Midlands, where it would wait for ten thousand years, to confront the perplexed archaeologists of the future with yet more evidence of their shit-worshipping ancestors.

Stephen dressed his charge, his fingers feeling like bloated sausages, as they grappled flaccidly with the fiddly straps and clasps. In its nylon all-in-one, the toddler looked to Stephen like some dwarfish employee of a nuclear inspectorate, ready to assess the toxicity of the Chernobyl that lay in wait outside. Backing and filling in the awkward confines of the flat – where bedroom, bathroom, kitchenette and living room all opened on to a hall the size of a mouse mat – Stephen manoeuvred the buggy with one hand while grasping glabrous scruff with the other. The borrowed buggy – what a risible, lopsided contraption. The buggy, with its collapsible aluminium struts, like a tragicomic boxing glove on an extendable arm, made to smack him in the face again and again and again. He could fold it up, but never put it away. Now it half-opened and jammed a door, and while he closed it up the prisoner escaped. But at the moment of recapture the double buggy fell open once more.

In the street Stephen married child and conveyance in a union of plastic clips and nylon webbing, then he sat on a low wall bounding a hedge and, feeling the sharp twigs scratch him through his thin clothing, he wept for a few minutes. It was here that Misfortune – that ugly, misshapen creature – saw fit to join him. And, when he rose and pushed the buggy off up the pavement, Misfortune went along for the ride.

'Inquitty,' said the toddler, registering the tinkle-thud of a falling putlock on a building site they passed by, and Stephen pondered how it was that, while everything had gone perfectly well with the child's development, now it was beginning to speak he found that it was he who was becoming autistic.

There was a bad thing waiting in the wings. There was an awful event struggling to happen. It was maddened already, battering against the windowpane of reality with its dark wings, like a bird caught in a room. I should never, Stephen thought as he pushed the buggy, have driven my wife insane by slowly increasing the duration of the car journeys we took together. I knew she had no sense of orientation, and yet I tormented her. If we had to go to friends' houses, or even to the supermarket, each time I'd take a different route, each time slightly longer. Naturally she'd protest: 'Stephen, I'm sure we didn't go this way last time.' And to derange her still more, I'd say, 'It's a short cut.' Now there was no car and no wife. Or rather, there was an ex-wife, and instead of circling each other like boxers in the confinement of their own home, the ring had expanded to fill the city, while they were still stuck in the same bloody clinch, mauling each other with short jabs to the belly.

At the bus stop Stephen waited with an old woman drinking a can of Special Brew and a dapper old man who leant against his cane at a jaunty angle. The old man sported a feather in his porkpie hat, his tweed suit was immaculately pressed. He looked as if he were watching for a field of runners and riders to round the corner and come galloping up the high street in a breaking wave of pounding sinew and frothing silk. He looked happy. Stephen sank down on one of the narrow, tip-tilting rubber seats; his misery stung him like heartburn. Misfortune, seizing the opportunity, played with the child.

Misfortune tickled its feet and the toddler chuckled, 'Chi-chi-chi.' Misfortune stroked a cheek and accepted the nuzzle of the frizzy head. Misfortune sympathised entirely with the child and took on its hallucinogenic impression of a sharp-smelling trough, full of toy cars, and bounded by neat piles of building blocks. Behind these were grey walls too high to touch, and over it all unfurled haunting skirls. The toddler, too young to know Misfortune, felt it to be an outgrowth of the parental absence slumped at its side, and accepted its distorted presence willingly.

'Fulub,' it said.

But the old woman, who knew Misfortune for what it was – who felt it congealed in her hair, smeared on her neck – cried out, hands shaking to ward it off, 'Gerariyer-gera –'

Lager beaded the little brow, Stephen jerked the handle of the buggy to roll it back a couple of feet and reached in his pocket for a tissue. The bus came.

In the time it took for the obtuse old man to pay for his ticket and climb up the bus to his seat, Stephen was able to load the human cargo, fold the buggy and stack it in the luggage rack. Misfortune, under the cover of the hiss of compressed air and the slap of the automatic door, slid on board too, and took up the seat behind the driver, the one allocated for elderly people or those accompanied by children. The old woman – if you can call fifty-three old – stayed on the bench, and watched, awestruck, as the bus stop slid away down the road, leaving the bus behind.

On the other side of town Stephen's ex-wife kept up a large detached Edwardian villa on maintenance. Stephen didn't know whether she had lovers – she hadn't vouchsafed – but if she did there was plenty of space for them in the generous rooms. The walk-in cupboards alone could've housed five or six closet Lotharios and, when Stephen wanted to make himself feel particularly bad, he imagined them in there, sitting comfortably in the close darkness, her dresses rustling around their shoulders, as they waited for her to select one of their number. Stephen's ex was beautiful. She was trim, raven-haired and sharp-profiled. She despised sexual incontinence in specific men – this he knew to his cost – but mysteriously, admired it in the generality of mankind. And so it was easier to imagine her with lovers than with a boyfriend.

Misfortune dogged his footsteps as he clunked the buggy over paving stones ridged with virulent moss. From the bus stop they went up the hill between flat-faced semis, then around the playing field at the top, with its stark goalposts like gallows. Then past the gasometer, down the short street walled with poky terraced houses, and finally along the parade of shitty little shops, each one apparently devised for public inconvenience. A grocer with only two kinds of fruit and three of vegetables; a butcher selling just sausages and mince, who counted on three boxes of dried stuffing as a tempting window display; an ironmonger's that never had anything you wanted. Stephen recalled asking for thirteen-amp fuses in it, for eggshell paint, for clothesline, for grout, but all of these were unavailable. Preposterously, the ironmonger's had been refitted in the last year, yet still sold nothing that anyone needed. Perhaps, Stephen thought, the ironmonger's existed solely to refit itself – not so much a retail concern as an evolved play on the whole notion of doing-it-for-yourself.

They turned the corner into Tennyson Avenue and passed by the Hicks' house (elderly bedridden mother, son on drugs), the Fakenhams' house (he a closet paedophile, she a pillar of the local church), the Gartrees' house (no human children but many cat babies). How could it be that he, Stephen, was exiled from this poisonous Eden, while so many serpents retained their tenancies? It occurred to him – not for the first time, not for the thousandth – that he should fake his own suicide, utilise the handy wreckage of a train he'd never caught, or the immolation of an office building he'd failed to enter, or simply leave his clothes, for once neatly folded, on a rock, and walk away from the CSA, from the children, from the pain.

Bending down to unlatch the front gate he caught the tang of urine emanating from the toddler. Best not to leave it – it would lead to a rash, and then he'd have to face its mother's wrath. Inside the gate he unbuckled the child and laid it down on the patch of grass behind the bins. He glanced up at the blank windows of the house, each with its cataract of net curtain, but saw nothing twitching.

'Anurk'a,' the toddler protested, as he ripped open the front of its all-in-one, yanked out its chubby legs, then held them open, spatchcocked, as he removed the absorbent wad.

While Stephen was groping for a clean nappy in the compartment underneath the buggy he heard the front door swing open, and looked up to see his ex-wife standing, radiating contempt. Behind her slim shoulders the hallway receded, lined on either side with hummocks of school bags, rows of shoes, stooks of sports equipment and piles of books.

'Huh!' she exclaimed, arms crossed, and Stephen, observing her quick-bitten fingers clutching at her elbows, and the anger that semaphored from her lantern eyes, could not forbear from remembering the exact quality of her rage.

'I've got fucking head lice!' Those same hands in frenzied agitation, as she sits on the side of the bed. 'Fucking nits! Fucking nits!'

He leaps from his side of the marital bed, in that instant grasping that he'll never lie down there again. His eyes search across the carpet for any certain object that they might anchor on in this suddenly fluid,

frightening world. But he sees only a nude Barbie doll, pushed
overboard by a passing child, its feet up beside its head, its pink plastic
pubis a disturbing juncture. How can this thing be — he's floundering
in stormy irrelevance — a toy?

'Kids!' Stephen's ex bellowed back into the house, and then
again, still louder. 'Kids!'

Stephen finished parcelling up the toddler and placed it
back on its side of the double buggy.

Now he has so few things he tries to treat them with the
respect others deserve. In the small flat on the other side of
town he washes up the toddler's plastic bowl with care, then
dries it and puts it away in the cupboard. He no longer has the
detached villa, with its innumerable corners, all of them
slowly silting up with the materiality of years of family life.

The six-year-old and the eight-year-old came down the
stairs to the hallway like surprised conspirators, reluctant to
admit their involvement with each other. Taking their anoraks from the pegs in the hall they put them on with an
orderliness and efficiency that struck Stephen as overwhel-
mingly pathetic. Then they winkled their feet into wellingtons, and he wanted to go forward and help them but
knew he really shouldn't. They came out of the house and
shuffled down the path to where he stood.

' 'lo, Dad,' said the older one, the girl, while the boy said
simply ' 'lo.' They both nodded to their half-sibling in the
buggy, as if this were a working situation, and they were all
being formally introduced for the first time. ' 'lo,' they said
again.

'Lorol,' said the toddler.

Stephen hunkered down and shuffled forward to encompass all three children with his outstretched arms. He smelt
Ribena on their breath, conditioner in their hair. Looking at

their pale faces he saw yet again the way his ex's incisive features cut out his weak ones.

Stephen's ex-wife reappeared in the hallway, dragging a protesting two-year-old by its arm.

'I'm not wanted it!' the two-year-old was complaining. 'I'm gonna' stayere, I'm gonna –'

'Doesn't he want to come?' Stephen called, half hoping.

'Oh no, he's going with you,' she replied, expertly stuffing the little boy into his anorak, then tripping him backwards over her foot, so that he sat on the floor. While she inserted his feet into wellingtons, she kept up an incantation of irritation: 'If you think I'm going to miss out on the only two bloody hours of the week when I have the house to myself . . . the only time I have to make a call, or even wash my bloody hair . . . You've no idea, have you? No bloody idea at all . . .'

While the boy, for his part, kept on dissenting. 'I gotta having this to show Daddy, 'cause . . . An' Daniel says I wasn't gonna 'cause . . . He tooken it, he-he –'

'Josh wants to bring his driving thingy,' Daniel explained.

'I told him it would be in the way,' his older sister, Melissa, explained.

'But I has to!' Josh cried out from the doorway.

'Then take the bloody thing! Take-the-bloody-thing!'

On 'take' she picked up the toy dashboard with steering wheel and gear stick attached; on 'the' she shoved it in Josh's arms; on 'bloody' she picked him up and placed him outside the door; and on 'thing' she slammed it.

In the frozen moment before Josh began to bawl in earnest, Stephen turned and looked away. On the opposite side of the road two nuns were passing by. They were both bespectacled, both wearing blue wimples and blue raincoats. From beneath their hemlines extended a foot or so of white nylon. The whole outfit, thought Stephen, gave them a look at once ecclesiastical and medical, as if they were on their way to nurse their Saviour in a specially equipped crucifixion unit. They flashed their lenses in his direction, and Stephen wanted to cry out, 'Suffer these little children to come unto you! You won't find a group of people more in need of help than us . . .' But instead he turned back to Josh who was keening, 'Erherrr-erherrr-erherrr,' his way into hysteria, 'waaaa!'

'ComeonowJosh, noneedt'cry, here we go, here we go . . .' Stephen kept up a prayerful murmur as he lifted the roaring boy and his toy up, carried him down the path to where the others were clustered around the buggy, strapped him into his side, balanced the driving toy on his knees, got the buggy out through the gate, got the older ones positioned on either side, small hands on handles, and with his shocked progeny four abreast, started off back up the road. Misfortune took up its position to the rear.

'It's OK, Josh, it's OK. We'll have a good time – you'll see . . .'

Melissa had taken over from him and although he was grateful to her, Stephen couldn't forbear from feeling sick with inadequacy, his own paternal dereliction melting into his shoulders like an irreversible jacket of napalm.

'So, kids,' he said cheerily. 'What're we going to do this afternoon? Museum? Zoo? Film? What's it going to be – you decide.'

'We wented to a film –'

'Went,' Stephen corrected Daniel – the six-year-old's grammar was always the first casualty of these emotional firefights.

'We went to a film yesterday.'

'Good?'

' 's' OK.'

'How about the zoo or a museum then?'

'Nah, boring,' the older children chorused.

'What then? It's a bit gloomy for the park, isn't it?'

Their silence said they didn't agree.

'D'you want to go on the four-swing walk then?'

'Yes, and you'll push us up an' up an' up –'

'So high, so high we'll go over the bar –'

'Or fly into space pasted the moon an' Mars an' everything –'

'To another galaxy –'

'Another universe, you mean.'

'OK, the four-swing walk it is then, but I can't promise you space exploration.'

Another universe – that was a good idea. Stephen didn't doubt that Daniel and Melissa wanted to go on the four-swing walk because they connected it with the time before he'd left. The older children had come into consciousness on these four sets of swings: two in the local playing field, then one in an adjoining patch of overgrown park, and the last, tucked away in a playground on a council estate. Perhaps they hoped that if they swung high enough they could describe a perfect parabola into the past.

'Swush,' said the toddler on the left-hand side of the buggy, and it was only then that Stephen realised it was autumn, for the child was mimicking the sound of feet and wheels sweeping leaves along the pavement.

Autumn, which explained this damp, oppressive sky, like a dirty grey clout waiting to be squeezed. Autumn, which located this sense of irretrievable loss in its appropriate context. Autumn, hence Stephen's aching weariness. He would've given anything to be able to lie down underneath that scarified hedge until spring. Autumn, which made sense of the silage beneath his feet, a mulch of lolly sticks, ring pulls and macerated paper cups, laid down during the long harvest of the school holidays. Autumn, when it had all happened.

'Come here! You come here! You come here and sit down by me. Sit here!' Her belly rounded and plumped up amidst the squashed pillows, her nightdress rucked up in angry folds.

'Melissa hasn't had them for months – for months! I comb her every day – every day! You sit here, you let me look in your hair. In your fucking hair!'

And so, like half-naked apes, they engage in a savage grooming that destroys all social cohesion. She scrabbles and yanks at his hair.

'There! There! You've got them too! And eggs – and fucking eggs! What is this, Stephen? You're fucking someone, aren't you?! Someone with fucking head lice. Who is she, Stephen? A schoolgirl?'

No, not a schoolgirl. At the time, still fixated on the disturbing juncture of Barbie's thighs, Stephen had considered that perhaps, had she been a schoolgirl, the truth would've been easier to acknowledge, because it would've been so grotesque, so singular. But of course it's lies that are singular; the truth – that she was Melissa's teacher – was merely prosaic.

At the shopping parade Stephen's engine, with its double-buggy cow catcher, clattered over invisible points and turned to the left, back up the hill towards the playing field. Misfortune was in the guard's van.

'Whoo-whoo!' said the toddler, and Josh, who sat beside it yanking on the orange plastic steering wheel, beeped his horn.

'So, how's school?' Stephen asked Melissa, because he thought he ought to.

' 's OK,' she replied.

'Good OK or bad OK?' he probed.

'OK. OK.'

And that was that, that was the full extent of his input into her education.

As soon as they reached the playing field the two older children broke from the sides of the buggy like swing-seeking missiles and headed off across the scummy grass. Seagulls lifted off in advance of them, crying unpleasantly. Stephen pushed the buggy along the path, past a zone of crappy benches where two adolescents were nuzzling. He felt an intense physical sympathy for the little goatee of pus and scab on the boy's chin. He wanted to touch it, but cancelled the feeling by staring at his feet as they negotiated the blobs and dollops of dog shit, some brown, some black, some desiccated white, some livid yellow. It was interesting the way that the two toddlers managed to ignore each other. Maybe in a few months' time Josh would turn to the other one and say, out of the blue, 'Are you capable of holding a conversation yet?'

At the playground Melissa and Daniel were already on two of the big swings. Daniel was kicking his feet out and leaning back, he'd gained quite a bit of height, but Melissa couldn't manage it, and merely dangled, twisting from side to side. Stephen got Josh out of the buggy and put him in one of the small swings, tucking his feet through the holes. Then he did the same with the other toddler and got them both swinging.

'Hold on to the front!' he ordered them.

'Come and swing *me*, Dad!' Melissa called over. 'I can't get going.'

'She can't swing!' Daniel cried out, delighted. 'She doesn't know how to, doesn't know how to!'

'Shut up, Daniel! Shut up!' Immediately Melissa was close to tears.

'She's eight and she can't swing!' he crowed as he swooped above her.

'Shut up – I mean it!'

'Now then,' said Stephen, leaving the two toddlers swinging. 'I'll swing you both.'

He got Melissa swinging using both hands, then shifted to shove the boy with one hand and the girl with the other. He pushed the seat one time and their backs the next. He felt their backs, the curvature of their spines, the warmth of their small buttocks. At the apex of the swings' curve he felt their bodies hover in his hands. And yet he felt no physical sympathy for these children – his children. Melissa and Daniel left themselves behind as they swung, left behind their preternaturally aged selves, they travelled in time – if not space – to a place of fun, that was simply and physically now. Stephen tickled them under the arms on the upswing and they giggled. He ran in front and like a crazy matador just avoided their feet-for-horns on the downswing and they screeched. He ran over to the toddlers on their little swing and got them going again, then ran back to the big kids and pushed them still higher. Back and forth Stephen shoved, round and round he ran. Now all four were laughing – even the stolid little toddler. Misfortune picked up a lost mitten someone had stuck on top of a railing and tried it on for size.

Then they stopped. Daniel squeaked himself to a halt, his rubber soles buffing the rubber tiling. He sprung off the swing before it came to a halt and walked over to the static roundabout. He knelt on the edge and leant his dark little head against one of the metal stanchions, as if praying. In that instant the whole desolation of the scene returned: the louring sky, the scuffed surface of the playground, rubber peeling away from bitumen, bitumen rubbing off concrete; the two-decade-old climbing frame like a garish steel pretzel for a metal-eating giant; the swings themselves, some of which had their chains twisted around the crossbar, evidence of adolescent mayhem, or maybe children genuinely catapulted into orbit. There was broken glass by the enclosing railings, there were lopsided crash barriers grouped around a depression in the concrete, which was filled with water and leaves, there was a bin all buckled in its bandolier of wooden struts. That such a rigid thing could have been vandalised at all was evidence, Stephen thought, of the most extreme population explosion.

Melissa got off her swing as well. The two toddlers were hanging, barely moving in their little swings.

'Come on, everyone!' Stephen injected enthusiasm into his voice as if it were a stimulant drug. 'Let's go to swing two.'

'Two!' the toddler cried out, loudly, distinctly, with perfect enunciation. They all ignored it.

Swing two was in the smaller, recently constructed playground next to the one o'clock club. The little army marched there across the playing field, a direct route that took them sloshing between the gibbet goalposts, each set erected in mud. The older two ran on ahead, the younger toddler rode in the buggy, Josh trudged carrying his plastic dashboard. Stephen remembered how Melissa and Daniel had clung to him so ferociously, demanding to be carried until they were well past Josh's age. But this two-year-old just plodded on, hunched up, clearly no keener to be touched by his father than his father was anxious to touch him.

It was the weekend so the one o'clock club was closed, steel shutters pulled down to the ground, and each horizontal line filled in with sloppy graffiti. The small playground was yet to be vandalised, its black rubber tiling was inviolate. Each beautifully appointed piece of equipment stood on its own inset carpet of green-rubber tiling. The sandpit was covered and padlocked. The climbing frame-cum-slide had a neat gabled roof, and ramps leading up to it with firm wooden treads, each one edged with more black rubber. Clover-leaf-shaped platforms stood about on coils of giant spring. The whole assemblage was so new and neat and padded. It defied the outside with its evocation of a safe domestic interior.

'It's so fucking claustrophobic,' Stephen muttered aloud, putting Josh and the toddler into another duo of swings. He felt this inside-out playground to be outside in the playing field, and the outside playing field in turn to be inside the city, and the city to be enclosed by the country, and the country to be jumbled together with other countries inside the world. A world like a vast and messy playroom, strewn with the broken and discarded toys of an immature humanity, who had been having an awful tantrum for decades. The terrible two millennia. Like the security camera atop its red pole in the corner of this playground, God observed it all from his own distant enclosure, a child-lover passively watching for paedophiles.

Stephen got the two toddlers swinging again, and then went over to the bigger swings and got the bigger kids going. The two sets of swings were facing, so four pairs of wellingtons were aimed at Stephen as he scampered around the red safety bafflers, desperate to keep the swingers all up in the air.

'I like this swing best,' said Melissa.

'I like swing three best,' said Daniel.

'This swing is faster,' said Melissa.

'Yeah.' Daniel cultivated the conversation as if he were attending an aerial cocktail party. 'But swing three is fastener – I can go fastener.'

'Sinee!' the toddler sang out.

'I'm thursday,' said Josh.

'You mean you're thirsty,' Stephen puffed.

'I'm very thursday,' the child reiterated.

They left the playing field through a short alley that became a cul-de-sac. Parked along the kerb were an abandoned car and two toppled motor scooters. The car had been both seared and eviscerated. All the windows were caramelised, the seats were cut into slices of burnt foam rubber. The dashboard had been cut out so that the electrical guts spilled all over the floor. All the wheels were gone, making it just the right height for Josh, who crunched towards it through the debris hefting his own dashboard. 'My car,' he said. 'My car.'

'No it's not!' Stephen snapped. He snagged him too hard and, picking him up, slammed him into his side of the double buggy. Josh began to cry, and the other three children turned their frightened faces towards him.

'I'm sorry, Josh, I'm sorry.' Stephen knelt down to bring comfort within Josh's range. 'Really I am. Look –' He peered at the accusatory faces. 'Look, you can all have drinks and sweets. How's that?'

There was silence save for sniffles for three beats, and then Daniel said, echoing the performance of some fifth-rate American actor which had become lodged in his own re-pertoire, 'OK, then, sure, whatever.'

They trundled on.

The four-swing walk wasn't going well – Stephen knew that. He had to stop stumbling through his life, he had to take all these children in hand – but how? How could he practise emotional hygiene in this filthy city? The scooters lay like the corpses of animals, each in a tacky pool of its own oil. The petrol stench of decomposing machinery was overpowering.

And by the walls of the abandoned shop premises they were skirting was a frozen wave of detritus, a fully evolved deco-system, where the squashed spine of an old vacuum cleaner was preyed on by the strut of an umbrella, which in turn was ensnared by a shred of gabardine, upon which suckered last night's discarded condom, which for its part was being eaten away by the white acid of bird shit. Stephen checked his watch, although he'd promised himself he wouldn't. Misfortune bided its time.

Down on the main road men stood about in Saturday afternoon poses outside the bookie's. One was throwing an empty lager bottle into the air and catching it again by the neck, another was savagely and methodically shredding betting slips, then letting the fake snowflakes flutter around his shaken-up world. Traffic coursed and thumped along the uneven surface of the road. After the stunned silence of the playing field, the way these vehicles honked and beeped seemed almost companionable. Stephen pushed the buggy right inside one of the shops, and the older children tagged along.

They were all the same – these shops – the same in their heterogeneity. They all sold small stocks of random supplies. Many shelves were empty – others bulged with useless plenitude. One shop would offer booze, fags, yams, ten-kilo bags of rice, cassava, sweets, fans and ex-rental videos; while right next door you could purchase seat covers, disposable barbecues, monkey nuts, sink plungers, aubergines, booze, dog chews, fags, sweets and sixteen-inch black-and-white TVs. One shop would be entirely sealed by an inner sleeve of steel mesh, so that customers had to transact their business in a sort of dog pen; while right next door it was all wide open, soda crystals and incense holders there for the taking.

In this one, a man with a V-necked cashmere pullover, blue stains beneath his brown eyes, sat behind a counter piled high with foreign-language newspapers, picking his teeth with a biro cap. Stephen let the children have what they wanted: Cokes and sweets. He even let the little toddler hold a big red can in its little brown paws. So much sugar – it wouldn't do any of them any good. Sweet guilt. Gummy, granulated, one hundred per cent refined shame.

'All right, boss,' said the man when Stephen paid him.

'Thank you, sir,' Stephen countered.

Neither of them knew if the other was being ironic.

Swing three was behind this parade, in a little misshapen scrap of park, a dumb-bell shape of overgrown grass and shrubbery, even more littered than the street. Stephen hated swing three most of all. It felt diseased here, with the backs of the shops exhaling their awful humours over a loose rank of overflowing wheelie bins, and five or so distempered chestnuts moping up above. But the children didn't mind, they were caught up in their sugar rush, rushing ahead, Josh hard on the heels of his older siblings, the toddler in the buggy screeching between slugs of Coke, 'Weeee!' Then they all pulled up short.

Sitting on the run-down swings that were their objective, kicking their feet and sharing a cigarette, were three teenagers. Two girls and a boy. They didn't look remotely threatening, but set beside the swings – which were small anyway – they were completely out of scale. Three teenagers. One of the girls was pretty in an over-made-up way, her lips a brilliant pink, her hair oiled and smarmed down into a series of precise curlicues across her coffee brow. The other girl was much more heavy-set and darker, her big breasts a veritable shelf, her large arse cut into by the swing's chains. She wore stretchy black clothing. The lad was in blue denim, a hip-length jacket buttoned to the neck, wide-legged trousers, the crotch of which was located in the region of his knees. A Los Angeles Raiders baseball cap was crushed down on his head, so hard that his hair formed frothy earphones. The pretty girl had a mobile phone in her lap, the hands-free set plugged into her delicate, gold-studded ear. She was toying with the keyboard of the phone, while the lad swung himself towards her and away, pretending to try and grab hold of it. The big girl ignored them, stared at her feet, smoked.

They didn't notice Stephen and the children for some moments. Moments during which he weighed up their timeless triangle, the priapic pipsqueak importuning the pretty one, while being silently warned off by this bulky black chaperone. The three of them, come here to the overgrown playground in an attempt to recapture an innocence that they'd probably never had. Then the pretty one saw Stephen and his kids. She stood, and trailing the lad by the flex – he'd snatched the mobile – she walked over to the seesaw. The big girl got up and followed them, goosing the lad with her hefty haunch. The pretty girl snatched back the mobile, the lad hitched up his mainsail trousers and sat on the middle of the seesaw, the big girl moved off to one side and stood, staring into a thicket.

Stephen's kids took their places. He helped Josh up on to the swing and began pushing him, the older two kicked and leaned, kicked and leaned. The other toddler still sucked on its Coke, buckled into the buggy like a fitful pilot, the whites of its eyes sharp in the mounting twilight. The rusty eyelets of the chains grated in their corroded bolts, 'ear-orr-ear-orr'.

Melissa gave up, and dropping to the ground walked towards the teenagers. She stopped a few feet away and examined them intently, then said, 'Hello.' They ignored her. 'Hello,' she said again, this time louder. The teenagers went on ignoring her, Stephen wanted to stop pushing Josh and go and pull her away, but he couldn't. 'Hello, my name's Melissa.'

'Y' all right, M'lissa,' said the lad.

'Y' all right,' the pretty one echoed him, and the big girl snickered, an oddly high-pitched 'tee-hee-hee'.

Melissa walked over to the buggy and stood there regarding the toddler for a while. She stooped, slid her hand inside the hood of its all-in-one and rubbed the curly mop of hair. The toddler said, 'Lissl.'

Then she came back to where Stephen was pushing Josh and, looking up at him with an expression minted by her mother, said, 'Dad, why's Setutsi black?'

The teenagers paid attention now, their six eyes sought out Stephen's pale face, the pale faces of the three older children, then wavered over to take in the pretty black eighteen-month-old girl in the buggy.

'Yeah, black right,' the lad exclaimed to no one in parti-cular. 'Black like me innit.'

And as if responding to some hidden signal, or perhaps to express a mutual disapproval of this miscegenation, the three teenagers gathered themselves into a little posse and strolled off. The last that was heard of them was the 'delaloodoo-delaloodoo-doo' of the mobile ringing.

Stephen stopped pushing Josh. He went over to the buggy and began unstrapping Setutsi. For something to do he got the changing mat and spread it on the damp grass. He got the wipes and a clean nappy. He undid the poppers of Setutsi's all-in-one, and pulled down the elasticated waist of her velveteen trousers. Her nappy was swollen with pee. He got it off, cleaned her with a wipe, then put a hand under her small, sweaty back and lifted her up so he could position the new nappy. As he fastened the Velcro tabs he looked up to see the three palefaces grouped around his shoulders.

'Isn't Setutsi toilet-trained, Dad?' asked Melissa.

'Well, she is really, but as we were out all day I put a nappy on her.'

'Josh is toilet-trained.'

'I know.'

'Mum says people don't toilet-train their kids 'cause they're lazy.'

'Well, maybe I am a bit lazy, but Setutsi's very good at going to the toilet by herself when we're at home.'

'D'you and Miss Foster sleep in the same bed?' Daniel asked, and before Stephen could reply he went on, 'Miss Foster doesn't teach at our school any more.'

'Can we come to your flat, Dad?' Melissa asked. 'Can we have supper there?'

'Have you got a video, Dad?' Daniel added. 'Can we watch TV while we have supper?'

Josh had knelt down by Setutsi and was half tickling her, half trying to do up the poppers of her all-in-one. Setutsi giggled obligingly. And even though his head was swarming with the ugliest of images – the bedroom like a bathroom where they spat and shouted and writhed – and his nostrils were full of her coconut conditioner – which had once aroused, but now nauseated him – he knew that this was a momentous breakthrough. That this rapid-fire inquisition was the beginning of an acceptance – for them, for him – of all that had happened. Of course Melissa and Daniel knew full well why Setutsi was black and exactly what that meant. But up until now Stephen had only offered instalments of this reality to them, randomly cut up, just as Setutsi herself had been a fleeting visitor, seen in blurred longshot through car-window screens. Now the older children had taken it upon themselves to construct a proper narrative, a story that involved them.

The questions kept on coming as he helped Josh to pee in a bush, then kissed him and set him on his side of the buggy. The enquiries continued as they left the grotty park and headed in the direction of swing four. And Stephen did his best to answer them truthfully, while observing the necessary economy of truth: Yes, he and Miss Foster did share a bed, and yes, he would ask their mother if they could come to the flat, but they mustn't be angry if she didn't want them to. And yes, he knew that Setutsi looked like him, even though she was black. And yes, she even looked like them, because she was their half-sister.

The leaden weight of Stephen's depression was lifted. He felt the physical sympathy he'd longed for for months course through him like electricity. He felt tears prick his eyes. He wanted to cuddle them all simultaneously. He pushed the two little ones in the double buggy, and felt the uneven tug of Daniel and Melissa hanging on at either side. He felt the joyful freight of his paternity. He paid no attention to the boarded-up windows of the flats on the estate they were walking through. He didn't notice the travesty of a recycling bin, which had been set on fire, so that its plastic bowel prolapsed on to the pavement. And he most definitely failed to register Misfortune, who, having taken a detour through the estate – to close the eyes of an overdosing addict, to clutch the aorta of a heart-attack victim, to clout the fontanelle of a suffering baby – chose this moment to rejoin them.

Swing four was floodlit by the time they arrived. A tiny quadrangle of black rubber under bright white lights. The wind was getting up and the cloud cover was breaking up. Most of the equipment here was still smaller than that at the one o'clock club, so small that the children of the estate disdained to use it, preferring to ride their scaled-down mountain bikes in the surrounding roadway, taking it in turns to jump off a ramp that one of them had propped against a speed bump. But there was one larger set of swings, and these were tenanted. A fat black boy, a year or so older than Daniel, dangled listlessly on one. He wore a green tracksuit several sizes too big for him, and assuming this was a hand-me-down, or a garment chosen by his parents to disguise his weight, Stephen pitied him.

As soon as they were all inside the gate the boy became galvanised and began talking at them. 'My name's Haile,' he said. 'I'm seven an' I'm big for it, yeah, an' I go to Penton Infants yeah, an' I like football an' I like Gameboy 'cept I ain't got one but I got my cousin's some of it, yeah. What's your name?' He asked Daniel first, but then he wanted to know all their names and their ages.

'I'm forty-six,' Stephen told him, laughing, although close to there was a disquieting air to Haile – his eyes bulged and he was sweating. Perhaps, Stephen thought, he has an untreated thyroid condition. It was only too likely.

Haile kept on harrying them, darting about the place, while Stephen got Josh and Setutsi out of the buggy, lifted them into the little swings. Haile then took it upon himself to push Daniel, staggering forward, his hands pressed hard into the younger boy's back.

Daniel said, 'You're hurting me!'

And Haile suddenly stepped clear so that the swing dropped and rattled on its chain. 'I gotten stay here most days, but also I get sweets from up by there.' Haile gestured towards the main road. 'D' you like sweets or chocolate?' He addressed Melissa, but before she could answer he embarked on a nauseating inventory: 'I like Snickers an' Starburst an' Joosters an' Minstrels an' all them little fings, an' chews an' lollies . . .'

But even though Haile was a bit crazed none of his lot seemed fazed. It's the new dispensation, thought Stephen, it's going to be like this from now on, my big multiracial family absorbing all and sundry, like a mobile melting pot.

He stopped turning every now and then to see what Haile and the older two were doing, and concentrated on the little ones, pushing them and tickling them, touching first Josh's nose and then Setutsi's, as if conjuring with their consanguinity. He looked over towards the flats where a couple of black guys the same age as Setutsi's mother's brothers were jump-starting a car; one of them was attaching the leads, while the other was gunning the engine of a second car which was drawn alongside. Yeah, thought Stephen, it's all going to be different now. I'm going to get along with Paul and Curtis, I'll go to the pub with them, stand them drinks, smoke a little weed. He lost himself in this new vision of familial accord, seeing the three of them, brothers-in-law, arms around each other's shoulders, full of mutual respect and amity despite their differences.

'Hey! Don't do that!' Melissa's voice cut through his reverie.

Stephen turned and couldn't believe what he saw. In the few seconds that had elapsed, Daniel had begun to swing so high and so vigorously that his swing was now twisting and plunging at the top of each arc, in a jangle of chain links. But Daniel seemed powerless to stop the violent motion, he kept on leaning back and plunging forward, the better to see what Haile was doing. The fat kid sat astride the crossbar of the swings, his plump legs hooked around them. He must've shinned up there, Stephen realised, although he didn't look at all capable of such gymnastics, and now he was there he was swaying dangerously.

'Daniel!' Stephen shouted, starting towards the swing. 'Stop swinging now! Stop swinging!'

Melissa had got off her swing and was standing well clear. Daniel began braking himself with his wellingtons.

Stephen walked below the crossbar. 'Hey, Haile,' he said, 'that's a hell of a dangerous thing to do, you should come down right away.'

'No bother if it is,' Haile said, ''cause I do it all times, see, t'pull the swings up.' And he began drawing one of the swing seats up by its length of chain.

'It's not a good idea, Haile,' Stephen pleaded with him. 'You could lose your balance.'

'Leave it, mister!' Haile shouted back, pulling up whole arm-lengths of chain now, looping first one about his shoulders and then a second around his neck, like some grotesquely chunky piece of jewellery. 'It's not fucking business, is it? It's not *your* fucking bloody business, you cunt!'

The final expletive propelled him backwards, the child rocked, then rolled, then fell. The chain loop rattle-yanked around his soft neck. Haile's head bulged. The neck snapped. His legs in the green tracksuit bottoms kicked once down towards Stephen's upturned face, then twice, taking the five-swing walk. Stephen, even in the mad numbness, could feel a tear struggling to detach itself from the trough of his eyelid, fighting the tension of this greater surface with its own need to become a moment. Then it was. It rolled down his cheek, dripped on to the rubber tiling. All hell broke loose. Misfortune expanded ten thousand times to fill the void.

CONVERSATIONS
WITH ORD

I was down to one friend, Keith, a former bank robber. We never talked about his bank-robbing days, just as we never discussed the fact that, although he'd long since said he would, he never got round to decorating his flat. A bucket, ladder, roller, tray and drip-stained cans of emulsion had stood in the hall for years, for so long, in fact, that arguably they now constituted the decorative scheme.

There was a dark, unpalatable truth hunched behind the unused decorating gear. Keith's flat was furnished with what had been the acme of modernity in 1973. An oval glass-topped dining table with steel legs like an inverted coat tree dominated the main room, the six matching high-backed chairs were too scary to sit on. A seating area had been contrived around a vinyl kidney of coffee table, and here a three-seater divan upholstered in vomit-coloured, oatmeal-textured fabric formed a right angle with a two-seater divan upholstered in fluffy electric-blue fabric. In the neglected portions of the poorly converted flat – its queered corridors and unnecessary half-landings – yuccas loitered, like the urban cousins of absentee triffids, willing to wound but afraid to strike. In the bathroom dusty, slatted cabinets harboured old liniment and when opened disgorged silvery tongues lumpy with aspirin. I never dared to enter the bedroom.

Keith, presumably, had thought his furniture, when he

bought it in the early 1980s, to be amazingly futuristic, quite simply out of this world. And it was out of his world, because he had – as he quietly reminded me when I made some unthinking aside about glam rock, Camden Lock, or Pol Pot – missed the 1970s altogether.

Keith and I had a certain rapport – we were both formidable mnemonists. Keith was the first man I've ever been able to play mental Go-Chess with. Mental Go-Chess is a game of my own invention in which, at any point during an orthodox mental-chess game, either opponent can suddenly change the game to Go. Both players must then transform the sixty-four-square internalised chess board into a three-hundred-and-sixty-one-intersection Go board, substitute the appropriate number (ten for a queen, eight for a castle, etc, etc) of Go stones for each of his remaining chess pieces, and then congruently configure them. Obviously, if you were black in the chess game you remain so in the Go game.

Keith was dead good at mental Go-Chess, something I couldn't help but put down to his many years of solitary confinement.

'Did you do a lot of systematised abstract thinking and memory exercises when you were in solitary?' I asked him after he'd beaten me at mental Go-Chess for the third time in succession.

'No,' he replied flatly and limped on along Battersea embankment – we invariably played while strolling – a great broken bear of a man, with a full beard and shoulder-length hair. I suspect that Keith thought his coif made him look like a rock star from the unnameable decade, but the truth was that he closely resembled a late-nineteenth-century patriarch, deranged by sexual repression and successful imperialism.

If we were tiring of mental Go-Chess we'd invent

imaginary dialogues. One Keith and I particularly liked was entitled 'Conversations with Ord'. Ord was a general, in his eighties, who had fought in every important campaign of the first fifty years of the twenty-first century. Flamboyant, openly homosexual, violent, brilliant, Ord had something to say about anything and everything. He had invented and then marketed his own range of militaristic skin-care products; he had synthesised all the Eastern martial arts into an exercise régime suitable for the fattest of Western veal calves, then sold millions of DVD manuals. During Ord's most savage and protracted campaigns he'd hung a sign on the flap of his self-invented, self-erecting tent HQ, which read 'I am ninety-nine per cent fit, are you?' His staff officers entirely grasped the meaning of this, and just as they surrendered themselves to his aggressive sexual attentions, so they also recognised his profound asceticism and radical scholarly bent. Ord had translated the Upanishads into the street language of Los Angeles's black ghettos. He saw himself standing in a long line of learned warriors, stretching back through Wilfred Thesiger, T.E. Lawrence and Count Tolstoy, to Frederick the Great, Akbar, King Alfred and even Marcus Aurelius.

I liked being Ord, but Keith was masterful. When he was being Ord and I played the role of Flambard – his reticent biographer and amanuensis – we could often stay in character as far upriver as Teddington Lock, or as far downriver as the site of the Millennium Dome.

But no matter how far we walked, these lateral journeys were the only relief we ever had from the suffocating confines of South London. Not for Keith and me were the cultured salons of the moneyed and the creative, where the high Regency ceilings opened out into an international atmosphere of sustained invention. Nor did we have access to the roof gardens of the beautiful people, where the platinum-plated pelvises of the rich paraded as purple parakeets trilled, each species mimicking the other.

No, we were confined to the horizontal. Keith and I inhabited a city of dusty parks, 1930s blocks built round scraps of park, 1950s blocks built behind oblong strips of park, and 1960s, '70s and '80s blocks built over-toppling, or actually within, parks. Degenerate parks with piddling water features and knock-kneed, demented loggias. Victorian parks, their faded imperial grandeur and once exotic plantations replicating the pattern of shoddy trade with former dominions. In Vauxhall Park – which was particularly favoured by street alcoholics – there was a crappy row of miniature buildings – house, church, cinema – done up crudely but durably with emulsion-slapped-on-concrete. Yet some way into our second season of walks I noticed that these had been subjected to miniature vandalism, the church's spire bent, the house's roof bashed in, the cinema's façade sprayed with a giant graffiti tag. Of course, this was as nothing to Ord, who in 2033 (and again in 2047) had seen the mud flats of the Dhaleswari turn to lava as his jet-helicopter gunships took out the shanty towns of Dacca. Nothing at all.

As for so many others the pretext for our park life was a dog, Dinah, Keith's shambolic Dalmatian. No one likes to admit that they like London parks pure and simple, so thousands have traditionally relied on a canine alibi. A few even go so far as to have children, in order to justify hanging out by the swings or feeding the ducks. Ord had trenchant things to say on the subject of dogs. His own genetically modified South African Ridgeback-Poodle cross had lived to the age of fifty-seven and reputedly killed as many men. Ord had doted on Robben, and after the hound died he became distinctly cynical about the species, viewing them as little more than effective parasites.

'Isn't it bizarre,' Keith said, in character as Ord, 'that you two – allegedly intelligent – grown men have gone even further than most dog owners of your era. With no significant livelihood, appreciable interests, or even viable relationships of your own, you've become the parasites of this parasitical creature. It would take a complete collapse in the social order to release you from your bondage.'

'Maybe . . .' I acknowledged, then donning Flambard's mantle I continued, 'Ord, presumably you've been in many war zones where dogs have reverted to their natural savagery, hunting in packs and so forth?'

But cruelly, Ord was not to be drawn. 'Dog's done a shit, Flambard,' he snapped. 'Best pick it up.'

I gloved my hand in a Sainsbury's bag and did the necessary, smearing runny faeces on the asphalt. What was Keith feeding her on?

'Perhaps you two should become faggots and hang out at the Hoist,' Ord sneered. 'You couldn't be more ensnared than you are already.'

Bondage of all kinds preoccupied Ord, although he professed to have no taste for it himself. Leaving Vauxhall Park we would pass by the Hoist, a club in the arched arse-end of the battered old railway viaduct. On a couple of occasions we did go in for a drink, and ended up sipping Red Bull and vodka, while watching the sado-masochists assess one another's heft. Epicene opera critics stood with us at the bar, awaiting the arrival of Jean-Paul Gautier and discussing the novels of Théophile Gautier. But it hardly mattered whether we swung in the Hoist or not, for it was almost always constricted and dark in this city of ours. It made no difference if we trolled around Battersea Park, or ranged along the underside of the Power Station, and the badlands of the Thames littoral, there was no escaping the bondage of our own claustrophobia.

Even in high summer the clear sky seemed particulate, as half-visible droplets of heavy metals drizzled down on us. To walk the dry ski slopes of Lavender Hill was like struggling into unfamiliar underwear. Everything grated. Sometimes, stopping for a meat patty at an Afro-Caribbean takeaway, and feeding a few scraps of virulent yellow pastry to Dinah's wet black maw, I would despair of myself. Why had I found it necessary to exile so many people I had once been intimate with, to the very periphery of my acquaintance?

To begin with the outer circle had been easy to abandon. A few unanswered phone calls, a flannelled date – not exactly a stand-up but almost – and these seedling friend-ships would shrivel then die. There were more established relationships which had required persistent neglect. It could take as long as nine months of evasions, unspoken intima-cies, unshared items of gossip, and unattended parties for these to wither by the roadside of life. But they did, eventually. And then there was the tangle of close con-nections that had to be actively hacked away at. So it was that I insulted those I had formerly embraced, I traduced those I had once exalted, and I resolutely failed to recognise former lovers in the bakery aisle of Nine Elms Sainsbury's. This went on until the awful ullage had occurred, and all that remained was bitter salt.

It was arrogance, naturally, an arrogance that was so solid within me I could feel it. I actually *felt* superior to myself – let alone others. I would hunch on the corner of the tilting heap of old mattresses which served me as a bed and pinch the slack flesh on the insides of my knees, whilst muttering, 'Not good enough . . . Not good enough . . .' like a child who has yet to appreciate the raw vulnerability of his own anatomy. I scrunched up my ears, bending their cartilage until it creaked. I popped my eyelids inside out, and pulled my scrotum up and around until it encased my penis in its hairy basket. On an average morning, as I was actually performing this ritual of superiority, my landlady, Mrs Benson, would call me from downstairs. 'It's Keith on the phone for you! He's wondering whether you'd fancy a walk.'

Ord had uncomfortable observations to make about my new living arrangements, for all that they amused him. 'Once you had too much space, a large house and an accommodating wife. Now look at you, the lodger of another family!'

I deserved his contempt – when my marriage broke up I rented this attic at the Bensons', a Tetra-pak of space, close in summer, distant in winter, in which the possessions salvaged from my former life looked like precisely that. As I lay on my springy, sleepy slab, fat-bellied planes wallowed in the muddy cloud overhead, threatening time after time to plop through the skylight. Even Keith was a relief.

'What d'you think of the balloon?' Keith said, one day in late summer when we were on our way to another MI6 cook-out. The balloon had been up for some weeks, tethered four hundred feet above Vauxhall Cross. But although it was on our beat we'd yet to visit its moorings. From where we currently were, crossing Battersea Park in a south-easterly direction, we could see its stripy awning of a belly nudging against the defunct cooling towers of the Power Station. Foreshortened London.

'Pssht! Dunno. It's a balloon, I s'pose. Can you go up in it?'

'Course you can; what would be the fucking point in

tethering a balloon four hundred feet over London if you couldn't go up in it?'

'Dunno. Observation of some kind – I mean it's right next to MI6.'

'You have distinctly primitive ideas about the secret state,' said Keith in Ord's camp, fruity and yet severe voice. 'Neither cloaks nor daggers are necessary at all when there are many many men – and women – who regard proximity, loyalty and even fealty as the mere small change of historic arbitrage. When I was suppressing the anarcho-narco warlords of Grand Cayman in '31, my death squads were penetrated to the very apex of their command structure. If I executed one of my traitorous officers another one immediately took his place and fed vital intelligence to the other side. Eventually I realised that the swine had penetrated us so deeply that I myself must logically fall under suspicion.'

'B-but what,' Flambard stammered obsequiously, 'd-did you do?'

'Simple, I too swapped sides. Taking control of the anarcho-narco forces I attacked the government and seized control of the State. With my hand thus massively enhanced' – Ord clenched his meaty fist and hit out towards the balloon – 'I could turn on the terrorist scum and finally eliminate them. Victory as usual!'

Still, whatever Ord said, the idea that the balloon was an observation platform didn't seem such an absurd notion to me. After all, if the not-so secret service could flaunt itself in a ludicrous postmodern wedding cake of an office building immediately abutting Vauxhall Bridge, then why shouldn't they have a hot-air-powered eye in the sky? Besides, I liked the MI6 building, its beige concrete façade and cypresses for finials suggested a kindlier apparatus than Ord's brutal vision, and there was also the tiny roomlet of riparian beach next to it, a notch of the way we were. The oddest driftwood and trash got snagged by the notch, then, at low tide, Keith and I would build little fires out of it. As dusk fell we'd sit toasting marshmallows and staring moodily across the ruched brown river to the Tate Gallery on the opposite shore, while Dinah frolicked leadenly on the compacted silt.

Sometimes, when night had all but closed in, the Frog Tours amphibian would come pitching and yawing upriver from Westminster. Going half-about in the ebb tide, its way-off-road tyres would skitter and then gain purchase on the concrete ramp which angled down from our beach. With a throaty roar of its diesel engine the bizarre vehicle mounted towards us, until with a splutter and a gasp it freed itself from the heavier element. Keith grabbed Dinah, and the three of us flattened against the vertical dunes of our refuge. Bemused tourists stared down at us from the cabin of the amphibian as it headed for the Albert Embankment. A terrified Dinah would howl, and once or twice Keith lost his cool, chucking shingle against the garish landing craft as it established its commercial beachhead. Then I had to assume the role of Ord and restrain him.

But on this particular day it wasn't the Frog Tour that concerned him. 'Nah,' said Keith as we circled the ornamental lake, 'the balloon's a tourist thing. It's a tenner to go up – maybe we should do it. We could leave Dinah with that nice Australian lad in Majestic Wine –'

'But why – why would we want to go up in it?'

'To see the city, you pillock. To orientate ourselves. Jesus, we spend most of our waking hours trudging round this bit of London – why not see it from the air?'

'No thanks, I feel hideously orientated already . . .' I felt a surge of anger and when I continued it was as Ord. 'About the only thing I could think of doing in that balloon is holding a debate –'

'A debate? Whaddya mean?'

For the first time in weeks I'd both grabbed the role of Ord and caught all of Keith's attention. I could tell this because it was his habit, when his massive Difference Engine fell properly into gear, to call Dinah over, put her on the lead, then walk with her closely to heel, as if he were a blind man entering his seeing-eye dog for Cruft's. Some baggy-clad adolescents stared at us as we worked our way over the Queenstown Road roundabout: big, little and spotty, side by side by side, was that what they were thinking?

'So, General, this balloon debate,' Flambard enquired as we marched under the railway bridge which spans the appendix of Prince of Wales Drive, 'would it be like a parachute debate?'

How I loathed Flambard's mock humility. He was like all biographers of the living, a ghoul standing by the road his subject was due to drive along, waiting for the inevitable crash so he could gawp and then write it down.

'Quite so,' Ord snapped.

'The loser would . . . what? Be thrown out?'

'I'd rather hoped they would have the decency to jump, but yes, if necessary they would be thrown. I well remember the balloon debate I had in '42 with Dickie Heppenstall and the Maharaja of Rawlpindi. That was during our pole-over-pole circumnavigation of the globe, and we had very little to do for weeks on end as our capsule was batted about the stratosphere by the trade winds. Madness to attempt such a journey, but then madness was always my forte . . .'

Ord paused, Dinah was straining at her leash, responding to

the chorus of anguished barks from the canine rejects banged up in the Dogs' Home. Flambard got her under control, and then as we went on he remained respectfully silent.

'We were up there for so long that I was able to interest both men in certain practices, but inevitably that led to pettishness, jealousy and eventually a terrible falling out as they vied for my affections. A fight of some kind was looking increasingly likely, so in order to appeal to both men's intellectual vanity I proposed we debate the motion: "This capsule believes that the man of action has more to contribute to the world than the man of learning." We all spoke . . .'

We turned the corner into Kirtling Street, and the dun peaks of sand and aggregate in the yards of the Tideway Works loomed into view, arid urban alps.

'And our contributions were judged from the ground by the then Professor of Metaphysics at Oxford, and Stig Öbernerdle, the powerboat-racing wunderkind of the interwar years.

'To give the Maharaja credit, when he realised he'd lost he went as quietly as a lamb. We dropped the balloon down to five thousand metres and he climbed out of the porthole. It was a dramatic scene, the sun rising over the Weddell Sea, the towering bergs throwing long shadows, and if I craned up I could see the tiny figure of the Maharaja crawling up the massive curve of the balloon above me, like a fly on a wine glass. Over it all scudded the cloud cover – awesome.'

'But tell me, General, what about this rather more lowly balloon debate. Had you a motion in mind?'

'Mmm.' Damn! Keith had wrong-footed me. Getting Ord back from the future was always tricky, and I felt my Ord mask slipping.

'And what about the participants?' Keith wheedled.

'Err, you – me, obviously; and . . . and . . . Sharon Crowd.'

'Ha-ha! I see, back to that, are we, Sharon-bloody-Crowd.'

'There's no need for you to get narked –' The Ord mask came right off; my face felt nude without it.

'Oh-no,' Keith snorted, 'not when you have so conspicuously already.'

There it was, out in the open, the nub of our friendship, and perhaps also the root of our dreary common isolation. Keith had an affair with Sharon Crowd. They broke it off, and, without knowing the whys and wherefores, I then had an affair with Sharon Crowd. In due course this ended and she went back to Keith. Hence the bloody between Sharon and Crowd. Tmesis, it's called, one word shoved between the legs of another. Months later, at about the last party I ever attended, a louring bear of a man came up and prodded me in the back while I was plopping guacamole on a paper plate, then he bellowed loud enough for the other guests to hear, 'Why don't you just put your prick up my arse and cut out the middle-fucking-woman!'

This was Keith, who was, by now, once more without Sharon Crowd. I never discovered whether he felt genuinely aggrieved about the loss of Sharon Crowd. If, like some true romantic, his flesh crawled from the wanting of her, his belly gurgled at the thought of her belly, and his eyes watered when he glimpsed the future stretching out ahead of him without her. I didn't want to believe that Keith was so sentimental – not about Sharon Crowd at any rate. It hardly fitted in with his background in violent crime, or his formidable reasoning powers, especially given the way she'd unceremoniously shafted him.

Bax, an ageing, hairy, dwarfish, and onetime very successful novelist, also knew Sharon Crowd, carnally and otherwise. Bax said of Sharon Crowd, 'You've got to admire her style. In the 1960s when you'd see girls weeping on the stairs outside parties, because they'd had some man do them wrong, you'd also see the odd smattering of doleful, lachrymose boys – they were Sharon's.'

'But Bax,' I'd objected, 'you can't champion a woman solely on the basis that she's a cruel deceiver.'

'Can, and do. Also she's clever and still remarkably handsome, which counts for something.'

At this juncture he'd leant forward to apply himself to rolling up a little turd of a cigarette, and dislodged the perilous quiff of hair that perched atop his head, so that it fell like a curtain over his puckish face. This was Bax's way of showing that a subject was closed.

But Bax had never been one of Sharon Crowd's lachrymose boys. Bax didn't do lachrymose, except – as he once confided in me – when he finished one of his novels, although whether this was because he felt keenly the loss of his intellectual companion, or he was already anticipating the indifference of the reading public, he never vouchsafed. Keith too had once had a promising little career – albeit his second – as an academic. But then Sharon Crowd had exposed the delicate embroidering of some of his research and Keith lost his job. What was it with Sharon Crowd? Professional jealousy didn't seem likely, even though she was a chalk-pusher herself. Why was it that she had so little respect for pillow talk? Because for me, well, there was the small matter of ten years' marriage down the tubes. I lost sleep with Sharon Crowd three times – we have no need of euphemisms here – and it felt worth it at the time. Hell, it still seems worth it now I'm accelerating at 32 feet per second per second. Her lovemaking was a peculiar combination of the tender and the athletic; frequently, having engendered a bruise, she'd lay her thin lips on it.

At a Christmas party in Clapham, given by friends with a mortgage the same size as our own, Sharon Crowd sidled up to Maeve, my then wife. The interval between our third bout and what I fervently hoped would be our fourth was already far longer than that separating the second from the third. At a punch-in-the-gut level I knew time out had already been called between us.

'Your husband's penis really is most astonishing,' was her opening. And when Maeve failed to respond to this sally, unable to recognise any connection between said organ and this stringy, washed-out, fiftyish blonde, Sharon Crowd continued: 'I mean the way that when erect it bends so exaggeratedly to the left, then tips up at the end. In a nose you'd call this aspect retroussé.'

Comprehension soaked into Maeve's face like spilt milk into kitchen towelling. 'You mean to say you've been fucking my husband?' Maeve made a fisheye lens of her wine glass through which to exaggerate the truth.

The conversation I'd been having near by with the host about free-range chickens was decapitated. It ran around for a few seconds then died.

'Yup. I've stopped now though . . . he isn't . . . he isn't very *versatile*, is he?'

That hurt. I'd fed it to her in every conceivable position. We'd copulate with her on top, with me on top, side-by-side, standing up, sitting down, leaning to and falling over. I thought I'd been leading this, but it turned out to be Sharon Crowd's merry dance.

'Face it,' she said to me months later when the lawyers'

letters had stopped coming, 'if the marriage had been any good it would've survived my intervention – so you'd have to say what I did was for the best. After all it's not as if there were children involved.'

Even at the time this struck me as the most Stalinist application of logic, allowing for the possibility of such alarming moral propositions as: If I hadn't killed you, you would've died anyway. Keith took an even more robust view. He was extremely fond of Maeve, admiring both her capability and her sociability. As far as he was concerned there was a child in the marriage, me, and this was my way of showing that it was time I left home and let my mummy get on with her life. In Keith's eyes Sharon Crowd remained mysteriously pure, apart from this little matter of destroying his career.

Two days after Ord had proposed the balloon debate, Keith and I went for one of our regular lunches with Sharon Crowd. Despite – or perhaps because of – her betrayals, the three of us remained close. One argument for this was that her flat was a convenient staging post on our walks. The other was that Sharon made us delicious meals. Pasta with ginger and tomato, fresh sardines swimming in lemon juice, artichoke hearts in melted butter, peppers stuffed with peppery stuff, and so on. White bourgeois woman tapas. She prepared the food in Le Creuset dishes, in her tiny galley of a kitchen, and brought it to Keith and me, where we sat, looking down the Wandsworth Road towards Nine Elms.

Sharon Crowd's flat was in a block next to her place of work, South Bank University. Ever since the balloon had arrived, and was winched into the municipal heavens, Sharon Crowd's dining area was the place to be if you wanted a spanking view.

'Have you been up in it?' Keith queried, poking a fork laden with bruschetta at the balloon, which from this vantage was well clear of the surrounding city, and motionless in the typically pewter sky.

'No, why should I?' Sharon poured me another glass of Côte Rotie – there was no faulting her as a hostess.

'He and I are holding a balloon debate.' The bruschetta wavered round to me.

'What's that – like a parachute debate?'

'Sort of, but instead of the winner getting the parachute the loser jumps from the balloon.'

'And what's the subject?'

At this Keith clammed up. It was one thing to disrespect Sharon Crowd in the privacy of our mournful promenades – quite another to do so to her face. I, however, felt a rush of delirious irresponsibility, a carefree loss of all self-protective instincts, and said, 'You.'

'I'm sorry?' Sharon Crowd's bone-china brow cracked.

'We're going to debate your conduct towards us – Keith and me, that is.'

'Conduct?' Her incredulity curdled the atmosphere. 'Let me get this straight, you troglodytes –'

'That isn't, "nyum-nyum", fair . . .' said Keith. The long years of imprisonment meant he was able to do indignation and tomato salad simultaneously.

'Nomads then. Yes, you two nomads are going to debate – to the death – my conduct towards you?'

'If Bax is to be believed' – having taken on the challenge I was determined to push this as far as it would go – 'many many hundreds of similar offences should be taken into consideration.'

Shaping words suddenly seemed too hard for our mouths

and they regressed to munching, squidging, cracking and lunching. From where I sat Sharon Crowd's sharp profile was etched against the painful concrete portico of South Bank University, which jutted out with brutal certitude. The two façades were not dissimilar, and Sharon Crowd's chin, although small, was impressively cleft, like facial buttocks.

'You never had any academic prospects to speak of, Keith.' Sharon Crowd's tone was brusque. 'Your research capabilities were negligible, and your ability to teach was severely compromised by the fact that the majority of your students were born in a decade of which you have no direct knowledge. I was doing you a fav —'

'What!?' Keith couldn't suppress this yelp.

'A favour. You don't know your own mind, you would've been humiliated. Publicly humiliated. You'd have found yourself worse off than you were already' — again the Crowd counterfactual — 'and certainly worse off than you are now.'

Keith hung his big head, bruised with the bumpy passage of the years. He had no ability to resist her. It was the same tactic she'd applied to me; by proposing an alternative — and still more negative — future, Sharon Crowd completely extirpated Keith's free will. He'd told me that on occasion she still came to his place and 'did things'. His imprecision matched my own unwillingness to imagine what such things could be, and I hoped my refusal to comment was interpreted by Keith as evidence that she still did things with me as well.

Now Sharon Crowd was the convenor of the business studies department at SBU, she undertook many lucrative consultancies and even appeared on late-night current affairs programmes, debating matters of public import. Her burnish, once merely institutional, was now digital and televescent. Her suits had always been severe but now they were mannish.

Her tits were non-existent. When we'd lost sleep together her nipples had been astonishing, smooth pink cones of erectile tissue rising straight from the grille of her ribcage, but perhaps they were gone now? I certainly couldn't visualise them any more – all I saw beneath her tailored breastplate was smooth, nippleless skin.

'And you, you're the originator of this motion?' She looked at me as if I were very small, a long way away and falling fast.

'You're a tyrant, Sharon,' I pronounced. 'You may even be corrupt.'

Her eyes zeroed in on the level of wine in my glass. 'You're probably drunk, and therefore not worth talking to – but let's say you are, you think I mistreated you, do you?'

'Sharon, given the benefit of hindsight, the passage of the years, after many a summer – and all that jazz . . .' I inhaled more wine, chiefly to wind her up. 'I can say with some authority, and all due respect, that at the end of the day you righteously fucked me over. Did it to me up the arse with a fucking telegraph po –'.

'You *are* drunk – offensive as well. Get him out of here, Keith.'

Late that afternoon we were back at the MI6 beach and I was winding up the security cameras which sat on poles and the tops of walls. If I paused behind a pillar, the camera, which was tracking my movement, became paralysed, wavering in the place I should've been. 'Like me and Sharon Crowd!' I shouted over to Keith who was dabbling in the tidal wrack with Dinah, their six legs tangled up in nylon twine, sodden newsprint, and water-smoothed wood.

'What?'

'The security camera – it thinks it knows where I ought to

be – but of course I'm not. Anyway, what I know – and it doesn't – is that it's only a machine . . . Well . . . I blew that, didn't I?'

I climbed over the fence, descended a flight of five concrete steps, crunched across the shingle to where man and dog stood.

'Not necessarily.' Keith sounded gnomic, he was in a serious mood, like when I accidentally referred to the unnameable decade.

'She's never going to go up in the balloon now, is she?' I felt teary carpets unroll on my cheeks. 'Not now she knows we want to chuck her out.'

'There are several considerations.' Ord picked up a length of old curtain rail from the beach; he used its tip to inscribe his battle plan in the silt. 'Firstly, she may not think we're serious.' His militaristic boot descended on a tessellated pane of glass set in a ruptured frame. 'Secondly, she may be so proud she wishes to defy us, and the third – and I think strong – likelihood is that she'll do it because Bax wants her to.'

'Bax?'

'I've dealt with people like Sharon Crowd, y'know. In the 2050s when I was stationed in Dar es Salaam, there was a very proud woman – a cult priestess – who became overly attached to my adjutant –'

But I wasn't in the mood to play Flambard. 'Bax?' I reiterated.

'Yes.' I couldn't tell if it was Keith or Ord speaking. 'I have considerable sway with him, y'know.'

I looked over my shoulder, through the defile between MI6 and Tintagel House, then across four carriageways to where the balloon crouched behind the Vauxhall viaduct. It was moored for the night, a cumbersome woman in a loud sundress who'd been mugged by gravity. It was hot all right, and it was bright enough still, but the light came welling up from an unidentifiable place, like the blood from an internal injury.

After a very long while Keith said, 'Come on then, let's play Go-Chess.'

'I don't *want* to play Go-Chess.' Why couldn't he acknowledge my pain?

'Let's have a dialogue then, I'll be Ord –'

'I don't want to do Flambard!'

'OK, OK, keep your fucking hair on, you don't have to, just let me be Ord and I promise I'll amuse you.'

So we passed on along Lambeth Walk and Ord regaled me with his tales of how he suppressed the Dog-Headed Jock-straps of Minnesota, the most feared motorcycle gang of the 2030s.

I met Bax in the Beer Engine, a pub in Stockwell. It was an awful dive, yet Bax frequented it so much that they kept his tankard hanging behind the bar. This was a ghastly miniature stein, with a witch's face bulging from the green glaze. Bax drank light and bitter from it, he was a one-man preservation league. I was having a particularly arrogant day. My arrogance was so palpable that my belly bulged uncomfortably, inflated by my superiority. Bax noticed the odd way I was canted on the leatherette bench.

'Whass the matter?' he slurred through smoke and beer.

'Arrogance.'

'Flatulence?'

'Arrogance. I've an inflated opinion of myself.'

'Whichever it is they're both calculated to drive people away.'

'I know that.'

Bax fell to building another roll-up behind his safety hair curtain and I fell to examining the wristlets he always wore. These protruded from the cuffs of his denim shirt and extended as far as his knuckles. They looked as if they were made of either very pale leather, or some peculiar rubber. It was impossible to tell whether they were a fashion accessory or an orthopaedic brace. A bit like Bax's novels really.

'Whassat?' He was sharp – horribly so.

'I didn't say anything.' I brazened it out.

'Sharon says' – he pooted the words out, together with irritating little dribbles of smoke – 'that she'll go up in the balloon with us on Sunday, this Sunday.'

'Really? And she'll take part in the debate?'

'Of course, that's why she's going. We'll debate the motion "This balloon considers Sharon Crowd to be thoroughly immoral". I assume you'll be proposing and Keith seconding?'

'S'pose so.'

'Sharon will reject the motion – obviously – and I'll support her. If you win, one of us takes the dive. If we win, the reverse will be the case.'

'I see . . .' This was a turn-up. I wasn't at all sure about Keith's reaction if his life was weighed in the balance with mine. 'And who did you have in mind to deliberate?'

'Why, whoever's operating the balloon, I s'pose, and whoever else is taking the trip with us, tourists and suchlike.'

I found Keith at the Vauxhall city farm. Dinah was tied up outside, but her master was down at the far end from the animal enclosures, past the new straw-brick pigsty, crouching in the small allotment section. I'd like to be able to say that with his beard and his weathered features Keith had a peaceful appearance in this bucolic – if diminutive – setting, but he didn't. Not even the three small children, who frolicked about him throwing handfuls of straw in the air, could lighten his mood.

'Bax says that whoever's operating the balloon, together with any others who're there at the time, should deliberate. On the matter of Sharon, that is –'

'Or you.'

'Or me, or you, or Bax.'

'Ah, but it isn't necessarily Bax or you, or Sharon or me, now is it?' His big boot rolled a small pellet of sheep shit around on the earth with surprising delicacy. 'It's me or you in the final analysis.'

I thought of big tie knots, droopy moustaches, the Rubettes, the Winter of Discontent and the death of Blair Peach. It was a lot for someone to have missed out on, and while I was thinking this Keith was gathering himself together and moving off.

'Yeah, yeah,' he flung over his shoulder, 'well, that's that then.'

'They'll never cooperate,' I called after him, 'the people in the balloon. They'll freak out.'

'I'll handle it.'

'Really?'

I caught up with him by the exit as he was untying Dinah. The Dalmatian had managed to wriggle inside and was straining at the leash so hard that her collar disappeared in the folds of her neck. Keith and I took a look at the doggy porn as well, a glass tank of ferrets scrabbling and flowing through sections of plastic piping.

'I'll *handle* it.' Keith rounded on me – I was reminded of Ord.

'Are you in character . . .? As Ord, I mean.'

'No, of course not, you prat.'

Off he went, Dinah's nails clicking behind him, as he traversed the cracked lozenge of paving beside the Vauxhall Tavern. Even at this early hour there was a scrum of bare-chested, bald-headed clones outside the grotty old rotunda. They goosed one another, snapping braces, nipping necks, while the techno broke over them in waves and the traffic roared past. The balloon was coming down for the night; from where I stood, it appeared to be settling in a giant egg cup of masonry. Foreshortened London – there was never any escaping it. Respectfully, I asked Ord if he had any comment to make on the clones, but for once he was silent.

The week before the balloon debate they began demolishing the Nine Elms Cold Store. This huge concrete box – which closely resembled a beehive of the cubic kind – had dominated the messy confluence of Nine Elms Lane and the Wandsworth Road for the last twenty years, shouting solidity and radiating chill. Presumably advances in refrigeration had done for it, the encroaching entropy. They bashed a big hole in its side and the wound festered as epidermal layers of asbestos swelled and the steel maggots squirmed out.

It was easy enough to get on to the demolition site, which, of course, Keith, Dinah and I did. We'd always got on to the Battersea Power Station site as well, dodging hard hats in order to wander, like post-apocalyptic communicants, into the towering chancel of red brick. Now the two massive structures were both being flung down, like the victims of summary war-time executions. At least the Cold Store was being dealt with with some dispatch, but the city had decided to make an example of the Power Station. The nave of the building, open to the dank sky, was profaned by abandon. Where once erg upon erg had been burnt into being, there were only pigeon droppings, and the strange cries of bungee jumpers, falling from a crane erected over the Thames, and shitting themselves as they plunged.

Ord had penetrating observations to make about London, its future and its fabric. During that last week he dismissed Flambard and gave me the full benefit of his long-term view.

'Let me say' – his voice was as clipped and peremptory as ever, radiating discipline and ferocity – 'that from the perspective of 2073 all your concerns about the removal of this building, or the implanting of that structure, seem trifling in the extreme. Take this stretch of the Thames littoral,' and he did just that, cupping the shimmering oxbow of the river in his callused hand. 'Apartment blocks with gull-wing roofs will rise up on the site of the Cold Store, then soar down again, a mighty Ferris wheel will dominate the Central London skyline for decades and then roll away. Some commentators may see the city as a peculiar entity, with its hillside suburbs and inner-city marshes as phrenological bumps and depressions, each revealing an enduring aspect of the metropolitan personality, but frankly this is bolderarckshifucklenoo.' Ord lapsed into the profane slang of the mid-future. 'London hasn't had any personality to speak of since the tube system, like some mighty course of electroconvulsive therapy, linked node to neighbouring node and shorted them out with hundreds of thousands of volts.

'That being the case –' He stopped to observe a queue of Somalians – golf-ball heads, golf-club bodies – waiting to send money orders from a small chemist's. 'You can't imagine what the Central Spike erected in 2035 will be like. Over a thousand storeys high, shaped like an immense termites' nest, its interior hollowed out into thousands of offices and apartments, hundreds of atria and gardens, and the whole mighty structure a permanent home and workplace for half the city's population, its many different streams of power, air and information both generated and regulated by newly developed bio-force.'

'No I can't.' I tried not to sound bitter. 'I can't imagine.'

In between walks I did my best to put my affairs in order. My will was a thin document: to Mrs Benson my pile of old mattresses, an envelope stuffed with foreign currency for a brother I'd neglected, boxes of old paperbacks and worn-out clothes to charity stores. Any money I'd once had had long since been frittered away. In an office crackling with static electricity and insulated with the papery record of the lives of others, I frittered away the rest.

'It's hardly worth your while to make out this will,' the solicitor said. 'It costs to have me write it, it costs to deposit it. To be frank – this stuff is near worthless.' Sweat plastered her white blouse to her white bra.

'I don't like the idea of the State getting hold of anything, anything at all.'

A desk fan creaked back and forth, ruffling the fates of men and women.

'I see.'

The water-cooler bubbled, perhaps it was boiling?

'I would scream in eternity if I thought a single battered paperback or mismatched sock was contributing in its material essence to the power of the State.'

'I see.' The solicitor was looking at me with mounting suspicion. 'Tell me, is there any particular reason why you should be making a will now?'

'No, no reason. Mortality bears down on us all though –
doesn't it?'

It was clear but gusty for late summer on the Sunday morning
appointed for the balloon debate. A pebble pinged against my
attic skylight. Standing unsteadily on my princess's bed, I
poked my head through and looked down to see Keith and
Sharon Crowd standing on the pavement.

Keith called up to me through cupped hands: 'Get a move
on!'

They reminded me of schoolkids come to fetch one of their
mates for a morning's skiving. I hurried down, grabbing the
parcel I'd spent the previous night preparing. This I slung over
my shoulder as I came out of Mrs Benson's front door, but
neither Sharon Crowd, nor Keith, appeared to notice. One of
the Benson kids shouted after us, but his words were caught
up and mangled by the passage of an early lorry. We walked
across Albert Square and down the Clapham Road towards
the Oval. At the mouth of Fentiman Road, Bax fell in beside
us and we walked on, in silence, line abreast across the
pavement, like band members in a pop video, or urban
Samurai. There was silence between us, a malevolent, brood-
ing silence.

As we marched around the curve of the Oval, then down
the grimy stretch of Harleyford Road to Vauxhall Cross, the
tension began to mount.

'Where're you gonna leave Dinah?' I asked Keith, who I
could hear inside my head, grinding his dentures.

'With the Australian lad in Majestic – obviously.'

'Oh yeah, yeah, sorry.'

'Why don't you leave him with the doorman of the Hoist,'
said Bax – they were his first words of the day – 'it's still open.'

It was. A metre or so of satiny fabric was attached to a hot-air blower in the doorway of the club. Its simulation of fire led me to picture a hell in which the torments were quite as ersatz. But Keith didn't deign to answer Bax, and the four of us trudged on as doggedly as Dinah.

The wind was smearing sheets of paper, strips of packing tape and dead leaves in broad brushstrokes across the stretched and primed sky, but the ulterior element remained daubed with its own plenitude. As ever, full of itself. It wouldn't be such a bad thing to leave this behind, this thick brick viaduct, these ancient pubs, these silent showrooms full of cacophonous motorcycles, these leprous squeegee merchants, and those Sunday saloons, stacked with life-size Playmobil figures, on their way to shop in Croydon. The whole pasta mash of Vauxhall Cross, with its myriad transport conduits noodling through the city.

While Keith and Dinah nuzzled one another under the kindly eye of the wine warehouse assistant, Sharon Crowd, Bax and I waited on the false hillock that runs along Goding Street. This was a barrow of scurvy grass, speared by sticks planted in wire baskets, and garnished with sweet shit. The balloon was being unlimbered for the day, its securing cables untethered by New Zealander travellers and Canadian postgraduate students. They worked efficiently.

'It seems fairly windy,' I said to Bax. 'Maybe they won't go up.'

'That would be a shame,' he replied distractedly, his yellow nails scrabbling at one of his wristlets. Sharon Crowd was looking magnificent. She'd elected to wear a brown Nehru jacket and matching brown trousers. The ensemble did her every compliment available. Her hair was scraped back severely, her lips were barely there at all. She and Bax went on ignoring my parcel.

When Keith returned we advanced down the hillock and crossed the park to the balloon enclosure. A Portakabin stood at a gap in the wire fence. Inside they were selling tickets and souvenirs to a clutch of tourists. I couldn't really take them in. I was getting very antsy. We all paid for our tickets separately, then filed out of the hut and along a plank walkway to the balloon's giant basket. It was not a basket as such, but an open square of walkway, the sides made of metal posts linked by five double strands of cable from waist to shoulder height, and below waist-level there were metal panels. It was Wright Brothers rather than Mongolfier, and when I saw it I realised I'd been hoping for a gondola with silk-embroidered panels, and in it a few show goats and a vicuña for company on our experimental ascent. But there was little time for quibbling, because one Kiwi took my ticket and tore it, another ushered me on board, then a third cast off.

The ascent was phenomenally fast, as quick as a lift.

On the far side of the platform from me, across a fifteen-foot gap, a child squirmed and protested in her mother's arms: 'Mummy, I'm scared aoooh! Mummy – I don't want to go up! Mu-uuummy!'

Fucking abuser, I thought to myself. 'Sadist,' I said aloud.

Then I noticed that Sharon Crowd and Bax weren't on board. I checked the other passengers: together with the abusing mother and abused child there were a couple of teenagers in white anoraks, while to my right there was a young Middle Eastern couple, and next to them was Keith. The Antipodean balloonist was isolated by the gate; he held a length of chain attached to the burner which he yanked from time to time, sending a great tongue of flame licking and roaring into the ever-tautening belly of the canopy. I looked down: framed in the square of the walkway was a rapid, reverse-zoom shot of the patch of Vauxhall Cross Park. It grew to encompass the Portakabin, the barrow, the Hoist, some boys having a kick-around, then the stand of vetch growing on top of the Vauxhall Tavern, and eventually the figures of Sharon Crowd and Bax, both equally tiny now, who arm in arm were striding towards the tube.

I was down to one friend, Keith, a former bank robber, although we'd never talked about his bank-robbing days. He was wedged into the corner of the platform, and as I looked on, awed, Brockwell Park disappeared below his shoulder, only to reappear beneath his feet. We were two hundred feet up and still rising.

'So,' Keith called over, 'no debate. Didn't think they'd go through with it. We may as well just enjoy the ascent.'

His knuckles were white, his arms bent back to brace him, his purple windcheater snapped in the stiff breeze. I was shocked by how precipitate the balloon trip was turning out to be – the platform bucked and heaved in the wind as if it were a crow's nest surmounting a flexible mast.

'Or perhaps you'd like a game of Go-Chess to distract you – how like a Go board London is, from this elevation.'

Keith turned to survey the city falling away beneath us, and I turned as well. The Antipodean chatting, the gas burner roaring, the Middle Eastern couple hand-holding, the child whimpering, all were as nothing when set beside its warty enormity. Already I could make out the burst boil of the Millennium Dome to the east and the greenery of Teddington Lock to the west. As we rose still higher, the streets of the city eerily unknotted themselves, straightening out to form a grid of many many poignant intersections, places where I'd laid the wrong stone.

'It is peculiarly like a Go board!' I shouted over to Keith, who was faint against the sharp sky. 'So we'll have to begin with –'

'Go!' shouted Ord, and I took this to be an order, as I'm sure it was intended. We understood our secret mnemonics – Ord and I.

I unslung the linen parcel from my shoulders. The Middle Eastern couple backed away from me muttering. The man tried to look me in the eyes, attempting the command of me with his own inner Ord. I evaded his control beams just as I ignored the woman's suitable beak and her black flapping chador. I unpopped the poppers of the duvet cover and took out the fitted-sheet parachute. The Antipodean called to the couple to move back towards me, they were unbalancing the platform. Ord gave a single bark of cruel laughter. How like the man. I got one foot up on the taut cable and swung myself over. The horizon tipped like a giant grey swell and I fell, screaming, towards the periphery of my own acquaintance.

RETURN TO THE
PLANET OF THE
HUMANS

Then he was back, suddenly and savagely. Not that he knew he was back, he simply found himself in a room full of monsters, lanky, pasty giants clad in disgusting nether garments, who, rather than beat him compassionately into stability, kept their distance and moaned. Their vocalisations were so low and febrile, so ghostly. They made no signs that he could comprehend and when he could bear it no longer he attacked.

They sedated him – that much he knew. When he came to again he was in a padded cell on the psychiatric ward of a hospital. While he had no clear memory of what lay either side of this nasty null space, he grasped that he'd been in a similar one before, for it felt familiar to him.

The monsters came and pressed their sharp muzzles against the tiny panel of toughened glass in the door. Periodically they entered the cell so as to inject him with drugs and he sprayed them. Once he was docile they wiped away the shit and piss. They told him that he had a history of this kind of thing, so they weren't inclined to pay any attention to his panicky vocalisations or frantic signing.

Fearing he was mad – for they were animals – he found that he could understand them, even though their long, thin, hairless fingers were so flaccid and insignificant. One of them took an interest in him, coming to sit beside him on the wipeable surface, pen and notebook in its static hand. When he tried to impart the whole story of what had happened to him with the intensity that it required, this creature reared back from his agitating fingers. If he managed to touch it, it hit a button and others came to restrain him, then probed him with the fat needle. But if he could keep back from the white-robed animal, while it watched him warily all the time, it grunted assent and feigned sympathy.

He told it that it and its kind were monstrous aliens to him, that they should have fur all over their bodies, not just on their tubular heads. He told it that to him their eyebrow ridges were grotesquely nude, while their exposed skin was repulsively soft. He told it that because their fingers were so still and their toes were sheathed in leather he could not fully believe in anything they tried to communicate. He told it that unless he could see their anal scrags and genital swellings he could not be sure they were like him in any meaningful way. He told it that their very odour was offensive to him, a thin stench blanketed with toxic chemicals which rasped his nostrils and made him gag.

When, in turn, it asked him what the dominant creatures were like where he came from, he told it chimpanzees, we are chimps. Chimpanzees inhabit the whole earth, chimps knuckle-walking in the streets, chimps displaying in the government buildings and brachiating through the trees in the public parks. The most vivid expression of social life was, he told it, a crowd of chimps mating and fighting, their fur erect. Then he implored it to touch him, to caress him, to groom him thoroughly as any caring chimpanzee would do, but still it remained aloof.

Instead of grooming him it told him that he was deluded, that his vision of a chimpanzee society was only that, a fantasy built up out of satirical books and science-fiction films. It told him that chimpanzees were animals, nothing more. That only a few tens of thousands remained alive in the wild, and their numbers were declining rapidly as they were hunted for food by the poor people who dwelled in the equatorial jungle.

Who were these 'pee-pul'? he asked. The vocalisation, so unfamiliar, so infantile, yet came to him unbidden. These people, it said, were humans, benighted humans but humans all the same. And like all other humans they could walk erect and speak many different languages. Humans possessed the most advanced technologies and performed great feats of construction. Humans had been to the moon and sent their machines still further into space. It was humans who ruled this earth and all other creatures were subordinate to them, mere gammas and deltas in the evolutionary hierarchy. Hearing these absurdities he yammered and howled and gnashed and threw himself about the cell in a frenzied display until the others came and they sheathed their fat needle in his scrawny, quaking flesh.

When they'd all gone he dragged himself upright and staggered to the door. In the glass panel he saw his own pitiful muzzle reflected. But could it be his, because like theirs it was scarcely lined. He had a tuft of fine hair on top of his head and sparse tufts sprouted on his muzzle, but apart from more thin patches around his hidden scrag and exposed penis his body was bare under his dirty robe. He felt weak, unbearably weak, and his awareness of the space about him was awfully hazy. His peripheral vision was almost non-existent and, even after this long period in this one room, he still couldn't grasp the positions of the few things allowed to him, the cardboard table and chair, the plastic piss pot.

Often, moving backwards, he knocked the piss pot over and sprayed his own urine into his frightened muzzle.

The humans told him that his weakness was good. They told him that the low cries he increasingly uttered were a sign he was recovering. They encouraged him to take the pills they gave him rather than waiting for the needle, and respectful – as all apes must be – of the hierarchy in which he found himself, he obeyed. As a reward they allowed him out of the cell and on to a ward of others who they assured him were like himself.

They were, in part at least. They gurned and howled like chimpanzees, and like chimps they tried to get their fingers in his fur. They yammered and fought like chimps, and on several occasions he even saw them attempt to mount one another, although this was frustrated by their absurd nether garments. Then the attendants came, as languorous as ever, limping on their rigid legs, and dragged them apart.

At first he couldn't tell which creatures were female because he couldn't see their sexual swellings or if they were in oestrus. But after a while he realised that the smaller ones with the longer, finer head fur tended to be females, and by thrusting his muzzle close to their crotches he could tell when they were ovulating. This behaviour, far from being appreciated, was met with bass cries of horror on the part of his captors, so he learnt not to do it and to cower away from the females.

After what must have been weeks on the ward he was allowed to visit the hospital cafeteria with one of the nurses. He was led out into the public areas of the building. Here he saw still more humans, buttoned up tight in their stupid clothing, ignoring each other and staring straight ahead with their oddly monocular gazes. The throngs on the stairways and in the corridors parted instinctively to allow the passage of the throngs coming in the opposite direction. The humans' movements were at once abrupt and languid as they wafted past.

He sat with the nurse in the cafeteria and ate their awful carbohydrate mush and rotten carrion. The only fruit available looked injection-moulded and stank of chemicals. Heading back to the ward they passed by the revolving door in the main hall. Slices of the outside world were cut up and flung at him: a red bus, a black cab, an orange milk float. Across the road he could make out a terrace of red-brick houses, and on one of them a street sign he recognised. It read 'Fulham Palace Road'. He didn't screech, he didn't cachinnate, he didn't lash out, but in the numb core of him something gave way and he was forced to acknowledge that it was true, that this was the world he'd always known, but now it was dominated by the loathsome animals. It was the planet of the humans.

After this day what his captors chose to call his recovery rapidly progressed. While his movements still felt stilted, crippled even, to them they were only side effects of the medication. He took very little interest in their world but he stopped spraying them when they brought him food. They told him that since he was getting better he should know that he was a person of some standing, that he had a family, friends and a career. They brought two infants to see him and told him that they were his. He sat on the far side of a Formica-topped table from the two sub-adult males and the female who they told him had once been his consort, but he felt no affection for them, or kinship. They looked like all the rest, with their brutish muzzles, their staring eyes, their jerky yet

251

slow gestures. He managed to display a few signs of interest in them, but was glad when they went. They didn't return.

It was the same with the other humans they told him were his friends and colleagues. He stared at them, they stared back at him. They groaned their pathetic reassurances, he groaned back his excruciating sense of total dislocation. To one or two of them he attempted an explanation of the other world he'd lived in, its exhilarating vigour and violent intimacy, its rank scents and sensual smells, its cathartic fighting and speedy mating. However, they looked either shocked, bored, or repelled, and sometimes all three. He was glad when these visits began to decline, and still more pleased when they ceased altogether.

They told him that he had to leave the hospital, that he was well enough now to manage by himself in what they called sheltered accommodation. He hoped this would be a great grove of trees, their branches cunningly interleaved, which he could disappear into and where he could build his nest, high above the threatening ground with its legions of bipedal ghosts. It turned out to be a mean little block of bedsitting rooms, single-storeyed and set around a square of dirty grass, smeared with dog shit and glittering with broken glass. The dogs frightened him; where he'd come from they hadn't been domesticated. The world outside his room frightened him as well. It was exactly the same as the city he remembered but a third larger to match the scale of its current lofty inhabitants. When he had to go outside, he preferred not to look up at the tops of the buildings, their vast size made him dizzy. He inched along the inside of the pavement, occasionally, despite himself, dropping to his knuckles and scuttling on all fours.

The nether garments he had to wear made him feel constricted, breathless. When he was certain he couldn't be observed – usually as he skulked on a patch of waste ground near the block – he'd loosen them and let his genitals flop out into the cool air. Fortunately he didn't have to go out that often. A human came to clean his room and would also shop for the plastic fruit he hated but still desired. The same human helped him to fill out the forms he needed to get money from the post office. These were the only interactions he could tolerate, for if he spent too long with any individual human – no matter how palsied and strange he still found them – he'd be compelled to grasp for their shoulder, thrust his muzzle close to theirs, while entreating them with agitated fingers to bury their fingers in his head fur, or mock-mate him, or hit him so as to convince him that he was still alive, still chimp.

Doctors came every week to give him injections. He obeyed them when they told him to take his other medication with unfailing regularity, for he found that if he didn't the world became a still more terrifying place, as his energy level rose and his perception widened, until he had an irrepressible urge to scamper up the façades of buildings, or force the humans he encountered to acknowledge his dominance by kissing his hairless arse.

The creature who'd first listened to him in the Charing Cross Hospital still came to see him from time to time, and at her suggestion he began to attend an art therapy group held in the community centre attached to his sheltered accommodation. She told him, this doctor, that she'd met him years before after his first breakdown. She told him that he'd once been a very famous and successful artist, and that she was sure the way forward for him – if not to total recovery at least towards some acceptance of his condition – lay through his art. Although he thought she was stupid this did make a peculiar kind of sense, for the world he found himself in was so grindingly itself that he could find no way of describing it in any other terms. A chair was a chair, a car a car, a house a house. If he wanted the other world back – the planet of the apes to which he hearkened with every fibre of his being – then he would have to paint it into life. Perhaps in the process he would discover an idiom which would make it bearable to speak of being human.

He went to the art therapy sessions and sat with the other sick beings. The brushes, charcoals and pencils felt familiar, but his own fingers remained alien to him, too long and bony, too weak for him to manage the fine muscle control necessary to render the depictions he envisaged. He wanted to make small canvases, thickly layered, which would portray the teeming world he'd lost, with its bristly figures so closely meshed that they'd appear as a single, heaving rug of warm connectivity. But when he tried to execute them his brush-strokes were too clumsy and the paintings turned out as muddy daubs.

The human who supervised the group tried to encourage him, saying that the paintings were different, a little unsettling perhaps, but definitely worth continuing with. He brought another human to see them, a female who said that she ran a small gallery of outsider art and she'd like to have two or three of them to exhibit. Outsider art. The expression made him howl with derision. How far outside she had no way of comprehending. Outside of time, outside of space, outside of this whole miserable world with its sexless, peg-legged, slick-skinned, feeble-fingered inhabitants.

Yet he went to see the gallery and met some of the people associated with it. He could tell how peculiar they found him, and often after he'd turned away his acute hearing picked up the things they said behind his back.

'Simon Dykes, y'know . . .' they said.

'What, the painter?'

'Absolutely.'

'But he was so well known at one time, there's stuff of his in the Tate, isn't there?'

'That's right, but he had a breakdown, two in fact, very severe as you can see. He's little more than a shell of a man, hardly anything left in him that's human.'

'Odd, most peculiar, and these mucky little things are his?'

'I'm afraid so, I think she only shows them for their curiosity value. Even compared to the work of other mentally ill painters they have no discernible merit. If they bear comparison with anything it's those paintings done by chimpanzees under the tutelage of animal psychologists.'

It was a time of war and oppression. From what he heard at the gallery millions of humans were being starved, tortured and murdered by their own species. How the gallery goers made him laugh with their talk of 'humanity' and 'human rights'. They thought themselves the very lords of creation as they supped their alcoholic grape juice with their fat wet lips. Standing there in their sagging bags of skin, never touching, never hugging, never – that he could see – mating, their very perception of the world a single cone of certainty, which projected out from their ugly muzzles, only to dip down to the ground within a few feet.

At one of these gatherings a female approached him and made signs indicating that she was interested in something else besides disparaging him. The odours were, as ever, masked with tight garments and smelly water, but he could tell she was in oestrus. When she suggested he accompany her back to her home and then encouraged him to join her in her nest, the thought of finally getting to grips with another – even another of another species – was too much for him to resist.

But oh the revulsion of the soft stroking and feeble palping she forced upon him! There was no intimate force or erotic vigour to this encounter. When she made it clear through her guttural groans that he should mate her, he found himself lapsing into more natural and cohering behaviour. He grabbed her head fur tightly, rammed into her tiny swelling deeply, then cuffed her with true affection. She moaned pathetically, dragged herself from under him, and backed into the corner of the nest with the insane look of a half-broken animal on her muzzle.

'It's my fault . . .' she whimpered. 'It's my fault.'

He returned to his sheltered accommodation, expecting the doctors to come for him, to net him and stab him with their poison-tipped spears. But they never did.

He gathered other things about his past from the female doctor who still came to see him. Apparently, after his last breakdown, he'd been treated by a very eminent, very well-known doctor. The doctor – a former colleague of the female's – had even taken him into his own group in an attempt to heal him.

He discovered where the doctor lived and went there. It was a hilltop suburb, where the windows of the large houses looked out over a stretch of open heathland to the grey city below. Crossing the heath to reach the doctor's house, he allowed himself to believe he was back in the world he loved, reunited with his tough and hairy body. He leapt for low-hanging branches and swung from them, he beat his chest and waa-barked in the gathering darkness, he tore at his nether garments and exposed himself to the night air. The few humans he encountered ran away from him, screaming in a most satisfying fashion.

When he arrived at the doctor's house his clothes were in tatters and he was bleeding in several places. He leapt over the garden gate and knuckle-walked up to the front door which he banged on with both fists. After a while the door swung open to reveal a fat male with sparse white head fur. The famous doctor looked at him with that expression – at once blank and meaninglessly quizzical – which he'd come to understand was typical of the species. The doctor uttered no vocalisation, nor did his twisted old digits make any sign. After a while he shut the door again.

He sat there on his haunches and his large ears picked up the sound of a telephone being dialled inside the house, then low mutters. Isn't it strange, he reflected, how when I had the delusion that I was human they couldn't do enough to help me, but now that they're certain I am one they don't care at all.

Then squatting down still further he readied himself for the arrival of the ambulance, the siren of which he could already hear, screeching its way through the alien jungle.